TROUBLE FOR TALLON

TROUBLE FOR TALLON

JOHN BALL

PUBLISHED FOR THE CRIME CLUB BY
DOUBLEDAY & COMPANY, INC.
GARDEN CITY, NEW YORK
1981

18708

Library of Congress Cataloging in Publication Data

Ball, John Dudley, 1911–
Trouble for Tallon.

I. Title.
PS3552.A455T7   813'.54

First Edition

ISBN: 0-385-17329-6
Library of Congress Catalog Card Number 80–1983

Dedication

*To Swami Kriyananda
and all of my friends at
Ananda Cooperative Village
Nevada City, California*

AUTHOR'S NOTE

Major assistance in the preparation of this book was given by Chief Jerome Gardner of the Cheney, Washington, Police Department and by many of its individual members. It was during a long, all-night patrol with Chief Gardner that many of the intricate procedural details were worked out. The fullest thanks are extended to Chief Gardner and to his charming wife, Patricia, for her unstinting hospitality.

Sincere gratitude is also tendered to Swami Kriyananda and many members of the Ananda Cooperative Village of Nevada City, California. Not only did the people of Ananda help in every possible way, but also Kriyananda was kind enough to read the entire manuscript in order to insure its accuracy in depicting the life style and activities of a contemporary spiritual community.

However, it needs to be added that this book is not intended to depict either the city of Cheney or Ananda, and no such relationship should be inferred. In particular, no actual individuals are portrayed from either of these two communities, or from the motion picture industry.

John Ball

PROLOGUE

Councilman Wilson Sullivan hoped with something close to desperation that no one would recognize him. He was in a part of the city where he was little known and the fact that the night was as dark as any he could remember helped too. As he walked down past the silent houses he was grateful for the steady row of shade trees that provided him additional cover.

He was in a foul mood. For many years he had been accustomed to getting his way by using people whenever necessary; that was part of the business he was in. The thought that he himself had been used was more than he could tolerate. He had been so angry it had taken him almost too long a time to work out his countermoves. No one could make a fool of Wilson Sullivan: he told himself that savagely time and time again as if he could gain additional strength from the meaning of the words.

Once, much earlier in his life, he had had to earn his living by doing construction work—manual labor. He had worked his way up from that through a series of deals: very small ones at first and then more important ones where he had always emerged the victor. He had cut the ground out from under a good many people, but that had been their lookout, not his. Business was business.

Then he had made one bad guess and he was now caught in his own trap. It had closed on him until he had reached the point of desperation; then he had discovered a way out. No one else knew it but him, but someone else was due to find out very shortly.

When he heard footsteps behind him, he turned but he did not see the face he had expected. A tiny sense of alarm ran through him, then he rallied. He was a hard, tough man and he had nothing to fear from anyone. Then he had the sudden feeling that the person he was facing was not alone. The night was so very dark, and the opportunities for concealment were much too good. The thing that had worked in his favor was now, silently and invisibly, moved to the other side of the ledger.

He had a firm, tough voice that suited his personality. More than once he had used it effectively to put someone in his place and to establish his own authority. When he had at last been elected to the city council, that power had become a reality; he had become an important man and others were in the position of having to ask him for favors. Whitewater was not a big city; it had less than nine thousand population when the college was not in session, but he was for the time being content to be a big frog in a small puddle. Because he knew something, something he had figured out for himself, and the information could, very literally, be worth millions. He was fully prepared to become a millionaire and more, but not by laying bricks or nailing studs into position. The people who did that were the pawns in the game; they would all work for him and the huge profits they would generate would become his because he had thought the whole matter through and had found the answer.

Because it suited his purpose to do so, he talked briefly with the person who had come to meet him. They walked together in the deep shade, then stopped while Sullivan laid down his terms. He was certain that no one else in Whitewater had the least idea what was going on. He issued his orders and demanded obedience because he was the kind of man who always saw himself as the boss. Most people, he knew, were sheep and would do what they were told by any strong man who gave them their marching orders. There had been a time when he had not been so confident, but he had convinced himself of his own mastery and he didn't care one iota whether anyone else liked it or not.

When he had finished, he turned his back and started to walk away, still very angry, but confident of his victory. He clenched his teeth hard together and renewed his sense of determination.

The sudden pain surged through him like an unleashed hellfire. He knew only that he had been hit, that he was in awful agony, and that his body was falling to the ground. A fresh burst of intense torment racked him and he opened his mouth to scream. He could not get the air into his lungs; not a muscle in his body would obey him. Then he was on the ground, prone, digging with his fingers against the hard concrete, trying to pull his body away from the thing that was consuming it with unbearable pain. For a few seconds things seemed to go black and he was conscious only of a great heat that filled his whole being.

When his consciousness returned, he pulled in air and let out a wild sob. It was a cry for help, for rescue, and for a miracle of healing compassion. His breath racked in his lungs and his mind told him that it might be some time before he would be found. He could not cry out loud enough to be heard; he could only endure the torture that engulfed him and hope with desperation that something, anything, would show him blessed mercy.

CHAPTER 1

In the quiet of early morning the bell sounded. It had a very clear, very liquid tone that suggested far-away exotic places. Its gentle, subtle sound was real, but it was amplified through carefully placed speakers so that it was heard over the many acres of the housing area and the guest cottages.

When she heard the bell, as she did every morning, Kumari opened her eyes and cast off the remnants of sleep that had remained with her. For a moment or two she enjoyed the comfort of her narrow bed, rolling her head on the hard pillow for the pleasure of feeling the motion. Then, dutifully, she got to her feet and stood in the tiny room that was almost half of her home.

Although it was hardly more than sixty square feet, Kumari had made it hers by setting her few possessions against the walls. In one corner was her guitar. She played it well, and sang even better.

The ceiling was very low because the A-frame construction was on such a small scale. She had lived in it for some time and had adjusted herself completely to its dimensions. She was a very neat and careful housekeeper.

For a short time she sat in meditation, then she bent her supple body in a few exercises designed to stimulate the circulation of her blood. That done, she stepped through the miniature doorway that divided the two sections of her home. In the second half she had a hinged table and an ancient reed organ that still worked quite well.

Up in the triangular loft was the tiny bedroom where her son had his cot. Because he was only six, he was able to sleep comfortably in the confined space. He did not seem to notice that there was only room for two upended orange crates that served as shelves to hold his books and toys.

He was called Jon, and Kumari loved him with an intensity that knew no limit. To her eyes he was a perfect child and his sturdy little body a great gift from God. Jon had heard the bell too and had gone into the bathroom. When he came out his mother kissed him before she took her turn. There was barely room for her to stand, but the structure, which had been added quite unexpectedly, the year before, was a marvel of efficiency. It had once been a restroom on an airplane; how it had been obtained for her use she did not know. Two of her friends in the community had installed it for her. The chemical toilet had been replaced by a small septic tank, so she had every convenience of the most sophisticated airline traveler.

When she had washed and combed her long, very dark hair, she came out to find that her son had already dressed himself. She had laid out his clothes the night before, as she did every evening, and he had put them on quickly. He had only three changes, but that was quite enough to meet all of his needs that she could foresee.

Kumari took the two or three steps back into her own bedroom and, with the door shut, dressed herself. It took her less than a minute to put on her underwear, the simple dress that was one of the four she owned, and the comfortable sandals that saved wear and tear on her only pair of street shoes. She used no cosmetics and needed none: she had a natural quiet beauty that was enhanced by a flawless complexion. She was thirty-two years old, but none of the supple grace of her late teens had deserted her. She took Jon by the hand and together they started out for breakfast.

As they walked together down the pathway toward the dining hall, she looked about her and once more drank in all of the unspoiled beauty that was so much a part of the Pacific Northwest. Every breath that she took was a quiet delight, the air was so sweet and pure. She had never noticed such things when she had been in school and had been plain Mary Goldstein. Now it was all enormously different, even to the point that at times she seemed to be living in a dream—one from which she hoped she would never awaken.

It was a quarter mile to the dining hall, but the short walk through the open field made her aware of how small she was in the great scheme of things. It was an emotion that came to her frequently, and in it she found a kind of fulfillment.

She had long ago forgiven the rapist who had brutalized her and taken her virginity. God had his own ways of dealing with such matters and he had compensated her vastly beyond her deserts.

As she and Jon neared the dining hall, she saw a car coming up the private road. At that hour of the morning it was unusual; the road was used little enough in any case. When it came nearer, she could see the Double Sonic unit on its roof and the large, distinctive police emblem on its side.

Her first thought was that someone was sick or had had an accident because there was no other reason why an official car would come on the grounds. Jon was animated by the sight and quickened his step, dragging his mother along so that he would not miss one iota of the excitement. Kumari came off the pathway just as the police car pulled up in the parking lot in front of the dining hall.

The man who got out was somewhere in his mid-thirties. Kumari noticed that he was quite handsome and the good clothes that he wore were perfectly suited to him. In contrast to so many of her male friends within the community, he was clean shaven and his hair was cut neatly short. Because of the car he was driving she had to assume that he was a policeman, but to her eye he didn't look like one.

He came over to them with a pleasant and calm manner, as though he understood where he was. Kumari had lived many years in the outside world and knew quite a lot about people. The way that the man approached her and looked at her, told her that he was a decent person, the kind they used to call a gentleman.

When he was close enough he spoke to her politely and informally. "Good morning. Are you one of the residents here?"

"Yes," she answered. She knew that his question had only been a proper opening. "I am Kumari. This is my son, Jon."

The man took a second to squat down and offer the child his hand. Jon took it gravely. Then the man stood up once more. "I'm Chief Tallon of the Whitewater Police Department," he said. "I'd like to speak to the swami, if you please."

Gently Kumari shook her head. "Swami is in seclusion," she told him. "It's impossible to disturb him; he is in deep meditation. Perhaps Narayan can help you. Please come in; you are welcome to share our breakfast."

"Is Narayan your husband?" the chief asked.

"No, I don't have a husband. I'm a renunciate."

"I don't quite understand," Tallon said.

"I am a nun."

He had not quite expected that. He glanced down at the small boy who was looking up at him intently and then wondered if some of the many stories that circulated in Whitewater concerning the nearby spiritual community might be true. He knew that a person's appearance was never a valid clue to his character or deportment; that was a hard lesson that some had paid dearly to learn. Despite this, his gut reaction was that the girl before him was not likely to be promiscuous.

It caused her no trouble at all to read his thoughts. "I was once physically attacked," she said. "It was very bad at the time, but it proved to be a great blessing, for God gave me Jon."

Tallon looked at her with fresh respect. "If I may meet the man you mentioned—" he began, and then paused.

"Please come with us," she said. "We do not speak during the morning meal. But Narayan will be glad to come out and help you." Tallon walked beside her at a suitable distance toward the dining hall. He did not want to give the least hint of familiarity; in his position, he could not possibly afford it.

Because of the discovery that had gotten him out of his bed two hours earlier, Tallon had not had time even for a cup of coffee, but he was determined not to impose on the community in any way. He therefore waited at the door while the girl and her son went inside. He had been there less than a minute when another young woman, this one dressed in a very simple garment and barefooted, came to him carrying a tray. With a gesture she invited him to sit down.

He took the tray and then realized that he could not simply stand and hold it. There were perhaps fifty people in the plainly furnished room; most of them were relatively young, but there were also older couples and several obvious family groups. None of them embarrassed him by looking in his direction. He sat down and poured milk over a dish of what appeared to be oatmeal. He had also been given a tall glass of an odd green liquid and a ripe banana. A small dish of brown sugar was also on the tray.

He ate quickly because time was important. He was handling this call himself since it was very delicate and none of the eight men on his staff was properly qualified to deal with it. A lot might be at stake—in fact, he was sure that it was.

He looked up to see that a man was standing before him. He was tall, six feet three at least, dark-complected, and bearded. He wore blue jeans and a peasant-type shirt that suited his narrow figure well. His hair was long, but it was tied back neatly. He had a pair of plain leather sandals in his left hand. Tallon noted that his nails were clean, although his hands gave evidence of hard work. His features were aquiline, but the darkness of his skin suggested that he might have been of mixed ancestry.

He nodded toward Tallon's tray, then at the door. As the chief got up, the man picked up the tray himself and led the way outside. Forty feet from the doorway there was a large shade tree with a picnic table set up underneath it. The tall man put the tray down and then spoke for the first time. "I am Narayan. Kumari told me that you have something to discuss."

The chief held out his hand. "Jack Tallon," he said. "I'm the police chief in Whitewater. Pardon me, but do you have another name?"

"I was Francis MacNeil before I came here."

"But you prefer Narayan now."

"If you please."

Both men sat down. Because he was still hungry, and also because the man who called himself Narayan had brought it out for him, Tallon ate some more of his cereal before he spoke again. "Mr. Narayan," he began.

"Just Narayan, please."

"All right, Narayan. How well do you know Councilman Wilson Sullivan?"

"I have never met him."

"But you have heard of him."

"Yes. We all have."

Tallon had another hearty spoonful of the cereal which wasn't bad. "Then you probably know that Mr. Sullivan was elected to our city council about six months ago."

"On January fourteenth, I believe," Narayan said.

"Then you also know that he's made it something of a personal crusade to try to get rid of your community here." Tallon made that a little abrasive on purpose.

Narayan looked at him passively. "We are quite aware of that."

Tallon changed his tack. "What is your function here?"

"It has pleased Swami to make me his assistant. When he is not here, or when he is in seclusion as he is now, then the responsibility for Dharmaville is mine. That is, insofar as the day-to-day operation is concerned. In all major matters we meet and discuss what is proposed. Then we vote. However, Swami is the final authority and we always accept his will."

"That sort of destroys the democratic process, doesn't it?" Tallon asked.

"Not in the least. In the first place, Swami is vastly better qualified than we are in most temporal matters. He is American-born, you know. Also, he never fails to give fullest consideration to our thoughts and ideas. We would be utterly lost without him."

"I see." Tallon ate for a few moments more until he had finished the last of the cereal. He put his spoon down and picked up the banana. As he peeled it, he spoke. "This past week Councilman Sullivan proposed an ordinance that could effectively destroy your operation. I presume you know that the city limits were extended a considerable distance last March so that part of your property is now technically in Whitewater."

"We recognize your jurisdiction here."

The way that was said surprised Tallon just a little, but he did not let it show. He kept to the subject at hand. "Councilman Sullivan first proposed that we require a ten-foot-high fence around your entire property," he said. "Since that was ridiculous, the council refused to even consider it. Then he came up with another ordinance that contains a number of provisions which he claims are for reasons of safety, public health, and morality. There is a possibility that that ordinance may be enacted."

"You have come, then, to investigate us. You are welcome. You may see whatever you like."

Tallon chewed and swallowed a piece of banana. "It's not quite that simple, I'm afraid," he said. "Last night Councilman Sullivan was attacked and severely beaten. He's in the hospital in very critical condition. He's in ICU and can't be interviewed, but when he was first brought in, he did manage to say that it was four men from your group who had assaulted him. He grabbed this from one of them."

Tallon reached into his pocket and drew out a looped Egyptian cross that he tossed onto the table.

Narayan looked at it. "That's mine," he said.

CHAPTER 2

While on his way to the Dharmaville spiritual community, Jack Tallon had thought about the piece of hard evidence he had in his possession. He had expected a blanket denial that anyone there had ever even seen it, a statement that would have to be intensively probed and possibly broken down. The sudden candor he had encountered instead threw him slightly off balance.

He recovered quickly, then nodded toward the looped cross that lay on the table. "Perhaps you'd better examine it carefully," he suggested. "You understand why."

"I understand perfectly," Narayan responded. "But that's mine. There's no doubt about it; I made it myself."

"Did you make it here?" Tallon asked.

"No, before I came. I had a workshop in my basement and I made it as an exercise. The ankh, or Egyptian cross, is a very ancient symbol and a very important one. You might compare it with the Star of

David. To save you the trouble of asking, I have no idea how it came into someone else's possession."

He looked Tallon directly in the face. "To put it on the record, I was not one of those who attacked Councilman Sullivan. I have no idea who the people were, but it's extremely unlikely that they were any of us."

"Why?" Tallon asked.

Narayan shifted his position so that he was facing his visitor squarely. "How much do you know about our community?" he asked.

"Very little, I'm afraid. Care to fill me in?" When he was gathering evidence, Tallon could be the most patient of men. The more people were encouraged to talk, the more they were likely to say.

"Of course." Narayan paused a moment, then he went on. "Dharmaville represents a dream Swami has had all his life. He spent more than twenty-five years in training and preparing himself for this. Along the way he gave up the chance to make a lot of money, even the comfort of a wife and family."

"He's a renunciate, then," Tallon commented.

"He is, yes. He studied under a great guru here, then he went to India and spent more years with the yoga masters there. He learned the language and eventually attained swamihood. For a non-Indian, that's a great achievement."

"I don't doubt that he's a very dedicated man," Tallon said.

"He's also a great teacher. He tours a great deal, lecturing and conducting classes in meditation, yoga, and spiritual awareness. The fees he earns go to our community."

"That's your principal support, I take it."

"No, we do very well with our industries. We grow much of our own food, we have our own dairy, and our own school; a lot of the nearby children attend it. We also have handicraft shops, a publishing operation, and we're planning to open a produce stand on the highway."

Tallon found that interesting in a general way, although it was not very much to the point. However, he stuck to his principle of letting his man talk on. Sooner or later patience was likely to bear fruit.

Narayan appeared to sense exactly what Tallon was thinking. "You'll find out very quickly that we're not hippies and that this is nothing like Jonestown. Dharmaville is a spiritual community where our religious life is built around yoga. It's a way of approaching God and nature through work, meditation, and studying the teachings of the great masters. The yoga exercises are our version of the police academy PT."

"That's very lofty," Tallon said, "but is it practical?"

Narayan refused to be nettled. "Most of us came here because we sensed an emptiness in our lives. Everyone does that sometimes; I'm sure you have. We live together as friends and we trust each other. There aren't any locks on our doors; among ourselves there's no need and there's hardly any temptation to thieves from outside. We use Sanskrit names because it suits the way we live here and because it helps us to feel a genuine unity."

"I see the point you're making," Tallon said. "How unlikely it would be for men from such a peaceful religious community to beat up a citizen in the main part of the city."

"Or anywhere else," Narayan added.

Tallon came back to the basics. "I need to see your swami as soon as possible," he said. "I understand that he's here. How large is Dharmaville, by the way?"

"Eight hundred and ten acres—plus a fraction. And I see your point: why don't we incorporate as a village and avoid any harassing ordinances that your council might pass? We've considered that; for the moment it's tabled."

"The swami," Tallon reminded.

Narayan laid his hand on the table. "I'll take it on myself to interrupt him. None of us have ever done that before, but it's clearly necessary. Would two this afternoon suit you?"

"Yes," Tallon answered. One more question remained in his mind and he asked it. "What did you do before you came here?" As he spoke he got to his feet to signal his departure.

Narayan stood up as well. "I was a corporate attorney," he answered. "Before that, I was a policeman."

Twenty minutes later Tallon walked into the Whitewater Police Department to find everything in good order. Francie, the department fixture who doubled as receptionist and as his secretary, was manning the front desk and the radio equipment. In his office his mail was waiting, the previous day's reports were on his desk, and the phone messages were noted on the proper form. He sat down to go to work.

It had been almost a year since he had come to Whitewater, but he was still adjusting to the drastic change from being a sergeant on the Pasadena, California, Police Department. He had put in twelve good years there and had been next in line to make lieutenant when Jennifer had finally broken down. She had come from a small town and the city pressures had been too much for her. Because it wasn't going to get any better, he had applied for the Whitewater job just to appease her. To his utter surprise he had been offered the opening, and when he had seen the tears of joy in Jennifer's eyes, he had taken it.

Now he was chief of police in Whitewater, Washington, population 8,500 largely peaceful souls. He had inherited eight officers of varying abilities, most of whom had never seen the inside of a police academy. He had corrected that by instituting his own training program, a step that had not been too popular. However, when a number of incidents had proved the value of his teachings, the whole department had begun to take on a new air. Now pride in doing a superior job was a well-established pattern.

He had left his office door open in case anyone wanted to see him. In his small organization, going through channels would have been an absurdity. Almost immediately Ned Asher, his plainclothes detective, tapped and came in. "I thought you'd want an update on Councilman Sullivan's condition," he said.

"Please."

"As of five minutes ago he's still in ICU and largely unconscious. There's no immediate hope of talking to him. Father Wilcox gave him the last rites a little while ago."

Jack digested that. "I take it that the prognosis isn't good."

"No, it isn't. I talked with Mary Clancy; she's been assigned to him full time. It's her feeling that he isn't going to make it."

Mary Clancy was a notably attractive RN who had been sworn in as a reserve member of the Whitewater Police. If she had told Asher that, she had had her reasons, because her medical ethics were sound.

Jack looked quickly through his mail and saw that there was nothing really important. He got to his feet. "I'm going over to the hospital," he said. "Pass the word." That meant that Sergeant Hillman, the watch commander, would be in charge until he got back.

The Whitewater Community Hospital was hardly five minutes away. It was a small facility, but it was well run and had an excellent reputation. Because the city was growing steadily, there was already talk of adding a new wing. It was the only facility of its kind within a sixteen-mile radius.

Jack parked in one of the three slots reserved for emergency and law-enforcement personnel and went in through the back entrance. That saved some time and did not advertise his comings and goings.

The nurse on duty at the emergency desk was very young and pencil slim, but she knew her job. Tallon was aware that she could deal with abusive patients if the need arose. "Good morning, Chief," she said as soon as Jack was within speaking range. "Dr. Lindholm was just here a couple of minutes ago. He wants to see you. I called your office and they told me you were on the way here."

"Did Dr. Lindholm take care of Mr. Sullivan when he was brought in last night?" Tallon asked.

"Yes; he still handles most of the emergency work. Shall I get him for you?"

"Please." As the girl picked up the phone, he added, "Anything new on Mr. Sullivan's condition?"

"Not that I've heard." She spoke into the phone and hung up. "Dr. Lindholm will be right down."

Within two minutes Lindholm appeared. He was young, probably still in his late twenties. He was moderately tall, clean shaven, and his blond Nordic hair was neatly cut in a no-nonsense manner. Tallon knew that he was competent, particularly in emergency surgery.

"Morning, Jack," he said. "Come on in."

Lindholm led him to his office where an automatic coffee maker was showing a ready light. He poured out two cups, then pointed to a shaker of sugar and a small bowl of powdered creamer. He sat down at his desk. Tallon fixed his own coffee and then took the only other chair.

Lindholm led off without invitation. "You know that we have Wilson Sullivan in the ICU and, as of ten minutes ago, his chances don't look too good."

"I've already got that," Tallon told him.

"If he dies, then it's murder because it will definitely be from injuries received last night. When he was brought in, he could still talk a little. Just a few words, and he was very anxious to get them out."

"It would help me a lot to know what they were," Jack said. He knew he was about to be told, but he had to make an official request. Ethics were involved and he wanted to give Lindholm full justification for anything he might say.

"Since grievous assault was committed, I'm giving you the required report, verbally. I'll put it in writing later."

"Go ahead," Tallon said.

"All right. Councilman Sullivan was brought in a little after eleven; the details are in the files outside. Before he was prepped, he made a statement. He said that he had been assaulted by four men, all young and bearded. He definitely identified them as members of the Dharmaville community. He had in his hand a piece of jewelry, if that's the right word, he had seized from one of them. I put it in a glassine bag and sent it over to your office."

"I got it," Tallon said. "I've already identified the owner."

Lindholm looked surprised at that. "You certainly worked damn fast. Now, there's something more that so far no one knows other than myself and Mrs. Prince, the emergency nurse who helped me last night. You know her: she's the heavy-set, fiftyish gal who's usually on nights. And a helluva good emergency nurse."

"I know her," Jack confirmed. "And I've good reason to know how able she is."

"Of course, I'd forgotten. The point is, Jack, sick and beaten up as he was, Sullivan lied—I'm certain of that. He may not have done it deliberately; people that are badly traumatized sometimes come up with some weird things. But Sullivan was clear and specific, as much as his condition permitted. He said that the four men had knocked him down only after a hard fight, and that all four of them had then kicked him."

"He said all that?"

"Yes. Not all at once, but in bits and pieces while we were undressing him and getting him set on the table. He repeated everything two or three times, as if he wasn't sure that we understood him."

"And Mrs. Prince witnessed all this."

"She did. After Sullivan was taken upstairs, we discussed it briefly. We both heard the same statements and we agreed that they couldn't be accurate. Granted, as I said, that Sullivan may have thought that they were."

"What are the odds on that?" Jack asked.

Lindholm worked his lips for a moment. "Possibly ten percent, no more. I think he was deliberately lying, even in his condition. You know how fanatical people can get sometimes."

"Hell, yes. Go on."

"Here it is in summary: Sullivan was attacked by only one person; I'll cover all bets on that. Someone who had a fairly short round weapon, such as a small piece of metal pipe an inch in diameter or less. He was hit four times with that, by a right-handed man. He certainly wasn't kicked as he claimed and the groin injury he complained of doesn't exist."

"Are there any signs that he fought back?"

"No—there are no marks on his knuckles, or anywhere else, to suggest that he put up a fight. Nothing under his fingernails that could be human blood or tissue."

Tallon drank the rest of his coffee. "Why would he do a thing like that?" he asked. "Lie, I mean."

Lindholm relaxed his professional manner, since he was no longer speaking as a physician. "That's your department, but it's widely known that he had it in for the people at the community. Maybe he's convinced that it's a sex colony. It's possible that after he got hit he decided to blame it on them. However, that doesn't explain the object he had in his hand. Can you handle that angle?"

Before Tallon could answer, the phone on the desk rang once, very briefly. Lindholm picked it up and listened. He spoke a brief acknowledgment and then hung up.

"Sullivan?" Jack asked.

Lindholm nodded. "You've got a murder case," he said. "That makes Sullivan's last statement a dying declaration, and you know how heavy that will be in court."

Tallon said what they both knew. "The very strong legal presumption is that a dying person will speak only the truth. Normally a dying declaration is almost unbeatable."

"Agreed," Lindholm said. "But in this case I'm prepared to take the stand and swear on medical evidence that he lied in his teeth."

CHAPTER 3

It was the first murder that Whitewater had had in years. A decade before a raging housewife had seized a gun and shot her husband in the midst of a violent quarrel. She had listened to a gossipmonger who had convinced her that he was having an affair with his secretary. Later, in the cool calm of a court of law, she had learned that the story had been baseless. She had pleaded guilty to second-degree murder and had been sentenced while she had wept for the man she had killed.

This time it was different: there was no ready suspect to confess and a severe challenge faced the small Whitewater Police Department. At Jack Tallon's request both Dr. Lindholm and Nurse Prince kept silent concerning the victim's statements. Despite this, the bony finger of suspicion tended to swing in the direction of Dharmaville. The community had been established for some time, but it had never been fully accepted.

Tallon put virtually his whole department to work on the case. He called in his senior sergeant, Brad Oster, and appointed him to coordinate the investigation. To assist him he assigned his detective, Ned Asher, and Officer Walt Cooper. Cooper, in particular, was sure to welcome this assignment as a break in the normally dull routine. Tallon knew that of all of his men, Cooper was the one most likely to give in to boredom. He had yet to learn that in police work the sudden need for action could erupt literally at any moment.

Oster's job was to keep track of every bit of information, all of the evidence that was gathered, and to tally it all up on an hour-by-hour basis. If holes appeared, he was to see that they were plugged if at all possible. He had been studying police science at home in his spare time and he was ready to take on the duty.

Asher and Cooper were sent to the scene of the incident, which had been blocked off exactly as the training program had specified. There they went to work carefully, taking measurements, rephotographing the site from every angle, and searching minutely for any possible clue. A small audience gathered to watch them, but they did not allow it to distract them from what they were doing.

Officer Gary Mason was detailed to search the immediate vicinity for the murder weapon. He took up his assignment with determination; it was his first opportunity to function as a detective and he was resolved to make the most of it. If the weapon was there to be found, he intended to find it. He took his time and examined every inch of the ground where it might lie.

Officers Ed Wyncott and Jerry Quigley, who had been off duty, reported in and were sent immediately to interview the occupants of every house within a two-block radius of the place where Sullivan had been attacked.

Tallon himself got on the phone to the Spokane Police Department and to the Sheriff's Office to check on any similar MOs that either agency had on file. When both answers came up negative, he put out a statewide bulletin and also notified Roger Lonigan, the Chief Resident Agent of the FBI in Spokane.

At regular intervals he checked with Brad Oster. With notable calm and efficiency, the sergeant had made up charts and was keeping careful track of each step of the investigation. He had prepared a listing of every address where the occupants were to be interviewed and was checking them off as the reports from Wyncott and Quigley came in.

Shortly after one, Asher and Cooper returned. They had completed their routine and had searched carefully for any possible additional evidence. Although their accomplishment was largely negative, Jack listened to their verbal report and gave his approval of what they had done. Then he authorized the removal of the barricades. After that he gave a brief interview to Nancy Snodgrass, the new reporter for the local weekly newspaper. Nancy was starting out well and she had just been appointed stringer for the largest paper in Spokane.

At one forty-five Tallon left for his appointment at Dharmaville. He had not had any lunch or time to think about it, so on the way he hit a fast-food drive-through and finished his trip with a hamburger in one hand and a milkshake held between his knees. He drove a little slower while he ate so that he would be finished when he arrived. Just before he turned into the community's driveway, he crumpled the waste paper he had left into the empty milk cup and put the whole thing out of sight in the glove compartment (which was a helluva name for that particular space in a police car).

A young woman was waiting to meet him. She was very simply dressed and her hair was loose so that it seemed to flow across her shoulders.

"I'm Chief Tallon," Jack told her. "I'm here to see your swami—by appointment."

"I know, sir," the girl answered. Her voice was unexpectedly low and well modulated. Those three simple words made Tallon glance at her again; she was obviously a cultured person. "May I ride with you?" she asked. "We have a little ways to go."

"Of course." Jack reached over and opened the right-hand passenger door.

The girl got in. "Why don't you call me Hannah," she suggested. "I have a Sanskrit name now, but it might give you some trouble."

"Hannah is just fine."

"Good. We have to take the road up the hill. Swami has his home there."

As he started up the narrow roadway that had been graded only as much as was necessary, Tallon turned the title "swami" over in his mind. He assumed it was a mark of respect for a kind of teacher in India. In the past a number of fake swamis had turned up in police reports. Some of them had been crooks working a variety of con games, some had been fortune-tellers, and one had sold a supposed miracle medicine. He remembered reading about a teenager who had been proclaimed a "perfect master" by his followers; they were keeping him in Cadillacs as partial compensation for his teachings. The Dharmaville swami was an American, a fact which might make his use of the title subject to question. Then he remembered that the man had studied for a long time in India, which could make a considerable difference.

Hannah, sensing his mood, said nothing until Tallon asked, "Was the swami upset when he was disturbed?"

"Not at all, sir. After you came here this morning, Narayan went to Swami's private retreat. Swamiji was in deep meditation, but when he became aware of Narayan's presence, he said to him, 'Something important has happened. Please tell me what it is.' That was all."

"I'm looking forward to meeting him," Tallon said. After that he gave his full attention to his driving as the narrow road continued to climb. When he reached a level area, where there were a number of geodesic domes of different sizes, Hannah pointed toward one of them. "Swami lives there," she said.

Narayan was waiting at the door to let them in. For a moment Tallon wondered if he was expected to take off his shoes, then he decided against it. He was ushered into a scrupulously neat room that took up a good section of the dome and invited to sit down. As soon as he did so he had a slightly odd feeling: he was definitely indoors, but the blue painted dome so high over his head gave an illusion of unexpected space. "Swami is on the phone," Narayan said. "He'll be with you shortly."

Four minutes later the swami appeared. Tallon had subconsciously prepared himself for some kind of a mystic, definitely not for the sort of man he stood up to meet. The swami could have been in his early fifties, but he seemed a much younger man. He was an even six feet, well muscled, and dressed in a good-quality sports shirt over a pair of light tan drill slacks. In contrast to his two disciples, both of whom had shed their plain leather sandals, he had on a pair of thoroughly presentable street shoes. He wore a beard that was neatly trimmed and his hair was well cut. There was nothing visible about him to suggest his unusual calling.

"Chief Tallon," he said as he extended his hand. "Please accept my apology for this morning. If I had known, I would have been at your disposal immediately. I hope that Narayan did everything he could for you."

"He did, Swami," Tallon answered. "My apologies for breaking up your period of meditation."

The swami sat down. "Meditation is a little like eating, Chief Tallon. We normally indulge ourselves at certain times, but no great harm is done if it has to be postponed, or perhaps missed altogether. Now I understand that Councilman Sullivan was attacked and badly beaten last night, and that our people are under suspicion."

His host's forthrightness caused Tallon to take a second or two to shape his response. "Substantially that's true, Swami. In particular, he had a piece of jewelry in his hand when he was found. I understand that it belongs to Narayan."

The swami nodded. "The ankh is definitely his, though how it came into Mr. Sullivan's possession we don't know."

"Swami, were you acquainted with Mr. Sullivan personally?"

The swami looked up quickly. "You used the past tense," he declared.

His host might indulge in meditation, but Tallon noted that he was not likely to miss too much that was going on. "Mr. Sullivan died of his injuries this morning," he said.

The swami looked toward Hannah. "Perhaps you'd better tell them," he advised.

In response the girl got up quickly and slipped out the door. A few seconds later, the swami explained. "We live by the yoga philosophy here: one of the basics is the brotherhood of all humanity. We know how opposed Mr. Sullivan was to our community, but in his time of need we've been holding a prayer service for him. You recall the Beatitudes."

Although he knew that it was not charitable, the news of the prayer meeting upset Jack a little. With his policeman's mind he had been hoping for a quick and easy solution of his case because the ingredients were all there: a group of irregular people, ample opportunity, and a strong motive. Plus, of course, a piece of hard evidence in the form of the Egyptian cross. The knowledge that at least some of the people of Dharmaville had been praying for Sullivan shot his easy theory down. And if the case came to trial, that piece of information would be bound to have a considerable effect on the jury.

He considered the possibility that it might be a bluff and then discarded it; the way it had come out precluded that idea. Also he accepted the fact that the swami, whatever his leanings, was nobody's fool.

"You realize," he said, speaking easily but carefully, "that I'm now investigating a particularly brutal murder. The surface facts are simple: Councilman Sullivan was fatally beaten last night and the only solid clue up to this moment is the ankh he had in his hand. Narayan has freely admitted that it is his. On that basis alone I'd be justified in detaining him for questioning."

"That's quite true," Narayan agreed. "You're welcome to question me here, or I'll accompany you to your office. I've already told you that I didn't attack Sullivan. Also, I don't believe that any of our people here did either, despite what he tried to do to us. You can call that a formal statement, if you like, and I'll sign it."

"Can you account for your movements last night?" Tallon asked.

"Yes, very definitely. If it comes to that, I'll give you a full statement with the names of witnesses."

That was good enough for the moment because Tallon did not want to push any of the Dharmaville people too far too soon. Complete alibi checking would come in due course.

He changed the subject. "How often do any of your people drive into Whitewater?" he asked.

"Only occasionally, I'd say. Some go into the markets on a more or less daily basis to buy supplies and food we can't grow ourselves. Tea, for instance. They normally use the supermarket at the south end of the city. Also they buy medicines if they are needed, dry goods, and hardware. It's our policy to buy locally whenever we can."

Tallon shifted to another angle. "If no one from here attacked Mr. Sullivan, can you suggest who might have done so?"

Narayan sidestepped that one neatly. "That's asking me to accuse someone of murder, Chief Tallon, and I'm not about to do that. I have no idea who might have attacked the councilman. I don't even know if he was robbed."

"Since we're here together," Jack continued, "I'd like to check further into that cross you made."

"I've been waiting for you to ask that," Narayan said. He glanced at the swami who was paying very close attention. "As I told you, I made it before I came here. I used to wear it regularly. After I found the path I had been searching for, I put it aside. I have an old bureau in my room. The bottom drawer is for things that I don't expect to need for some time; I seldom open it. I put the ankh in there and that is the last I saw of it until you showed it to me."

"How long ago was that?" Tallon asked.

"A little more than a year, give or take a month or so."

"Who has access to your room?"

"Anyone who wants to come in at any time. We have no locks on our doors here."

"Outsiders could come on your property . . ." Jack began, but Narayan cut him off.

"We do have many visitors, some who come to stay here for a while. But for anyone who doesn't belong there to go into our living areas unobserved isn't very likely. Also, none of us keep valuables in our rooms, such as money."

The swami added to that. "We have an old hotel safe in our office; all of the resident members have a lockbox there."

Satisfied with that, Tallon pulled out a small notebook. "Swami, I have some requests," he said. "Insofar as you can, please try to establish where all of your people were last night, say from ten to eleven. That includes any visitors you may have had. Also, I'd like a summary covering the use, or nonuse, of your available cars during the same period."

The swami nodded. "I'll do my best," he promised.

"Do any of your people customarily walk into the city, or ride bicycles?"

"No, that would be a seventeen-mile round trip at the least on foot, and we don't have any bicycles that I recall. However, I'll verify that. Is there anything else?"

"Later I may ask you for a roster of all of your people here. I presume you have records."

"Certainly—if necessary. I would like to point out that much that is on file is restricted. Since I am an ordained spiritual leader, I cannot break certain confidences. The roster, if you need it, is open to you."

Tallon hesitated for a moment and then decided to be frank. "I understood that the word 'swami' more or less meant 'teacher.' "

"That's true; I believe that 'rabbi' has the same connotation. Like a rabbi, I perform marriages and discharge other religious duties. Sometime when you are free, I would be most happy if you would have dinner with me and we can talk about it. Since we are now in your jurisdiction, it would be mutually beneficial, I believe, for us to have a line of communication."

"That's a very good idea," Tallon agreed, "and I accept with pleasure." He tore a page from his notebook. "Meanwhile, here is what I am asking from you."

The swami took the slip of paper, but did not glance at it.

At that moment an idea came to Tallon. He considered it for a second or two and then made a decision. "Could we speak privately for a moment?" he asked.

Narayan excused himself with no evidence of taking offense.

"What I'm about to say," Tallon began, "is in confidence—the same kind of confidence that I extend to other members of the clergy. I ask that you don't repeat it."

The swami spoke calmly. "You may rely on that."

"Very well. This hasn't been made public because it might be harmful to your community, but when he was brought into the hospital for emergency treatment, Mr. Sullivan stated clearly and more than once that he had been attacked by four men. He definitely identified them as members of Dharmaville."

"Did he mention any names?" the swami asked.

"No, he did not."

"Then he must have been remarkably perceptive to know four of our members when he had never met them, bearing in mind that we don't wear distinctive dress of any sort."

The swami paused for a moment, either to think or to allow his point to sink in.

"Swami," Tallon said, "you can save me some time and perhaps materially help a murder investigation by answering one question."

"Suppose you ask it."

"I assume that you have some knowledge of the backgrounds of all of your people. In a place built on trust, as this one is, you'd have to do that. I'd like to know if any of your members, or constituents here, has a criminal background. I'm not concerned at the moment with petty theft or juvenile infractions, but in such things as murder, rape, armed robbery, arson—you understand what I mean."

"I do understand," the swami answered. "I'll answer your question, but I'd appreciate it if you would this time respect my confidence as far as your duty allows."

"I'll do my best," Tallon promised.

"At present we have about a hundred and fifty people here. Three of our young women have been rape victims, including Kumari, whom you met. Ninety-eight percent of our members have clean, unquestioned backgrounds to the best of my knowledge. That leaves three others. Of these, two are on parole, reporting to me. There is a judge who knows of our work and who has confidence in some of the things we accomplish. The third person has a record of several misdemeanors before he was tried for a felony. The jury returned a verdict of not guilty."

Tallon was very careful with his next remark. "Swami, I realize that any subsequent conversations you have had with that individual are privileged. I accept that. But since he hasn't been named, I'd like to ask if, in your opinion, he is being rehabilitated."

"I will only answer that in a general way," the swami said. "If I were not convinced that he is overcoming his problems, he would be off our grounds before morning."

"What was the original charge, rape?"

The swami shook his head. "No," he answered. "Before he came here, the person in question was accused of being a mugger. The charge on which he stood trial, and of which he was declared innocent, was felonious assault."

CHAPTER 4

At four that afternoon Jack called a meeting of his entire department. Sergeant Wayne Mudd, whose turn it was to be on patrol, sat near the door in the event he might have to answer a call. Francie, who was not a sworn member, remained at the front desk to handle the telephone and the radio; sometimes sheriff's units in the vicinity would contact her on the Whitewater frequency. Even Mary Clancy, the nurse who had been sworn in as a reservist, was present.

The only person absent was Officer Gary Mason who had been assigned, some hours before, to search for the murder weapon. Asher and Cooper reported having seen him while they were conducting the on-site investigation, but they had been occupied with their own duties and hadn't noticed where he had gone. It was suggested that he might have taken time off for a meal, which he was certainly entitled to do. Tallon was slightly annoyed that Mason was not present, but there was a good chance that the young officer would walk in at any moment. With that in mind, he got down to business.

"As you all know," he began, "most murders are walk-throughs—cases so simple that the solution is obvious. The domestic quarrel is a favorite, as is the mercy killing of someone incurably ill. I don't want to go into all that now. What we have on our hands is a first-class homicide with no immediate suspects and no clear motive."

Because Tallon encouraged his men to use their heads, Brad Oster did not hesitate to interrupt with a question. "Chief, I thought the motive was pretty clear: Sullivan was giving that religious community, Dharmaville, a very hard time. And there's the looped cross that definitely comes from there."

Tallon was by nature an informal person. He put one foot up on a chair. "You're perfectly right that there is a clear motive visible there, but is it a motive for homicide? You have to ask yourself that. Also, and I want you all to remember this, the first motive that appears in a problem homicide like this one is not necessarily the right one. Unless we get a break that resolves the whole thing, we're going to have to do an in-depth investigation. The first seventy-two hours after a killing are the most important, so we can't wait to see if someone is going to come in and confess. And if someone does, we still can't accept the confession until we check it out. Has anyone seen Mason, by the way?"

There was no answer to that.

Tallon went on. "I'm going to give out some assignments. From now until we wrap this thing up, we'll all be working double shifts: twelve hours on and twelve off. That includes me. There is another route: I can admit that we can't handle this one and call in the sheriff to take it off our hands. He has homicide experts and everything else. It's our jurisdiction, but he has overriding authority."

"To hell with that," Sergeant Hillman said. There was a general murmur of approval.

Ned Asher, the plainclothes detective, also asserted himself. "It's our baby and, unless you say differently, we'll rock it."

Tallon flushed slightly, gratified that he had that much *esprit de corps* on his side. "Let me say that I agree with that," he said. "We'll give it our best shot. If we can't pull it off, then I'll have to ask for help. Now for the assignments. First, we'll try to keep at least one car on patrol, as usual, because we still have to protect the community. I'll try to set up four hour shifts on that so that no one gets stuck for too long away from his added duty.

"Ed Wyncott and Jerry Quigley will work together on a background of Councilman Sullivan. What I specifically want is a forty-eight-hour history of the man just before his death. And I want it literally hour by hour. I want to know everything he did, whom he saw or talked with, where he went, every detail of his life during those hours. Don't assume a thing, such as presuming that at three in the morning he was asleep. Check it out so that every one of the forty-eight hours is covered. If you hit something that requires you to go back in time, do it. Talk to every single person who even saw Sullivan during that period. Am I clear?"

"Every possible detail," Quigley confirmed.

"You've got it. If you need any additional authority, see me. If you uncover anything that is in the least way irregular, you are to inform me at once, day or night."

"Uniform or plain clothes?" Wyncott asked.

"Your choice," Tallon answered. "As of this moment, every one of us is working detectives—robbery/homicide."

His officers were mature men, but he sensed the small charge that went through them as a result of that statement.

He turned to Sergeant Oster. "Brad, you'll continue to keep track of every phase of the investigation. Because you'll be the one man seeing all of the evidence as it comes in, keep a very sharp eye open for the least indication of anything unusual. We once caught a killer in Pasadena because he switched his brand of mouthwash."

"Will do," Oster responded. He said it calmly, but Tallon knew how sincerely he meant it.

Tallon turned next to Sergeant Hillman, his radio expert. "Ralph, I want you to head up a team of yourself, Gary if you can find him, and Mary to do a complete background on the swami out at Dharmaville. Mary, I know you're busy at the hospital, but we may need a female on this one and you'll have to be it."

"That's fine with me," Mary answered.

"I want to know everything there is to know about the man. Check his record. Get all you can about his purchase of their land. In particular, find out if he is entitled to call himself 'swami' and exactly what that title means. You may have to dig some of that out in the Spokane library. Do whatever you have to, to get the information."

He stopped for a moment, but no one had anything to say.

"Next, I've got a big job for Ned Asher and Wayne Mudd. The subject is Dharmaville. Find out all that you can about it: when it was founded and where, before it came here. I want all the background you can get on the organization itself. It had to be in existence for two or three years at least before it could be strong enough to buy more than eight hundred acres of land, and it had to have a good credit rating. Check into that. Find out who loaned the money and on what terms."

Wayne Mudd had a question. "Some of that might be a lot easier to get if we could talk with the people out there. How about it?"

"Talk to them, of course," Tallon answered. "They know that there's a murder investigation going on and so far, at least, they have been cooperative. Whatever they tell you, double-check it at the source. If you need any authorizations, I'll get them for you."

"Good enough," Asher said.

Tallon turned to Walt Cooper who was waiting expectantly. "Walt, you and I will be working on fill-in wherever we're needed. Some of the time you may have to go it alone because I still have the department to run and that job isn't going to get any easier. For openers, there's a man out at Dharmaville called Francis MacNeil, a.k.a. Narayan. They rename a lot of their people. I want a complete check on him from the day he was born. He claims to have been both a policeman and a corporate attorney. Interview him if you want to, but keep your guard up because he's pretty sharp. He has no alibi for the time of the beating and the Egyptian cross the victim had was made by him and is his property. He claims that someone took it out of a drawer in his room, time unknown. He says that he hadn't seen it for months."

"Perhaps someone saw him wearing it," Cooper suggested.

"Good—check that angle and every other that you can. If he's sleeping with any of the girls up there, I want to know which ones and how often."

Cooper actually smiled. "If he was a policeman, there's a background check on him on file. I'll get that and everything else that I can."

Tallon was pleased. "Good. Now, I know that, with the exception of Ned, you haven't been working detectives. If you get in a corner and don't know where to go from there, come and see me. We'll work it out together. Don't be afraid to ask for help. One more thing: I want the interviews Ed and Jerry are doing completed before anything else.

Check every single occupied house within a two-block radius of the murder scene and talk with every resident or visitor ten years of age or older. If you happen on anyone who might have been passing through the area at the right time, get their story. That goes for everyone; we need a witness badly."

He stopped because he couldn't think of anything more to say. The tension was a little too thick, he sensed it and forced a quip. "If any of you investigators runs across Mason, tell him to report in."

It was feeble, but it was enough. He got a mild laugh and a good way to conclude the meeting. Since it was already late in the day, Walt Cooper volunteered to take out the early evening patrol assignment. He left the station in the one unit that the Whitewater Police Department would have out in the city during the night to come. Jack went back to his office to sign his mail and to take care of some of the other things that demanded his attention.

He was at it for more than an hour, vaguely aware that he was keeping Francie overtime and not letting that fact disturb him. Police work was frequently demanding of sworn and unsworn personnel alike. Crime was not a forty-hour-a-week proposition; neither was keeping it under control.

At twenty minutes to seven Officer Gary Mason pushed open the front door and came in. His uniform was muddy and the shine that had been on his shoes had been completely obscured by grime; his tie was loose. Tallon had never seen him in such sloppy condition.

He laid a short length of metal bar on Tallon's desk. It was the type of rod commonly used in re-enforcing concrete. "There's your murder weapon," he said, in as common a tone of voice as he could manage. "I'm sorry it took me so long to find it, but it was in a drainpipe under the road about three blocks from the scene."

Tallon admitted to himself that he was impressed. Mason had been sent to do a job and he had stuck to it until he had succeeded. "How did you locate it?" he asked.

Mason was clearly so tired he could hardly stand on his feet. I just kept looking," he answered. "It was my first assignment as a detective, and I didn't want to blow it. I just examined every place that it could possibly be. It was almost in the middle of the drain, under the center of the street, and I had a time getting it out. I couldn't help handling it, so any prints have probably been destroyed."

Tallon looked up at him quickly. "You did a superb piece of work finding it at all," he said. "Don't blame yourself for what couldn't be avoided." He looked again at the piece of metal and saw the dark brown stain visible at one end. That was almost a relief because it meant that Mason wasn't in for a crashing disappointment. "That kind of surface probably won't take prints anyway," he added. "And those marks certainly look like bloodstains to me."

"They are," Mason said. "Before I brought it in, I stopped by the hospital and showed it to Dr. Lindholm. He confirmed that it's blood, all right. He also told me that it fits the marks on Sullivan's body."

There were many things Jack wanted to say, but none of them would form themselves into words. He had a second important clue, and the location where it was found provided a third. It was a major step forward. He looked at Mason again, and for a moment envied the youthfulness of his face. "Did Dr. Lindholm take a sample of the dried blood?" he asked.

"Yes, sir, he did. He's going to type it."

"Good. Now go home and get yourself some rest. You've earned it."

Mason managed a controlled grin. "See you in the morning," he said.

Tallon let him go without telling him about the assignment he had been given. There would be plenty of time to do that later, and he was pretty tired himself.

Officer Walt Cooper reported in promptly the next morning and then set out on his assigned task. Tallon excused himself from going along. There had been a major domestic disturbance during the night and the wife was in the hospital with a possible concussion. The interrogation of the husband was about to begin and that had priority. It was understood that Tallon would handle that himself; no one else in the department was qualified for that kind of work.

As he drove down the highway, southward toward Dharmaville, Walt Cooper had many thoughts buzzing through his mind. For some time he had been planning to resign from the Whitewater force, largely because of the unvarying routine and the lack of any real action. He had put out some feelers for a lateral transfer to another, larger department, but he had run into a hard obstacle: he had not graduated from any recognized police academy and that, apparently, was a basic requirement.

It was true that when the new chief had come to Whitewater things had picked up a little. The training program that had been instituted had shown Cooper one thing: how far he still had to go to become a full-fledged, professional police officer. But under Tallon he was learning new things every week, and in time he might be able to submit experience in lieu of the formal training he had never had. He knew that he was definitely getting better at his job, and in that he found some genuine satisfaction.

He reminded himself that he had just been given an important assignment in a major murder investigation. The thing that TV was always calling Murder One. All right, there were eight officers in the department, not counting the chief, so he had a much better than 10 percent chance to be the one who would uncover the vital clue, the one who would solve the case. And if he did, he knew that Tallon would not rob him of the credit. The new chief supported and backed his men, and that meant a helluva lot.

He swung out and passed a slow-moving truck with crisp efficiency. In a sense he was play-acting for his own benefit, but he liked what he saw. He remembered that Frank Smallins, who had been a several-times-passed-over sergeant on the Whitewater force, was now Chief of Police in River Falls, and everyone knew that it was Tallon's recommendation that had gotten him the job.

Cooper straightened himself a little behind the wheel and began to think like a cop. Maybe this would be *his* chance. If so, he was ready to make the most of it.

Swami Dharmayana, dressed in a long robe, sat near the center of the large blue geodesic dome that was his home and, when he so desired, his retreat from the rest of the world. On the north side the pattern of triangles that made up the dome was largely filled by glass so that there was a panoramic view over the fields and rolling hills of the Pacific Northwest.

Because the dome arced so high overhead, the feeling of being enclosed was greatly diminished. The central room of the dome seemed to be half indoors, half outdoors, and the illusion affected almost everyone who was invited inside.

Seated on the floor, in front of the swami, was a small group of his followers. They were all residents of Dharmaville and most of them were on the community's council. Kumari was there, as was Narayan. Next to them sat Shanti, who was the most advanced of the swami's disciples, and Benoye who was well over sixty. To represent the newer members, Santosh had been invited.

The whole group was silent, waiting for the swami to speak. Outside, the sound of gently running water added its quiet music to the stillness and made it even more potent by its invisible alchemy.

"My dear friends," the swami said, "I have asked you to come because we now face the most serious challenge we have ever been called upon to overcome. You know how many years we worked to accumulate, little by little, the funds we needed to establish this community, and the months we spent looking for the proper place to locate it. Then at last, thanks to God's blessing, we were able to take possession of this property and to open it for our true spiritual purposes.

"Once we were here, it was not easy to stay here, for there were many calls on us that we did not foresee. Our mortgage is a crushing burden and meeting it is a fresh crisis every month. The cost of building supplies, of food, and everything else that we have to buy outside has risen to the point where it is more than three times what we had planned on when we first signed the deed for this property.

"I have hoped that we would find friends in the nearby residents, and in the city of Whitewater, but this has been very slow in coming. We are suspect because we follow the teachings of yoga and of the masters from India. If we were a community of Catholics, or a Protestant church school, we would have been readily accepted, but the great truths that inspire us are still rejected, through ignorance, by almost all of those who live around us."

"That will change," Santosh said softly. Because he was new, and intensely dedicated, he was silently forgiven for interrupting the swami in the midst of his thoughts.

"I was about to propose that we open a small shop on the highway, in Whitewater, to sell some of our arts and crafts," the swami continued. "Now I think it best that we wait on this until the murder of Councilman Sullivan has been solved and we are found free of blame. Meanwhile, we must expect that we will be harassed and interrogated by the Whitewater Police, and later by the sheriff's department or other agencies that may be called in.

"So I wish to set out what I think best for us to do. If you do not agree, I ask that you tell me so and give your reasons. That is why you are here. We are sure to be asked many questions. We should answer those that are fair and reasonable as best we can. Questions as to our faith and religious practices are not a proper part of the investigation, but it is possible that if they are asked, we will be able to make it a little clearer why we are here and what we are striving to accomplish. Do you agree, Benoye?"

The older woman lifted her head without the least show of anxiety. "Yes, Swamiji, I agree. If I may, I suggest that there are some things that are confidential that have nothing to do with the murder and these we should keep to ourselves."

The swami nodded his approval slowly and with dignity. "I was about to speak on that next. Our private affairs are our own. I am protected as a religious leader from answering unwelcome questions. If you are asked any, or any member of our family, please refer the matter to me. I shall deal with it." He paused and tossed a loose fold of his robe over his right shoulder. "I do not need to tell you what things may be said and which should be kept to ourselves."

"I will call a meeting of the full membership," Narayan said. "We should all gather as soon as possible. But I am sure that, in the meantime, none of our members will talk of things they know to be our private business."

"That's a very good idea," the swami declared. Perhaps unconsciously he sat a little straighter and his inner strength could be sensed by all those present. "We have worked and struggled too long to make this possible," he continued. "You, as well as I, know that if all of our undisclosed information were to become known to the city council and the police of Whitewater, we might find ourselves in a very uncomfortable position."

Narayan rose to his feet. "I will call the meeting at once," he said.

CHAPTER 5

When Officer Ed Wyncott came to work the following morning, he found his assigned partner, Jerry Quigley, patiently waiting for him. Quigley had dressed very neatly in a coat and tie.

Wyncott realized immediately that he had committed a tactical error by choosing casual attire. "I'm going home to change," he said. "I'll be back in twenty. Meanwhile, suppose you call Mrs. Sullivan and set up an appointment. For this morning. Don't let her put you off; you know what the chief said—time is damn important right now."

Quigley was not anxious to make the call, but it was his obvious duty, so he agreed and went to look up the number. On the way he passed the open door of the chief's office and saw that Tallon was already at his desk. He tapped and entered.

"You said we could ask for instructions," he said. "Ed and I are going out to see Mrs. Sullivan this morning, in civvies. Would it be all right to represent ourselves as detectives from the department? It might go over a little better."

"Why not—it's the truth," Tallon answered.

That helped a lot. Quigley located the number in the directory and then went into one of the few private offices that the Whitewater department could boast. He shut the door and dialed.

The phone was answered by a teenaged male voice. "I'd like to speak to Mrs. Sullivan, please," Quigley said. He did his best to sound agreeable and authoritative at the same time.

"She isn't taking any calls now."

"This is Detective Quigley of the Whitewater Police Department. My partner and I are investigating Mr. Sullivan's unexpected death. It's very important that we see Mrs. Sullivan as soon as possible this morning."

"Wait a minute." There was the sound of a phone being put down. During the next few seconds Quigley congratulated himself on his choice of words. He had almost said "murder," but "unexpected death" was a great deal better.

The youthful voice came back on the line. "What's your name again, please?"

"Quigley. Detective Quigley of the Whitewater Police."

"She says that, if you must come, you can now but please keep it short, will you?"

"We'll do our best," Quigley promised. As he hung up he was glad that he had checked with Tallon about the use of the word "detective." That reminded him of something else; he almost ran up the short corridor to the front desk where he told Francie about his temporary change of title. If anyone called back to check, she would be prepared to cover.

Ten minutes later Ed Wyncott was back, dressed in a dark suit and with a sober tie knotted over a plain white shirt. Quickly his new partner briefed him on what had happened during his absence. "Let's take one of the marked cars," Wyncott suggested. "It'll look more official."

"We'd better, since that's all we've got," Quigley answered. "Incidentally, this is the first time that I've ever worked with a partner."

"Me too," Wyncott said. "So let's go out and solve this damn case. Shall we, partner?"

"Right, partner!"

The drive to the Sullivan home did not take very long. It was in one of the better parts of Whitewater, but not in the genuine high-rent district. As he drew up before the residence in his new role as a detective, Ed Wyncott noted that it was moderately well maintained, the grass and shrubbery were neatly trimmed, but there were two or three signs of minor neglect. One downspout had come loose and had not been replaced. Also, the house was overdue to be repainted by at least a year. The concrete walkway had a small broken area that should have been repaired and, since Sullivan had been a builder, Wyncott considered all that to be a little surprising.

The door was opened by a girl who appeared to be about eleven. She was red-eyed from crying, but she seemed in possession of herself. "Yes?" she asked.

"I'm Detective Quigley," Jerry told her. "From the Whitewater Police. This is my partner, Detective Wyncott. We're expected."

"I know. Come on in." She turned her back and led the way through a small foyer into a well-furnished medium-sized living room.

"Wait here," the girl said.

As she left, Quigley glanced at his new partner and reached a silent understanding. Since he was the taller, and wore glasses, he would start the questioning. Wyncott had very light blue eyes that detracted a little from the strength of his features. Both men remained standing until Mrs. Sullivan came into the room.

She was not what either of them had expected. Although it was still relatively early in the morning, she was dressed in a simple, but clearly expensive outfit. She was a tall woman with a narrow, almost aristocratic face. Her high cheekbones were emphasized by her blond hair which was drawn severely back and fastened in a bun at the nape of her neck. Few women would dare to wear their hair like that, Quigley knew. He glanced at her nails and saw that fresh polish had been applied. He also noted the dark circles that shadowed her eyes and read the tension that was still very much in her.

"Please sit down," she invited. Her voice was practical, but also carefully cultivated.

As soon as she was seated, Jerry Quigley started the conversation. "Mrs. Sullivan," he began, "I'd like to express our sincere sympathy and that of our whole department."

"Thank you." Her words said just that, and no more.

"Since Mr. Sullivan was the victim of a violent attack, you understand that his death is a police matter."

"Of course. Ask me what you have to."

Jerry carefully took out his notebook. It was a fresh new one he had drawn from stock that morning.

"There are several detectives working on this case, Mrs. Sullivan. Our particular job is to put together a complete record of Mr. Sullivan's movements during the last forty-eight hours of—before he was attacked."

"I can't see any possible point to that," the woman said, a tinge of anger in her voice. "Mr. Sullivan lived an absolutely blameless life and there is nothing whatever for you to find out." By the time she finished speaking, she was clearly hostile.

Ed Wyncott stepped in. "Let me explain why we do this," he began in an even, quiet tone. "In most cases of this kind, something that occurred during the last forty-eight hours of a victim's life had a direct bearing on his death. Our only purpose is to catch the person or persons who attacked your husband. I'm sure you want to help us accomplish that."

Mrs. Sullivan was not mollified. "You know perfectly well who attacked Mr. Sullivan. If you want to find the people who killed him, go out to that sex colony he worked so hard to clean up. It's obvious that they became violent when someone decent went after them. That's where your murderers are!"

Wyncott surprised himself with the way he handled that. "Some of our detectives are out there right now, because the chances are very good that your husband met someone, or took some other innocent action that brought violence down upon him. By knowing just what Mr. Sullivan did, and whom he saw, we can help put together the proof that we need to make the arrests."

Grudgingly, Mrs. Sullivan saw the point. "Well, all right," she conceded. "On Monday and Tuesday Mr. Sullivan went to work as usual. He was frequently out of his office to meet with buyers and to show his properties. Monday night he worked late and didn't get home until after midnight. That wasn't at all unusual: he was negotiating for some new property and the owners were reluctant to sell. His secretary can give you the details. He was home as usual Tuesday evening. On Wednesday morning . . ."

"We understand," Quigley said quickly. "We won't take up any more of your time now, but may we have your permission to make some routine checks into Mr. Sullivan's affairs? If it becomes necessary."

"If you must."

Ed Wyncott got to his feet and Quigley followed suit. "Thank you very much, Mrs. Sullivan," he said.

"Will you be coming back?"

"It's hard to say at this point, but we will bother you as little as possible."

On the way back to the station Quigley managed a satisfied smile. "You certainly handled that coming back part very neatly," he said.

"And you got her consent to check into Sullivan's affairs. We didn't need it, but she'll feel better because she was asked. But did you notice one thing?"

Quigley, who was driving, kept his eyes on the road. "If you mean that she didn't offer any explanation at all why her husband was out on the street late at night, well away from his office, and in a not-too-good neighborhood, yes, I did," he answered.

Sergeant Ralph Hillman had on his uniform, not so much to display his rank as to show that members of the police force were on duty and guarding the city, should anyone be interested. Gary Mason, who had been assigned to work with him, showed up in his best sports outfit which he saw as befitting his new role as a detective. When he caught a glimpse of Hillman on his way in, he went to the rear of the small department and put on his own uniform without regret. He was only twenty-four years old and the authority that it symbolized, and the responsibility, still meant a great deal to him.

As soon as he reported to Hillman, the sergeant sat down with him to lay out a plan of action. "You know our assignment: to run a thorough background on Swami Dharmayana. Have you ever worked on a background check before?"

"No," Gary admitted.

"As a sort of standing rule, interviewing the subject is one of the last steps in the process—not the first. One reason is that few people being investigated know it, and we don't want to tip them off."

"I see," Gary said.

"So let's start at the library. It's small, but it may have something we can use. Then we'll check on spiritual communities, yoga, and whatever else that's related in Spokane. He may even have published something himself that we can dig out; Books in Print will tell us. As soon as we find out his real name, we can check on the sale of the property to him or his organization."

"If we look up the real estate records, won't that give us his real name?" Gary suggested.

"That's certainly possible. Now let's get going."

The Whitewater Municipal Library was housed in a single storefront in the small downtown area. Although not wide, it was quite deep and housed a good many books in near perfect order. The skill of a professional librarian showed in three special displays near the front: one of recent additions, one specifically on child care, and the third devoted to popular sports. A half-dozen people were in the library; two of them were seated at a table loaded with bulky reference works.

The sight of the two uniformed officers brought the librarian from behind her desk. "Can I help you, Ralph?" she asked.

"Yes. Sarah, do you know my partner, Gary Mason? Mrs. Weintraub."

The librarian smiled. "Gary comes in quite often. What do you need?"

Ralph Hillman lowered his voice. "This is very confidential, Sarah.

We're looking into the background of the swami out at the religious community."

"You mean Dharmaville; Swami Dharmayana."

"Yes. Have you anything that will help us?"

The librarian kept her voice down too, but she had a prompt answer. "We have a lot. When Dharmaville opened, a man named Narayan, or something like that, presented the library with a full set of the swami's books—eight of them altogether. One of them is the swami's autobiography."

Gary let a slight note of excitement tinge his voice. "Do you know if it's in?"

"I'm quite sure that it is," the librarian said. "Let me get it for you without too much fuss." She walked down the stacks and returned shortly with three books in her hands. "Here it is," she told them. "I brought two others by him that might help. Just take them with you and return them when you're through."

Gary took the books and stole a look at the one in the middle. The portrait of a bearded, but well-groomed, man was on the cover. "He's an American, you know," Sarah Weintraub said. "He's been in a few times; a very gentlemanly person."

Gary nodded as he noted the title: *The Path of Love*. It sounded faintly pornographic to him, but that was not his immediate concern. During the short drive back to the station, he checked quickly through the pages. "It's all here," he said, reveling in the find. "His whole life story. We'll have to check it out, but this makes it easy."

"I hope so," Hillman responded.

When Walt Cooper arrived at Dharmaville, he followed the small signs to the office. There he was met by a young woman in her early twenties who wore an old-fashioned dress and had her hair pinned back in the style of another day. To complete the picture, she had on a pair of granny glasses. The aura of virginity clung very close to this girl.

When she spoke, her voice was thin and a trifle high in the bargain. Despite all this, she managed to put some warmth into her greeting. "Good morning, sir," she said. "I am Bhakti. How may I help you?"

Walt Cooper had never been in Dharmaville before and the idea of using a name like that upset him slightly. He realized in time the need to play the game, and he did his best. "Good morning," he replied. "I'm Officer Cooper of the Whitewater Police."

The girl took that unblinking. "Then you wish to see Swami?"

Cooper tried his best to think of her as a girl despite the outfit she had chosen to wear. A nice, datable girl. He gave her his best smile and hoped to brighten her life a little with some attention. "Actually I came to see Mr. Narayan, if he's free."

The girl who called herself Bhakti smiled back and revealed that she was potentially datable after all. Presumably she had some other clothes. "I wish I'd known," she said as though she meant it sincerely. "I could have saved you a trip. Narayan is in San Francisco. He handles most of the business affairs for our community. But can I help you in any way?"

"Perhaps," Cooper answered, a little cautiously. "You probably know that we're conducting a murder investigation."

The girl put her hand across her breast in a gesture that might have been in the repertoire of Sarah Bernhardt. But despite that, Walt Cooper took it as quite sincere. "Is Narayan in any trouble?" she asked, her voice tight with concern.

"No, not at all, as far as I know," Cooper hastily reassured her. "I just wanted to get some information."

The girl got up like Meg in *Little Women*. "Please sit down," she invited. "I may be able to help you. Would you care for a cup of tea?"

It was in character: if she had said "coffee," Walt Cooper would have been aware that something was out of tune. "No, thanks," he replied, "but let's talk a little bit. You understand that I don't want to pry, but there are some things we have to find out."

Bhakti came from behind the small counter and took the other of the two chairs that made up the sparse furnishings of the reception area. "Swami has told us we are to cooperate completely," she said, without once suggesting that any limitations had been imposed on that policy. "So, please, what is it you wish to know?"

He decided to try an easy one first. "What is Narayan's real name?"

"That depends on what you call real," Bhakti answered. "We all think of him as Narayan, and so does he. Before he earned that name he was Francis MacNeil."

So that checked out. "I heard that he was an attorney."

"Yes, he still is. He does our legal work for us."

"Is he a member of the bar in Washington?"

"I think so; I know that he is in California. He worked there a while, as a lawyer."

"Do you happen to know who for?"

Bhakti nodded and named one of the nation's most impressive conglomerates.

"That's big-league stuff," Cooper commented. "If he worked for them, as a corporate attorney, he really must be good."

"He certainly is," Bhakti agreed.

"He told Chief Tallon that he was formerly a policeman."

"That's right, too."

"Can you tell me anything about that?" When he sensed a certain hesitation, Walt was verbally fast on his feet. "Please understand, these are things I have to ask. They'll go into my confidential report. They won't be made public unless it's absolutely necessary." That wasn't the entire truth, but he could take steps to protect any real confidences she might give him.

Bhakti folded her hands in her lap. "You're sure you wouldn't care for some tea? We have some very good Darjeeling—from India."

"Now that you've asked me twice, yes," Cooper answered. He didn't care for hot tea at all, but if it would make the girl more comfortable, then she might be willing to talk even more.

Bhakti got up with a certain grace and retired into what was apparently an anteroom. She came back within a minute or two with a small tea service on a tray. It was very plain but functional.

With careful movements she poured out two cups and then handed one of them to Cooper. He took it silently and spooned in some sugar when it was offered to him. His hostess took hers plain.

"Narayan was a detective, and a very good one," she said as though there had been no interruption. "He was with the Los Angeles County Sheriff's Department."

The policeman in Walt came forward. "What did he work? Burglary? Robbery/homicide?"

"Missing persons, I think. He was on the Marsha Stone case for some time."

Walt Cooper raised his teacup to his lips to cover his expression. The disappearance some years before of one of the cinema's newest, and most talented, actresses had been covered heavily for weeks, and at intervals for months after that. It had been a little like the Patty Hearst case: Marsha Stone had been reported seen in hundreds of different places, but she had never been found. Walt Cooper could not honestly tell himself that he remembered the names of the detectives who had been publicized as having worked on the sensational case, but MacNeil could well have been one of them. She had disappeared from her beachfront home in Malibu; nothing had been taken from her home and there had been no suspicious circumstances. Except for the fact that she had just signed a contract that had put her at the very peak of future stardom.

No body had been washed ashore, her financial affairs had been in order, and she had left no shattered romance behind her. She had simply vanished. It had been one of those things, like the unsolved killing of Elizabeth Ann Short—the Black Dahlia.

Various relatives had come forward to claim what she had left behind her, but the Court had ruled that she was not legally dead and would not be for several years. Although her attorney's relationship with her had been privileged, he had testified under oath that he had had no foreknowledge of her disappearance and no instructions to follow should such an event occur.

All this came back to Walt Cooper who had been avidly interested in the more exciting aspects of police work since his early teens. Invisibly the man now called Narayan rose in his esteem because he had actually worked on the case. Furthermore, if he had had such an important assignment, his own tracks should be very easy to trace.

He finished his tea. "I'd like very much to discuss that case with him some time," he said.

Bhakti shook her head. "Normally he won't talk about it at all," she said. "Of course, if it's official, then he might."

Cooper knew immediately that it would not, and could not, be official, but he decided to try anyway. In his mind the idea of Narayan as the guilty man receded well back. Narayan was a professional detective of high stature; such men are not normally murderers.

"He is in San Francisco, you say," he repeated.

"Yes, and we don't know when he will be back. It is something to do with our property here."

That could be a new lead and Cooper snatched at it eagerly. "Are you in any danger of losing it?" he asked. He made it sound as innocent as he could.

"I don't think so. If that were the case, it certainly would have come up at our community meeting. And it hasn't." She refilled his teacup, a favor he did not especially want. Cooper felt that he had gotten about as much out of the interview as he could and he was anxious to start in on some of the generous leads he had been given—including the reason why Narayan was in San Francisco. That ought not be too hard to find out.

"Officer Cooper . . ." Bhakti began.

"Walt." She, thank God, wasn't a murder suspect.

She gave him a thin little smile that was warm nonetheless.

"Walt, then. We like to go by first names here—until we earn a better one. Swamiji has instructed us we are to help the police department in every way. And we will. But there are some things we don't like to talk about—such as our reasons for coming here, in some cases. You understand?"

"I think that's true of everyone," Cooper said.

"Please, you will protect us as much as you can? We know that the people of the city haven't accepted us—don't trust us. But we are good people. There are just some things we'd like to keep to ourselves."

At that moment she was human and warm—another person who was reaching out to him. He put down his cup and held out his hand. After a few moments she put her smaller one into his.

"Bhakti . . . what does that mean, by the way?"

"Devotion."

"Are you one of the nuns they have out here?"

"Not yet. Later, I think."

"All right, Bhakti, I'll give you a promise. I'm a policeman and I have a job to do. Now it may be that when I get back it will be all over and the killer will be in custody. Or it may be that before this murder investigation is over, a lot of well-kept secrets will be out in the open. But I will promise you this: I won't do anything to harm your community, or your swami, if I can avoid it. You have the right to your own life style. Is that fair enough?"

"Walt, do you really mean that?"

He smiled at her, because he really liked her then. "I must and I will do my duty. But I won't go beyond that."

"You promise."

"I promise." He wondered how in the hell he had gotten himself into such a position with this girl. It was his job to lead the conversation and to keep control of it at all times. Somehow, she had taken it away from him.

As she sat across from him, she took off her glasses and put them on the tea tray. Reaching behind her head she released her hair so that it cascaded down. At that moment the plainness was gone and she was quite lovely. With a few cosmetics, some suitable clothes, and one or two other things, she could be a very nice date. Cooper wondered if she were doing this in order to suggest just that. He was about to test that theory when he remembered that Dharmaville and all of its people were for the time being suspect. Dating one of them in the midst of the investigation would be totally out of line and he knew it.

She looked at him with wider and more intense eyes. "I'm taking you at your word, Walt. Because you might have found out some way. Please don't tell anyone that I'm Marsha Stone."

CHAPTER 6

Sergeant Wayne Mudd was still trying to get used to his new dignity in the department. When he had flunked out of the LAPD academy, he had assumed that any chance for a police career was gone forever. On the second time around, he had made it in the state of Washington, where the stress was not quite so great, and he had found a job with the Whitewater Police Department. There he had applied himself so well he had earned his sergeant's stripes and, with them, the goodwill of every one of his colleagues.

Now he was to enter into a new phase, that of being a detective. Ned Asher was the official department detective, but that in the past had largely been a titular designation. However, Ned had had the experience, such as it was, and therefore he was the best partner that Mudd could have hoped for, apart from the chief himself. The assignment they had been given was a stumper: the entire population of Dharmaville, apart from the swami and Narayan.

Wayne chose his wardrobe carefully. Since Ned always wore plain clothes, a uniform would be out of order. Dharmaville, however, was a very informal place; he doubted if there was a tie worn anywhere on the premises. He decided on his very best sports shirt and a pair of neutral slacks. The shirt was worn outside, which covered his weapon neatly, and still looked informal. When he arrived at the station, he discovered that Ned Asher had opted for a coat and tie.

No matter: Mudd doubted very much if the Dharmaville group paid much attention to what people wore. Ned's personal car was often used for police business and was fitted with an official radio; that made it the logical vehicle for them to take. As he got in beside his new partner, he tried to visualize the spiritual community that was still much of an unknown factor to most of Whitewater. "I assume the man we want to see is the personnel director," he said.

"If they have one," Asher agreed as he pulled out of the lot. "Some-one out there must keep track of their people."

"What if they tell us that their records are confidential?"

"Then we come right back and get a court order. Judge Howell will certainly go along with that."

An unhurried fifteen-minute drive took them to the entrance to Dharmaville. Just inside there was a sign that showed the way to the reception center and to the main office. Since the office was clearly what they wanted, Ned followed the indicated road for a quarter mile to a very plain and unpretentious building. It had been freshly painted and there was a small parking area marked out for visitors. Ned snapped off the radio that had been silent anyway and, with Mudd at his side, walked up to the door.

It was opened for them by a young man in blue jeans and an ordinary work shirt. His hair covered his ears, but he was clean-shaven and clearly personable. He was well built on an average-sized frame and moderately fortunate in his appearance. Ned surmised that he got along very well with the girls.

"Good morning, gentlemen," he said. "Is this an official visit?"

"Yes, it is," Ned answered. "I'm Detective Asher; this is my partner, Detective Sergeant Mudd."

The young man showed some surprise. "From the Sheriff's Department?" he asked.

"No," Mudd answered. "From the Whitewater Police."

"I'm sorry; I didn't know they had detective sergeants locally. Please come in. I'm Santosh." In the somewhat cluttered room that was the main office, he gathered three assorted chairs and set them in a group. "Sit down," he invited, "and tell me what I can do for you."

When they were settled, Mudd took the lead. "We'd like to see your personnel director, please."

"We don't have a personnel director; we keep the list of our permanent residents, and also the temporaries, here in the office."

"May we see them, please?" Asher asked.

"Yes. Normally we don't allow that, but Swamiji told us to cooperate in every way possible with your investigation. You are here about the Sullivan case, aren't you?"

Ned nodded. "That's right, and it's good to hear that we won't have to go to the bother of getting a court order. For openers, how many people do you have here?"

Santosh drew his eyebrows closer together. "I can't give you an exact figure offhand," he said. "Most of our population is permanent, but there are others who come and go. Some try out our way of living and decide that it isn't for them. Also, we have quite a few who come here for periods of a week to six months or more."

"How about a ball park figure?" Mudd suggested.

"As a guesstimate, a hundred and eighty, counting all heads."

"And how many of those would be permanent residents?"

"A hundred and forty—plus. We have some temporaries now who may decide to join us permanently."

Ned Asher put in a question. "Have any of your people left here since the murder?"

Santosh was prompt with his answer. "No, definitely not. Swami himself asked about that, so I know."

Asher took up the conversation once more. "On the night of the murder, were there any special events here? Any meetings or parties?"

Santosh was very quick in grasping the nature of the question. "You're thinking of alibis," he said. "Yes, we did have a meeting, and a lot of people were there. We had some films of India that we all wanted to see—our whole philosophy here is based on Indian teachings."

"I'd like to see India some day myself," Ned said, "so I understand. How many people would you say attended the meeting?"

Santosh paused a moment to think. "It's hard for me to give you an accurate estimate, because I never thought of counting the crowd. But at least a hundred and fifty. Probably more. Almost the whole community was there."

"Could you, for example, give us a list of the people you saw at the meeting?" Asher asked.

Santosh nodded. "That would be easy. Probably twenty people or more who are good friends of mine. I'm a little new here and I don't know everyone by name yet, but I know enough to give you a pretty good list."

Mudd had thought it out. To be sure of his ground, he asked a question. "Is it possible that there is anyone here at Dharmaville who hasn't been entered in your records yet? What I'm asking is, is the list you have here a complete one?"

Santosh was entirely comfortable with the question. "I'm sure that it is because any people who didn't belong would be noted pretty promptly. Basically we're a close-knit group; we're all friends and even the temporaries are well known to almost everyone. When anyone checks in, a card is made out and they're put in the file even before they're given a place to stay."

Mudd spoke openly to his partner. "Ned, we'll need a copy of the complete list of residents. Then we can conduct some interviews and identify as many as we can who attended the meeting."

Santosh got up. "There's no problem there," he said. "We keep a current list typed up. I'll make a copy for you."

He pulled a folder out of a filing cabinet, took it to a duplicating machine, and fed in a series of pages. When he had finished, he stapled the copies together and handed them to Mudd. "Please, as far as you can, keep that information confidential," he asked. "We'd appreciate it very much. Some of our residents aren't anxious to advertise where they are."

"Understood," Mudd told him. "Now, how many of these people can you identify as having been at the meeting? People who not only showed but who stayed to see the films."

Santosh took the list and read down with some care. With a pen he ticked two or three names on each page. When he had finished, he had identified twenty-four people. "I'm prepared to swear that all of those people were at the meeting and stayed to the finish. In fact, no one at all left that I saw."

"That's a big help," Asher acknowledged. "Now can we interview some of these people?"

"Of course," Santosh answered. "You pick the names, and I'll take you to see them."

At four-thirty that afternoon, Jack Tallon called a meeting of his full staff in the courtroom directly adjacent to the police department in the same building. Except for Mary Clancy, the full roster of sworn personnel was present. No one was on patrol, but Francie remained at the front desk to take any calls. If a policeman were needed, Jerry Quigley was in uniform and ready to respond.

"We'll go down the list," Tallon began, "because it will help if we all know how far each team has gotten. Ralph."

Hillman was ready. "Gary and I secured a copy of the autobiography of Swami Dharmayana." He opened his notebook in his hand. "The swami's real name is Arthur Van der Water. He comes from an old eastern family that's been in the chips for generations. He went to Harvard and graduated magna cum laude. He took his master's in the School of Business and a PhD in ethics and comparative religion. His family had him pegged to become an Episcopalian minister; his grandfather was one. Instead he took off for India. He'd become interested in Indian religious thought and he wanted to learn more about it firsthand." Hillman stopped and looked around quickly. "This is his account, of course. Tomorrow we'll start checking on it."

"Go on," Tallon said.

"He stayed in India for almost ten years. That didn't sit well with his family; they thought he was throwing away the best part of his life. He states that in yoga he found the thing he wanted. By that time he'd learned the language, so he entered an ashram run by a famous master, or guru. His last five years in India were spent there. At the end of his term he 'was accepted into the brotherhood of the initiates' and given the title of Swami Dharmayana."

Tallon was impressed. "He's certainly no fake if he did all that. Tomorrow check on those Harvard degrees. He should be in Who's Who. See what you can find out about his training in India and the man who was his teacher there. That will be harder, but give it a shot."

"Will do," Hillman said.

Tallon turned to Cooper. "Go ahead, Walt," he invited.

Cooper had his notebook ready too. "My subject is Francis MacNeil, no relation to Marion McNeil, the councilwoman. MacNeil is a.k.a. Narayan at Dharmaville where he's the second in command. I went there to interview him, but he was in San Francisco. I talked with a girl there known as Bhakti. MacNeil's father is Negro and his mother is a Hindu. He's a member of the bar in both Washington and California, in good standing in both places. He does most of the business and legal work for the community. Before he joined it, three years ago, he was a corporate attorney for one of the biggest conglomerates on the West Coast. Before that he was a deputy sheriff in Los Angeles County."

"Any idea why he left?" Tallon asked.

"I was just coming to that, and here's where it gets interesting. He was working missing persons when he was assigned to the Marsha Stone case. She's the screen star who suddenly disappeared just after her career had really gotten started. The case went on for some time; Stone was never found. While MacNeil was working on it, he graduated from law school and passed the bar. I talked with the captain who was in charge of the case. He stated that MacNeil had been a real comer in the department and was expected to go all the way. His resignation had come as a complete surprise and when interviewed he refused to give any reason."

"Have you any ideas?" Tallon asked.

Cooper flushed slightly before he replied. "Not yet. That's all I was able to dig out in one day."

Jack was quick to mollify his man. "That's plenty, and all good solid stuff. Obviously Mr. Narayan is someone we're going to have to handle very carefully." He turned to his one regular detective. "Ned, what did you and Wayne learn about the people at Dharmaville?"

Asher had been waiting his turn. "We started off with a good break. On the night of the crime there was a meeting at Dharmaville that began a little before eight and lasted until after eleven. Most of the people were there. We talked with a Mr. Santosh who gave us a current roster of all the Dharmaville people. We saw him take it from the records and I'd say it's valid."

"We've been asked to keep the list as confidential as possible," Wayne Mudd added.

Asher continued: "We spent the rest of the day working on the list. Mr. Santosh checked the names of twenty-four persons he specifically remembered seeing at the meeting. We interviewed seven of them, and from them got some more names. There were many duplications, but so far we've identified eighty-nine people who were at the meeting, assuming that the witnesses are credible. Tomorrow we'll continue the interviews."

"Did you get good cooperation?" Tallon asked.

"The best," Mudd answered. "We were told that the swami had passed the word to cooperate fully. Either they're doing just that, or else . . ."

"Or else what?"

"Or else they're a damn skillful bunch of liars up there."

CHAPTER 7

For reasons best known to himself, Jack Tallon ended the meeting at that point. He informed everyone that Francie had assignment sheets covering the next three days. The city had to be patrolled and plans provided for meeting any police emergencies that might arise. Gary Mason changed into uniform and took out a unit to cover the first shift. Once in a while it was possible to have a brief meeting of the whole force, but any prolonged absence of patrol cars would be very promptly noted and that was a risk Tallon was not prepared to take. Murder or no murder, he had a city to protect and barely enough people to do the job under normal circumstances. Sergeant Brad Oster took over as watch commander and at least the appearance of normalcy returned.

Tallon went to his office where Ed Wyncott and Jerry Quigley were waiting for him. He dropped into his desk chair and slid his feet out of his shoes. "You asked to see me," he said.

Jerry opened the conversation. "You told us to come to you when we needed help."

"Have you hit a snag?"

"I think so," Jerry answered, using his gift for understatement. "We started out by calling on Mrs. Sullivan and asking her permission to look into her husband's affairs. We both thought that it would be better if we asked her first rather than just get the necessary court orders and go ahead without telling her."

"From a PR standpoint, I agree," Tallon said.

"She wasn't enthusiastic," Quigley continued, "even when we pointed out we were trying to catch the person who killed her husband. She's very much got a mind of her own. From her place we went to the bank to check on deposits, withdrawals, and whatever we could get on credit cards. Even though Mrs. Sullivan had given permission, the bank manager wanted a court order."

"Judge Howell will issue one, certainly."

"He will; we've already asked him. But now comes the sticky part. Sullivan had a secretary, a Mrs. Harriet Riley, and she's the problem."

As if on cue, Ed Wyncott took over. "She wouldn't tell us a God-damned thing. We approached her very properly and explained what we were trying to do. She absolutely refused to cooperate. We suggested that she call Mrs. Sullivan, but she wouldn't do that. Then Jerry asked her if she knew what was going to happen to her job now that Sullivan's dead. She told us that that was none of our affair. She said that she was a confidential secretary and nothing that we could ask her was going to get an answer."

"That's unusual," Tallon commented.

"That's how it struck us," Wyncott continued. "We pointed out very carefully that Mr. Sullivan is now dead and that the main consideration is catching the person who killed him."

"Maybe the answer is another court order," Tallon suggested.

"We discussed that, Jack, but we agreed that if we got one, she'd answer just what it required and no more. And that won't do. She's one of our basic sources; Mrs. Sullivan even suggested that we see her, but she won't give an inch."

"So what you're getting at, you want me to tackle her."

"If you would," Quigley said. "We made a deduction and wonder what you think of it."

"Let's hear it."

"Mrs. Riley's boss is dead and there's no prospect of anyone to take over the business. He didn't have a partner and we both feel on the basis of what we have so far that he wasn't doing overly well. Now maybe Mrs. Sullivan called her and told her that her paycheck would keep on coming, but that still wouldn't account for her stone-wall attitude."

"Your idea is," Tallon supplied, "that someone got to her and put the clamps on."

"Exactly," Quigley agreed. "Nothing else makes sense. Confidential secretary or not, she has to know that an investigation is inevitable. Tax reports will have to be made out. And, sooner or later, she's going to have to find another job. So why give us such a hard time during an official call?"

Tallon rotated back and forth a few degrees in his chair while he considered that matter. Then he sat up straighter. "All right," he announced, "I'll have a crack at her in the morning. You keep on with your reconstruction of Sullivan's last forty-eight hours."

"We'll need her to do that," Wyncott pointed out."

"I know, but you can follow up at the bank, check what he may have taken out of the library, and go after the credit-card angle. You'll have plenty to do. See me about noon."

As soon as Wyncott and Quigley had gone out, Walt Cooper appeared at the door. "Are you busy?" he asked.

The question itself told Tallon a lot. "No," he answered. "Come in, sit down, and tell me what's on your mind."

Cooper carefully closed the door before he seated himself at the side of the desk. Tallon turned to face him and nodded that he was ready to listen. He kept himself relaxed and informal to encourage Cooper to unburden himself.

Somewhat to Tallon's surprise, his man came directly to the point. "While I was out at Dharmaville today, I was given a piece of information. In general terms, a rather well-known person is staying there and doesn't want it known. It would make the newspapers if it came out. I was asked to keep it totally confidential. As far as I can tell, this piece of information has nothing whatever to do with our investigation. My own inclination is to respect that person's wishes and keep my mouth shut, but I don't want to fall down in my duty." He stopped there: the story had been told and there was no need to state that he was asking for an opinion.

Tallon considered that matter for a few seconds, partially because a too hasty answer might appear superficial.

When he did speak, he was careful with his words. "First of all you're right in line. In police work we're constantly called upon to keep confidences. If we didn't, we'd be out of business. Also, you're doing the right thing in asking me about it."

He stopped and read out that Cooper was with him that far. "For the time being," Tallon continued, "keep the confidential piece of information out of your report. Also, don't discuss it with anyone unless, in your judgment, it will help the investigation. Then see me and I'll decide whether you have to reveal it or not."

"Thank you," Cooper said.

"Now, would you say that you were given that confidential piece of information personally, or as a police officer."

"Putting it that way, personally. But the person who gave it to me was a stranger before today."

"If you feel comfortable about it, I'd appreciate your telling me what it is. In return, I'll agree to keep it fully confidential unless it is no longer possible. And I'll cover you if it ever needs to come to light."

"Is that an order?" Cooper asked.

"No, I'll leave it to your judgment. But I do know how to keep my mouth shut."

"I know you do," Cooper said. "Wayne Mudd is a close friend of mine. He told me how you kept something off the record for him."

It was quiet for a few seconds, then Cooper spoke again. Once more he went to the heart of the matter. "It's Marsha Stone," he said.

Tallon leaned forward and his casual manner disappeared. "You mean the screen star that disappeared—the one MacNeil was looking for when he was a cop?"

"That's the one," Cooper answered. "I told you it would make the papers if it got out."

Tallon slowly nodded his head. "Did you actually meet her—talk to her?"

"Yes."

"Did you recognize her from her pictures?"

"No."

"But she trusted you with her secret."

"Yes."

"I presume she's going by one of their Sanskrit names."

"That's right."

Tallon let those facts sink in. "Her name will be on the roster that Ned and Wayne picked up."

"I doubt it. She's too well known. She may be down by her real name—that is, if Marsha Stone is a screen name."

"I'll tell you what," Tallon said. "First thing tomorrow go into Spokane, check the library and the newspaper morgue there, and see if you can find out what Stone's real name is. Without giving away the show, of course. I'll check the roster we have."

"Will do."

It was getting late and Tallon was tired. Invisibly it had grown dark outside and his stomach was reminding him that he had not eaten in some time. He wanted to go home and see Jennifer, and take his ease in his own living room far away from police matters—unless the phone rang. But his mind was still functioning and an obvious fact stared him in the face.

"So when MacNeil, or Narayan as they call him now, was a cop he spent weeks trying to track down Marsha Stone. Apparently he did find her, after all."

At twenty minutes to ten the following morning Jack Tallon walked unannounced into what had been Wilson Sullivan's office. He had deliberately allowed time for mail to be opened and for the formidable Mrs. Riley to realize once more that her employer was dead and would not be issuing her any more orders. He had formed a mental image of a determined, middle-aged woman who took her duties with the utmost seriousness. And who had a tongue in her head. Mr. Riley, whomever he might be, would not have his sorrows to seek.

Tallon found himself confronted by a slender brunette who was unusually tall, definitely comely, and in all probability under thirty. She looked up at him with no expression whatever on her face. "May I help you?" she asked.

Jack Tallon knew perfectly well that he was what most women would call good-looking. And he was still very much on the right side of forty. He tried his most winning smile without giving away too much. "Good morning," he said. "Are you Mrs. Riley?"

The brunette rose to her feet and Tallon saw that she was at least five feet ten in her shoes, possibly even a fraction more.

"What is it that you want?" she asked.

"I'd like to sit down," Tallon answered. "I'm Chief Tallon of the Whitewater Police." He waited until Mrs. Riley reluctantly did so, then he seated himself in the one available visitor's chair.

"It's quite obvious that you don't require an invitation, Chief Tallon," she said. Her voice was not icy, instead it was expressionless, to match her face.

"I presumed you would extend me that courtesy," Tallon said. He kept his own voice bland. He was about to add to that, but the secretary spoke first. "Two of your officers, or detectives, were here yesterday. I told them that I had nothing whatever to say concerning Mr. Sullivan or his personal affairs. Obviously they told you that or you wouldn't have come here yourself."

"That's all quite right," Tallon said. Then he casually crossed his legs and noticed that Mrs. Riley had a half-filled coffee cup on her desk. He let her note his glance, but she made no move to offer him anything at all.

"For the record, you were the private secretary of Mr. Wilson Sullivan?" Tallon made it a question.

"*Councilman* Sullivan. Mr. Tallon, until things are better clarified, I am not about to give you any information of any kind whatsoever. I trust that is sufficiently clear?" She reached into a desk drawer, pulled out two sheets of paper and a carbon. She made up a sandwich and rolled it into her machine, ignoring Tallon as pointedly as possible.

Very calmly Tallon reached into an inner pocket and took out a document. He unfolded it slowly, got up, and laid it on top of the typewriter keys where it could not be ignored. "Since that is the way you want to play it, Mrs. Riley, I am hereby serving you with this court order. You will note that it directs you to answer any and all questions concerning Mr. Sullivan, *and* his personal affairs, so long as they have a bearing on the investigation of his murder."

Harriet Riley looked at him with an expression of intense determination. "And who is to be the judge of that?" she asked.

"I am," Tallon answered. "If any question arises, then I am to call Judge Howell in his chambers and he will decide whether any particular line of inquiry is proper or not."

Mrs. Riley picked up a phone and punched out a number. When it was answered, she said, "Mr. Cohen, please. This is Harriet Riley."

There was a pause of several seconds, then a voice came on the line. Mrs. Riley was careful to hold the phone close to her ear so that Tallon could not catch a word of what was said at the other end of the line. "Mr. Cohen, I have a man in my office, who came without appointment, and who says that he is the police chief here. His name is Tallon. He has just served me with a court order requiring me to answer any questions he may put regarding Mr. Sullivan's business or personal affairs. That is, provided the information has any possible bearing on his death. Mr. Tallon states that he will be the judge of whether or not his questions are suitable."

She listened for a few seconds, then she read the text of the court order over the phone, including the signature.

Mrs. Riley listened for a good half minute before she hung up. Then she turned to Tallon as emotionless as before. "Mr. Cohen suggested that you come here at two this afternoon when he can be present." She did not say who Mr. Cohen was, nor did Tallon have to ask.

"That's not convenient," Jack told her. This time he put some bite into his voice. "You now have a choice: you can comply with that court order, here and now, or I will place you under arrest and take you to jail." When he had let that sink in, he added to it. "There is a third alternative, and I recommend it. We can go back to square one. I can withdraw the court order in exchange for your reasonable cooperation in our investigation."

"And if I refuse?"

"Contempt of court is a serious charge. Furthermore, it's an open-ended one; Judge Howell can impose any sentence he pleases and continue to reimpose it until his order is obeyed."

"Very well, Chief Tallon. Since it appears I have no alternative, what do you wish to know?"

He was very tempted to ask her outright if she had been the dead man's mistress, but he knew better. Since he had her at least partially broken down, he deliberately made things as easy for her as he could.

"Mrs. Riley," he began, "in any homicide investigation, one of the most important procedures is to trace in the greatest detail possible the last forty-eight hours of the decedent's life. More often than not, that line of inquiry will turn up crucial information. Now, on the Monday before he died, did Mr. Sullivan come to his office?"

Mrs. Riley looked at him as though she were about to challenge him on the councilman title once again, then she apparently realized there was nothing to be gained by doing so. "Yes, he did," she answered.

"And on Tuesday he was here also?"

"Yes."

"And on Wednesday?"

"He was here—for a time."

It was the first crack in the wall; the first piece of information she had given without a direct question. Tallon took out his notebook and sketched a grid. "Do you recall at what time Councilman Sullivan arrived at his office on Monday?" He deliberately gave her that, in fair exchange.

If she noticed, she gave no clue. "At about nine forty-five."

"Was that his usual time, considering that it was Monday?"

"No, he was usually in before that. Between nine-fifteen and nine-thirty."

"Did he say anything to indicate why he was delayed?"

"I don't recall that he did."

"In your opinion, Mrs. Riley, did he appear to be in normal good health?"

"I would say so." For the first time she hesitated, obviously making a decision in her own mind. "I'll have to qualify that," she said. "You will undoubtedly find this out anyway, but Councilman Sullivan suffered from a serious ulcer."

Tallon nodded sympathetically. "I remember his mentioning it at a council meeting. He put three sugars in his coffee and then explained why."

There was a brief awkward pause, then Tallon went back to his questions. "The councilman arrived here on Monday at about nine forty-five. Did he remain here the rest of the morning, or did he go out somewhere?"

"He stayed here until he went to lunch—at about twelve-thirty."

Tallon drew in a line on his impromptu graph. "Did he have a lunch date?"

"Yes, a prospective buyer."

"Do you happen to know where he lunched?"

"Yes, at the Wagon Wheel Barbecue."

"Then I take it that his lunch date did not know Councilman Sullivan very well."

The girl looked a question at him, but did not speak.

"For a man suffering from an ulcer condition, a barbecue restaurant might be the wrong thing," Tallon explained.

She saw that he had made a point. "The Wagon Wheel is very popular," she said. "Consequently Mr. Sullivan did have to eat there fairly often—with clients. He had an arrangement with the management. I always called when he was coming and they prepared something special for him."

"How about the bar?" Tallon asked.

"Mr. Sullivan always ordered a Golden Cadillac. He was served with a glass of light cream, without any liquor. That was a private arrangement he had at several different places."

Tallon considered telling her that she was being very helpful, but decided in time not to press his luck. She was still under compulsion and acutely aware of it. "Do you recall who he lunched with?"

"A Mr. Morganstern. I've never met him."

She was giving information much more freely and Tallon guided her with great care. "He came back alone to his office, then, I take it."

"Yes, at a little before three. It was a long luncheon."

"Now I must ask your opinion, and this is quite important. Did Councilman Sullivan seem pleased when he returned, or did you get the feeling that he might have been disappointed?"

"Am I required to answer a question like that?"

"Probably not," Tallon admitted, "but it would be most helpful if you would."

"Since you put it that way, he was probably disappointed. If the lunch had gone well, he would have said something about it. He always did."

Very carefully Tallon led her on, probing a bit and then easing off with totally innocent questions when he sensed that she might be tightening up. He extracted details concerning incoming mail, and phone calls, that might have had an effect on her late employer's business affairs. He let her tell him several times that he had no enemies at all, that he had been in the building business for some time, and that he had a very good reputation. The moment that he felt she was tiring under his questions, he broke off the conversation and released her. He thanked her with just the proper amount of warmth for her cooperation and then drove to the office of the city building inspector.

He left there twenty minutes later with some very specific information. Wilson Sullivan had started out by building some good quality homes that passed the various required inspections with ease. More recently the situation had changed and his work had become marginal. He had been privately warned twice that he was skating too close to the edge of the building code.

Satisfied, Tallon drove to his office and went inside. It was a quarter to twelve and he was ready to talk with Wyncott and Quigley. He had had the advantage of the court order, but he had also had more than ten years of experience in conducting interrogations.

As soon as he was seated Francie came in, her hands weaving patterns in the air; a sure sign that everything was not as she wanted it to be. "Are you waiting for Ed and Jerry?" she asked, knowing perfectly well that he was.

"That's right."

"Well, they won't be in for a while. Ed said something about something . . . I mean they've hit on something. . . ." She stopped and let her hands flutter to reflect her confusion. "Anyhow, they've gone into Spokane and won't be back until later."

"Thank you," Tallon said. "Bring me in the roster of Dharmaville residents that they got hold of yesterday. Brad Oster probably has it, since he's coordinating all the evidence."

Francie hurried out and came back with it less than a minute later. Tallon dismissed her and then quickly checked the several pages of names. They were in alphabetical order and there was no Marsha Stone among them. In a few cases, only the Sanskrit names were given, a nice method of keeping identities secret if that was the intention. Tallon rather thought that it was, but he admitted to himself that the Dharmaville people were probably justified in concealing the presence of someone who expressly wanted to avoid any publicity for legitimate reasons. Marsha Stone would fall into that category.

He left his office and a little grimly told Francie that he would be at the Hawaiian Gardens for lunch. He didn't especially want to go there because the food, at the best, was undistinguished, but Whitewater was a small place and he knew the value of patronizing all of the local restaurants from time to time.

When he reached the place, there were only two other cars outside. He parked his and taking a hand radio with him went into the restaurant that had once hoped to become the glamour spot of Whitewater. Now the few fishnet decorations and the tired plastic flowers were dust-covered and inert, unable to yield the least hint of the subtropics for which the place had been named.

Tallon slid into a booth and surveyed the frayed menu that had been modified by new prices posted for each item. The dollar and a half luncheon special was long gone and the real choice was limited. He settled for a chow mein plate and then made a conscious effort to relax. His session with Mrs. Riley had taken a lot out of him simply because of the need to watch every move that he made, every word that he spoke. He reflected on the fact that he had gathered a good deal of information and had opened the path for more.

When his food came he ate faster than he should—a fault he had been trying to overcome for years. It was a result of too many quick meals snatched at fast-food stands and eaten on the hood of his patrol unit as he listened with the radio turned up. That was all behind him now, but the old habit stuck.

He was genuinely surprised when Walt Cooper walked in with a grin on his face. "Is it OK if I join you?" he asked.

"Glad to have you," Tallon answered. "You look like you've got something."

"Let me order first," Cooper said, "then we can talk."

As soon as the lone waitress had departed at an unhurried pace, Walt Cooper unloaded. "I just happened to think of something. It wasn't part of my assignment, but when it popped into my mind, I decided to go after it. You weren't around to ask, so I went ahead."

"You've wound up, now pitch," Tallon said.

"OK. You know that for some time the idea of legal gambling in the state of Washington has been coming up. Now it looks like it might be close to passage. However, I remembered reading, some time back, that a compromise had been proposed. Because of the opposition from church groups and others, it was suggested that instead of making gambling legal throughout Washington, it might be authorized in a few scattered localities. One over on the west coast where most of the tourist traffic is, one in the southern part, and one on this side of the state."

"I saw the same thing," Tallon told him. "At the time it was just an idea, no more."

"Well it's more now. On a wild hunch I made some calls and did some checking. Nothing has passed the legislature yet, of course, but the tentative sites have been selected. That's being kept under strict wraps because if the word got out, you can see what would happen to real estate values in the gambling approved areas."

"Don't tell me that you found out!"

Cooper all but smirked. "I do have a few friends here and there. One of them, knowing that this is a murder investigation, gave me some highly secret stuff. All I asked for was the tentative location in this area. And I got it."

"That's damn good work," Tallon said. "I'm sitting down; break the news."

The waitress reappeared at that point and remained long enough to keep Tallon on tenterhooks. When she finally left, Cooper took a mouthful of food. Then, realizing that he had overplayed his hand a little, he talked with his mouth full. "How does the site now occupied by Dharmaville grab you?" he asked.

CHAPTER 8

When the city council met at two that afternoon, Jack Tallon was present by invitation. Since he was frequently asked to sit in, he felt no special concern when he took his usual place near the foot of the table. He would never admit it to anyone, but the death of Wilson Sullivan had resolved the only real problem he had ever found in the civic administration. Otis Fenwell, the elderly city attorney, frequently did not see eye to eye with him, but Fenwell liked to argue for the sake of argument. In most cases he had been willing to listen to reason in the end.

As she frequently did, Councilwoman Marion McNeil sat at his right. Marion had a mind of her own, but it was a good one and she was not afraid to face up to any issue that might arise. Across the table City Treasurer Bill Albrecht had his cost sheets ready in a neat pile.

Next to him City Manager Dick Collins had his hands clasped in front of him on the table, ready to field any questions he might be asked. Fenwell came next; opposite him there was an empty chair. At the head of the table Dr. Arnold Petersen, the still youthful and effective mayor, was ready to preside.

Petersen opened the meeting with the calm, businesslike manner he always used. He was well liked, partly because he delivered a considerable percentage of the babies born in Whitewater and partly because it was commonly known that he gave all of his municipal paychecks to the hospital.

Otis Fenwell asked for the floor and got it. He rubbed a bony hand across his angular features, which was a device he used to gain attention in the courtroom. "We all know that a member of this body was struck down a few days ago," he began. Then with an effort he suppressed his tendency toward old-fashioned oratory. "Wilson Sullivan was a good friend of mine and I think we should pass a resolution deploring his death and offering our deepest condolences to his wife and family."

"I'll second," Marion McNeil said. Everyone present knew that she and Sullivan had almost invariably been on opposite sides of the fence, but death carried with it its own forgiveness.

The vote was taken without dissent. Petersen picked up a typed letter. "How does this sound?" he asked, and read aloud. It was a beautifully phrased expression of sympathy and admiration for the man who had been a council member for such a short time. When he finished, there was unanimous approval. "I'll sign it and send it by messenger," he said.

Once more Otis Fenwell asked for the floor. "Now that that's been properly done," he said, "I want Jack to tell us when he's going to arrest those people from the colony who are responsible for Wilson's death."

Jack Tallon had had enough experience with the testy lawyer to know how to handle him. Basically Otis was a good man, but he held certain prejudices, and unconventional life styles was one of them.

"I'll answer that absolutely straight," Jack said, "with the proviso that what I say is strictly *sub rosa* for council members only."

"Understood," Petersen told him.

"A high percentage of homicides are what we call walk-throughs: there's no doubt as to who did the killing, and why. But sometimes that isn't the case. As of this moment, we don't know either who killed Councilman Sullivan or the motive for his death."

"Come off it!" Fenwell exploded. "You know Goddamned well who killed him: those freaks out at the colony. Furthermore"—he shook a long finger in Tallon's face—"I've got it on good authority that you have a piece of hard evidence that proves it already in your possession."

Tallon kept his temper. "Otis, if you had to go into court with the evidence I have now, you couldn't convict Santa Claus of wearing a red suit. Furthermore, the motive for the killing isn't at all clear. I know as well as you do that Sullivan gave the Dharmaville people a hard time, but that isn't enough provocation to incite murder—not under normal circumstances."

Fenwell dropped his voice with courtroom cunning. "But they aren't normal people. Did you know that some of them even claim to be monks and nuns? It's an outrage even to compare some of those dope-smoking females they have out there to the dedicated sisters who give their whole lives to the church."

Unexpectedly Bill Albrecht was heard from. "Otis, in all fairness, I've got to say that we've never seen any evidence whatever that the Dharmaville people use dope, or allow it on the premises."

He intended to say more, but Fenwell cut him off. "My wife met one of their women in the south side supermarket. She said that she had never been married and that she was a nun. And she had a small boy with her that she said was her son."

Tallon began to lose a little of his calm, but he kept it from showing. "I know her," he said. "Her name is Mary Goldstein and she's a rape victim. The rapist made her pregnant. But rather than have an abortion, she had her baby and kept it. I checked on her story and it's true; I have a copy of the police report on the case in my office."

"Sounds like a gutsy gal to me," Marion McNeil said.

"She is," Petersen said. "Since the matter's on the table, she's a patient of mine and I can confirm what you just heard. Anything more would be a violation of ethics."

"We're getting off the topic," Dick Collins interrupted. "Jack said he didn't know what the motive was. You all knew Wilson and you know he was determined to drive those people out of our city. From where I sit, that's a helluva motive right there."

Marion spoke up. "Jack, one question. Have you found *any other* reason why someone wanted Wilson dead?"

"No," Tallon admitted.

"Another question," she continued. "Was he mugged in the common sense of the term? In other words, was he robbed? You see what I'm driving at."

"Yes, I do, Marion," Tallon answered. "Sullivan wasn't mugged, although he was certainly assaulted. A mugger usually robs his victim, but doesn't harm him unless he resists."

"Wilson would have resisted, you can bet on that," Dick Collins contributed. "He wasn't what you'd call an even-tempered man."

Jack tapped a finger on the table. "All right. For your information only, Sullivan wasn't robbed. His wallet was on his body and he had some money in it. His watch wasn't taken, and it's a fairly expensive one. So the idea that he was a chance victim of a prowling criminal won't hold up."

Mayor Petersen spoke quietly, but firmly. "Jack, without breaking any confidences, I happen to know that one of the people, at least, out at Dharmaville has a record as an accused mugger. Were you aware of that?"

"Yes, I knew that," Tallon said.

"Then have you been able to establish what that particular person was doing at the time that Wilson was murdered?"

"No," Tallon answered. "I can tell you this: we are checking into every person at Dharmaville. So far we have been able to establish sound alibis for eighty-nine persons out of approximately a hundred and forty. The ex-mugger isn't one of them, but our investigation isn't half finished out there."

"Which proves that they don't give a damn who they take!" Otis Fenwell snapped.

"I'm not going to defend them," Tallon countered, "but it is a religious community, whether we happen to agree with their beliefs or not. And there's plenty of precedent for religious institutions acting as rehabilitation agencies. Boys' Town, for example."

"Let me ask this," Dick Collins interjected. "How many more convicted criminals do they have out there? Is Dharmaville a halfway house?"

"I haven't completed a full check on the Dharmaville population," Tallon answered, "but, so far, the man in question is the only one I know of who has been accused of a felony. I'm familiar with the backgrounds of some of their people and those I know about we're glad to have as citizens."

Otis Fenwell was still smoldering. He had frequently voted with Councilman Sullivan and obviously was convinced that the murdered man had had the city's best interests in mind when he had tried to "clean out" the community. "Jack," he began slowly, "it seems to me that you are being unusually soft on these people. I know you're a compassionate man, but there are limits. Also, it's no fault of yours that our police department is small and certainly inexperienced where major crimes like homicide are concerned. I move, therefore, that you be asked to call in the sheriff who has jurisdiction and who has trained people to handle this investigation."

"I'll second," Albrecht said, somewhat reluctantly. Clearly, he was considering the cost.

Mayor Petersen looked down the table. "Jack?" he asked.

Tallon could have blessed him for that, but he was in no mood to be generous. "I don't have a vote here," he said, "but if I did it would be against the motion. I know our department is small, but every man in it is working a double shift and they're doing a fine job. They may be inexperienced in this kind of thing, that's true, but I'm not, and until you decree otherwise, I'm the police chief here. When and if I need the sheriff to take over, I'll be the first to ask for his help. But you have got a police department and we draw our pay because we know our business. It's our jurisdiction."

"I'll call for the question," Petersen said.

As soon as the motion was defeated, Tallon left the council chamber with his temper barely under control.

Ralph Hillman was waiting to see him in his office. The soft-spoken sergeant had been with the department nine years and was the resident electronics expert. He did all of the maintenance work on the radio equipment. The units in the cars were off-the-shelf items, but he had built the station transceiver himself and it was the best one of its size in the state.

As Tallon came in he read the signs, but it was too late to back away. Jack dropped into his chair and made a careful effort to be calm. "What have you got, Ralph?" he asked.

Hillman was very careful to keep things on an even keel. "I'm reporting for Gary and myself; he's out on patrol. I'll be joining him shortly to cover the kids coming out of school."

Tallon nodded, but said nothing.

"We've been checking into the Dharmaville property. The swami is the legal owner under his real name of Arthur Van der Water, but in trust for the Dharmaville Yoga Fellowship. Apparently he was smart enough to do it that way so that if his community didn't work out, he wouldn't be in a legal bind over the land. Because some of the property is unusable, the previous owner sold it to him for eight hundred dollars an acre; I already told you that she made it easy for him to buy it. She accepted a ten percent down payment, so he put down sixty-four thousand, eight hundred dollars. The interest is only six percent, so the swami has to come up with something like three thousand a month to meet the payments."

"What about income?" Tallon asked. He took comfort in the fact that his man was doing a good job; it was a reassurance he could use.

"I was just coming to that. He has a hundred and forty permanent residents who pay eighty dollars a month to live there. That includes food and lodging, which is dirt cheap. Then they have a special deal for families that's even less. He probably takes in between nine and ten thousand a month that way. Then they have a school, they run a small market, and sell their own publications. In addition, they take temporary visitors who pay for room and board plus a fee to study yoga, meditation, and things like that."

He turned a page in his notebook. "The community raises a good part of its own food, which is all vegetarian. I talked with one of the officers at the bank whom I know pretty well. In general terms he told me that the community is paying its bills and has a good credit rating."

Jack sat up in his chair, feeling a little better. Hillman's information was a sound addition to the allover picture that was being built. None of it was spectacular, but much of the best police work never is.

Hillman closed his notebook and looked up. "I have a little more," he said. "About six months ago, a group of the residents out there set up a home-construction business. That was just about the time that Sullivan joined the city council."

"In direct competition?" Tallon asked, just to be sure.

"Yes, exactly. They have a registered architect and good experience putting up their own buildings, so they decided to solicit some outside contracts. They got one for a block of six houses on a parcel of land of about an acre and a half. They're being built out on Meadowbrook Lane."

"East of the college."

"That's right. They underbid Sullivan for the job and he made quite a fuss about it. He claimed they weren't qualified bidders, but they did have all the proper licenses and they're now performing under the contract. I saw the building inspector and he told me that their work is superior. I asked him if that meant better than Sullivan's and he said, 'Yes, but don't quote me.'"

Tallon was definitely impressed, enough so that his mood took a sharp turn upward. "Which explains why he was after the community so hard in the city council," he said. "That's very good work, Ralph. I didn't know about the Dharmaville construction contract, and that could be important."

Hillman stood up to go. "I've got to hit the bricks," he said. "While I'm driving, I'll check by those houses under construction. I just might learn something more."

"Good idea," Tallon agreed.

Officer Gary Mason had been on patrol for more than an hour and a half without an incident of any kind, but he was not bored. As he drove mechanically, up one street and down another, his mind was fully occupied by the sensational crime he was trying to solve. He forced himself to remember that he was protecting the city, and incidentally letting the citizens know that the Police Department was on the job.

There was a rumor that Whitewater might be one of the three areas in the state to be designated a site for legal gambling. If that worked out, then the Whitewater Police would no longer be a small and quiet department, but a very vital one.

When he had covered the center of the city and the three-block downtown area, he turned north and headed up toward the limits. That gave him a chance to drive up the highway in a more or less straight line before he would have to begin weaving his way back up and down the streets where most of the better middle-class homes were located. It was not an area that generated very much crime, but it was good for the patrolling unit to be seen there two or three times a day. It gave a sense of security to the residents, and that was one of the things they were buying with their taxes.

A little north of the city limits he turned around and began to check on the outskirts. The few buildings were scattered and none of them was very important. Two blocks from the main highway he saw a thin column of smoke beginning to climb; someone was apparently burning trash or weeds. Because of the frequent rain there was little danger of a field or brush fire, but he accelerated nevertheless, just to make sure that everything was under control.

Within seconds he knew better.

He saw clearly that the smoke was coming from a corner of a wooden building and that it was gaining rapidly in size and volume. He gunned his car forward and took the mike out of its clip at the same time. He wasted no time identifying himself when it was unnecessary; in quick, careful words he reported the fire and gave the approximate address.

In a matter of twenty seconds he reached the location and saw that the building was indeed on fire. He saw more than that; behind the structure he caught a quick glimpse of a motorbike being kicked into action. Without a moment's hesitation he spun his patrol car off the pavement and headed it directly down the side of the burning house, ignoring the few thin plantings that his wheels were destroying. He burst into the unfenced backyard barely in time to see the motorcycle taking off ahead of him. The rider turned for one quick glance and Mason saw a heavy face almost totally disguised by uncut hair and a wild, unkempt beard. As the rider bent forward, Mason could see that he was solidly built and of much bigger than normal size.

He wanted to radio in, but he needed both of his hands on the wheel as he cut across the open field in pursuit. Twice the man on the bike abruptly changed direction and each time Gary stayed right with him. He did not even have time to turn on his roof lights, but he did hit his siren just in case a sheriff's unit might be in the vicinity and hear it.

Under the training program that Tallon had instituted, and taught himself, Gary's driving had vastly improved; he had learned pursuit techniques that he had not known even existed. He used every bit of his new skill in keeping his wildly bouncing car under control, but despite his efforts, the motorcycle was pulling steadily away. Gary strained his eyes trying to get even a partial make on the license, but he was unsuccessful. To add to his frustration, he knew little about motorcycles and therefore could not identify the make. He had a poor view of the machine; he only noted that there was a metal frame that extended upward behind the rider to protect him in case of a fall. Then, abruptly, the bike and its rider disappeared from sight.

Gary knew that he could never catch the bike going across the semirough terrain, but he had been hoping that the rider would spill and make his capture possible. A sudden obvious drop of the bike gave Gary a fierce hope; he took another violent bounce and aimed straight for the place where his quarry had vanished.

He was almost there when the bike and rider dramatically reappeared, coming out of a deep ditch beside an unimproved road. It had been a deliberate trap and Gary knew it two or three seconds before his plunging car gave one last convulsive shudder and then plunged nose first into the sharp hollow. He felt the impact and the sensation of his safety harness biting into his chest. Then it was suddenly quiet and he wondered if he were still alive.

Within a few seconds he decided that he was. He looked through the top of the smashed windshield and saw the bike and rider escaping up the road. The rider turned once more to look back and despite the distance and his mass of facial hair, Gary felt that he was laughing.

Sudden, uncontrollable rage took hold of him. If he had been on the spot ten seconds earlier, he could have caught the arsonist. As it was, he was still strapped into what had been the newest and best patrol car belonging to the Whitewater police. White steam was escaping from under the hood, the front grille was half buried in the dirt embankment, and the engine had abruptly ceased running.

Perhaps the radio would still work if the battery hadn't been ruptured. Grinding his teeth together in total frustration, he unclipped the mike, pushed the button, and tried to make his voice normal. "Whitewater One," he said.

By some miracle of mechanical survival, he got a prompt reply. Francie's voice came out of the speaker. "Whitewater One; go ahead."

He was so relieved he could have kissed her. "I'm about a half mile north of the fire," he reported. "Near a dirt road. I'm in the ditch and wrecked."

"Are *you* all right?" Francie might be vague at times, but let a real emergency come and she was a pillar.

"I don't know. I guess so," Gary answered truthfully.

"Whitewater One, stand by."

To Gary the next few seconds were dead and lifeless, just like the car that still held him. Then Tallon's clear voice came out of the speaker. "Mason."

"Yes, sir."

"If you're sure you're unhurt, get out of the car and stand by. If anything is broken or feels numb, remain still. The ambulance is rolling."

"I think I'm all right," Gary said into the mike. "I was chasing the arsonist." He remembered suddenly that he was still a cop. "There may be evidence," he added.

"Hang in there, I'm coming. Meanwhile, cut the ignition and turn off the radio."

As soon as the order was given Gary understood. He had needed the radio, but he had forgotten all about the ignition, and he had been taught to cut the fire at once in the event of any kind of a crash. He did what he should have done on his own and then checked his limbs. They seemed to be all right, so he loosened his seat belt and got the door open by throwing his shoulder against it. Gingerly he climbed out and made his way up the soft soil to the surface of the narrow roadway. When he got there he looked back at the car. There were only four, and he had just wiped out the newest and best.

He was too far away from the fire itself to see very much, but red units were rolling up, lights flashing. Considering the fact that the fire department was located in the center of the city, they had made good time.

Another siren cut through the air and he saw red lights coming directly toward him. He waved his arm above his head to show where he was. Within seconds he was aware that it was the hospital ambulance, and with the realization came a chagrin that there was no need for the emergency code-three run on his behalf.

The ambulance pulled up and three people got out: the driver, the regular attendant, and Dr. Lindholm. The doctor strode over to where Gary was standing, glanced at him, and then at the car in the ditch. As he did so, the two ambulance men took out the gurney and prepared it to receive a patient.

"I don't need that," Gary said, a little heat in his voice. He was not going to show weakness, no matter what. "I'm perfectly all right."

"You should see your face," Lindholm told him. "You're on your feet, but I can see mild shock and there may be other things."

"The chief is coming," Gary declared. "I'm not hurt and I'm going to meet him on my feet."

Lindholm might have issued an order, but another car was coming up the road, also in code-three condition. It pulled up sharply and Tallon was out almost before the vehicle had stopped rolling. "How is he?" he asked the doctor.

"Mild shock and who knows what else. I want to check him over."

"Take him." Tallon turned to his youngest officer who was still defiant. "Gary, for insurance reasons I want you to go in and have a checkup. That's no reflection on you, so hop to it."

As soon as the ambulance had left, with Gary Mason reluctantly lying on the gurney inside, Tallon checked over the car. He saw at once that the patrol unit was wiped out, at least for the time being. It had dug hard into the soft dirt of the embankment; if it had been a solid surface, then his patrolman might have been very seriously hurt.

He went back to his car and called the city wrecker, giving directions. The fire, he noticed, was still going strong. There weren't any hydrants in that area and the house was probably doomed. He was grateful that one of his men had tried so hard to nab the arsonist; obviously Gary Mason had not thought at all about his own safety when he had taken up hot pursuit across such unfavorable terrain.

Another unit, running code three against regulations, came up the road and, as expected, Ralph Hillman was in it. "How's my partner?" he asked as soon as he was on his feet.

"Gone to the hospital for a precautionary checkup. Otherwise he seems OK," Tallon answered.

"Then in that case, let's see what kind of evidence there may be here. He was after a motorbike, so there should be some good tire tracks."

That was the kind of thing Tallon liked to hear—first things first. After that there was police work to be done.

CHAPTER 9

Tallon's thoughts were churning as he drove rapidly back the short distance to where the fire department was doing its best against impossible odds. The flames were still strong and coming from every part of the structure. A crowd had gathered, but he noted quickly that two of his men were on hand to maintain control. He got out of his car and almost on the run joined the fire captain. "Any casualties?" he asked, his breath short and tense.

"No, thank God," the captain answered. "Two residents were inside, a boy eleven and a girl about eight, but we got them out quickly."

"Why didn't they get out on their own?"

"They were trying to fight the fire—with water from the kitchen sink. Gutsy kids all right, but they never had a chance."

"You know it's arson."

"Of course. A guy on a motorbike."

Tallon did not stop to ask how he knew that. "One of my men chased him in a patrol car across the fields. He lost him when he went into a ditch."

The fire chief had a tight jaw. "There are times when I could do murder with my bare hands."

Tallon well understood the feeling. "I can't promise you we'll get him," he said. "But we'll give it a damned good try."

"Have you got enough people? With the murder and all."

"No," Jack admitted. "I'll handle this one myself."

He had known automatically that no one else was available. In no way could he afford a personal vendetta, but the arsonist had wrecked his best patrol unit and sent one of his men to the hospital.

He got back into his car and started to drive back to his office. On the way he put out a broadcast to the sheriff's department concerning the wanted man on the motorbike; there was a chance that he might still be intercepted on the highway. He was thoroughly uptight when he strode into his office. There were things waiting for his attention, but he brushed them aside. Using his private line, he called the Spokane Police Department and asked for everything they had on a hairy arsonist on a motorcycle. They would know to try all the possible combinations to see if they could come up with something. Next he called Captain Long of the sheriff's department and gave him the same information.

"We know a lot of hairy motorcyclists," the captain said, "and a good many of them are oversized individuals. Offhand I don't know of any of them who has a reputation for arson, but it could have been a paid hit. We'll do everything for you we can here." Long knew very well that the Whitewater department was overloaded and he expected that Jack would have to ask for the sheriff's help at any time. But whether he did or didn't, he would still get all of the cooperation possible.

During the next hour Tallon conducted an intensive telephone investigation into the house that had been torched. It had been owned and occupied by a Herman Landville and his two children. The man himself was a widower with no police record and no traffic violations for the past three years. He was a driver for a large interstate bus line. His employment record with his firm went back eight and a half years and was a good one. He had no known bad habits, he was above average for reporting in for his runs on time, and had been involved in only one accident during the time of his employment, one that had been determined not to have been his fault. He had only a few friends, and more or less kept to himself, but no one regarded him as unfriendly or hostile. He had no known enemies.

A carefully handled call to the bank provided the information that his finances were in order and the payments on his home up to date. He had borrowed money once to buy a medium-sized motor home, and he had met the obligation promptly.

The real estate dealer who had sold him his home recalled the transaction. Mr. Landville had not had a great deal of money to put down, so his choice of a home had been somewhat restricted. He had picked an older building with a fair amount of property rather than something smaller in a better neighborhood. Only about a year after he had bought the house he had lost his wife. The tragedy had hit him very severely. Afterward he had arranged with a neighbor to look after his children. The neighbor, a Mrs. Savatini, liked him very much and considered him an excellent father. Nowhere did Jack find any connection between the burned-out homeowner and either Wilson Sullivan or the Dharmaville community.

He had just reached that point when Francie appeared in the door of his office to tell him that a Mr. Landville wished to see him. Tallon got to his feet immediately and went out to meet him. Landville, who was waiting outside the counter, was in his driver's uniform. He was an even six feet, well built, and under normal circumstances probably personable. He suggested a man who could take care of himself. He was obviously very distraught, as he had every right to be.

Tallon held the counter door open. "Come in, Mr. Landville," he invited. "I'm anxious to talk to you."

The bus driver walked into Tallon's office and dropped into a chair without invitation. "You're Chief Tallon?" he asked.

"That's right."

"Chief, I don't know who in hell would want to do a thing like that to me." The man was in no mood for any preamble. "I haven't had any fights, I don't owe anybody, and I haven't been messing around with anyone else's woman."

"Where are your children?" Tallon asked.

"Outside in my car. They'll stay there. Chief, we've lost everything—our home and everything that was in it. All the pictures I had of my wife. The kids' clothes and their school books. Everything." He rubbed his hands across his face as if that action would somehow lessen the strain.

"Putting first things first," Jack said, "do you have a place to stay?"

"Not yet. I haven't had time to think of anything. But we'll make out somehow."

"Do you mind answering some questions?"

"No. I guess that's why I'm here."

"A lot of people get very sore over traffic incidents—sometimes very minor ones. You're a professional driver. In the past month or two, have you had any kind of a flap that might have made someone mad? Think hard about that. You drive a conspicuous, easily identifiable vehicle."

"I meet looneys on the road all the time," Landville answered. "So do all the guys. But the company policy is always to give way—and we do. It's very seldom that anyone beefs one of our drivers. Our aim is to get where we're going and we leave the traffic regulation to the cops." He stopped and pulled back into an acute realization of what had just happened to him. At least, that was the way Jack read it.

"Were you adequately insured, Mr. Landville?" Tallon asked. He made it almost a gentle question.

"I guess so. The people who hold the mortgage issued the policy. I don't know about the contents of my house."

"Usually the contents are insured for half the value of the house," Tallon said. "So you might have as much as, say, thirty thousand of protection there."

Landville shook his head. "The house itself wasn't worth sixty, even on today's market. A lot of the value was in the land. I've got a full acre."

Jack let him score the point. "You're right about the land, but I don't see how you could receive less than twenty on the contents of your home. That won't bring back some of the things that were precious to you, but it will help to cover the cost of replacement. If the mortgage holder issued the policy, you can be pretty sure that your house is fully covered."

Landville returned to his first statement. "The thing that gets me: there's no one in the world I know who'd want to burn me out of our home. I haven't had any offers to sell, and I don't have enemies." He paused a moment. "I'm sure of that," he added.

Jack tried to be reassuring. "I'm taking on this investigation myself," he said. "There's one possibility right off."

"I know," Landville said. "Someone just wanted to start a fire and they picked on me. For no reason at all."

Jack nodded. "Now, how can we help you while you're in this bind?"

An unexpected voice came from the doorway. "Perhaps I can answer that."

Tallon looked up, angry. He never wanted anyone to have access to his office, or to hear his conversations, without his knowledge. Just outside the room, dressed in ordinary street clothes, Swami Dharmayana stood with his hands held together in front of him.

The swami was very quick to catch Jack's displeasure. "I beg your pardon for intruding," he said. "I didn't realize. There was no receptionist at the front desk, so I took the liberty of coming in. I shouldn't have done so."

Tallon was definitely not in one of his best moods; too many things had gone wrong that day and his patience had worn through to the breaking point. Francie should have been at the desk, but if she had taken a short break, the swami wasn't too far out of line. He made a hard effort not to allow himself to lose control. "What can I do for you?" he asked.

"I was driving back from the airport," the swami said, very calmly, "when I saw the fire. By the time I got there, the house had been destroyed."

"That's right." Tallon noticed that Landville had stood up, which made an introduction necessary. "This is Mr. Landville, who is the fire victim. Mr. Landville, this is Mr. Van der Water who owns and operates the Dharmaville community a few miles south of here."

If the swami was annoyed by the use of his real name, he was careful not to let it show. "I came here because I knew that someone, some family, was temporarily homeless. I wanted to tell you that we have comfortable guest accommodations at Dharmaville." He turned to the man he had just met. "Mr. Landville, we would like very much to have you and your family as our guests until you can make other arrangements. How many of there are you?"

"Three," Landville answered.

"Please come and stay with us. We can put you up very easily in one of our vacant cabins; they accommodate up to six people. We serve quite good vegetarian meals, also, if you care for them."

As he listened Jack realized that the swami was solving one problem for him, one that he hadn't even had time to consider.

Landville hesitated. "That's very kind of you, sir, but I don't know . . ."

"You understand," the swami added, "that we would like to have you for as long as you wish to stay. We'd like to help mitigate your misfortune just a little, if we may. There's no obligation whatever."

Landville still had trouble; the shock of his loss had hold of him and wouldn't let go. "The kids are in school," was all he could think of to say.

Clearly the swami understood all that as well as Tallon did. "If you have another place to stay, we certainly won't interfere," the swami continued. His voice contained a kind of reassurance Jack could not pin down, but it was effective. "If you don't, let me call down and have your cabin prepared. Your children will be welcome at our school; we have a lot of students who don't belong to our group."

"We don't have any clothes," Landville said, as though he had just become aware of that fact.

"I'm pretty certain we can help you there too. Understand that you won't be asked to take part in any of our community activities unless you want to. And no matter how long you stay, there won't be any bill."

"That's not right," Landville said.

Tallon had heard enough, and he knew without asking that Landville did not have any close friends or relatives to whom he could turn. He pushed over his phone toward the swami. "Make the call," he said.

As soon as his office was clear, Francie looked in. "I'm terribly sorry," she said. "I was away from my desk when he came in, and no one else stopped him."

"It's just as well," Tallon told her. He thought for a moment and then said, "Call Jennifer and tell her I won't be home until late."

"She'll hand you your head," Francie warned. "And you're bushed. Go home and hit the sack."

Tallon got up. "No, I couldn't sleep if I did. Who's down for the early evening patrol?"

"Asher."

That was mildly interesting because Asher was the one man who didn't drive a patrol unit under normal circumstances, since he was the designated detective. "Tell him to knock off," Tallon said. "I'll take it myself."

He went to the back where the lockers were and took out his uniform. From the jacket he carefully removed the insignia that marked him as the chief of police. There was a small lettering to that effect on his badge, but most people wouldn't notice it. Things had reached the point where he instinctively knew that he had to take some action himself, to help lift the load that was pressuring his department so hard. His men were doing splendidly, but he couldn't expect to sit in his office and not lift his own hands to resolve things. He was, after all, the best qualified member of his department and a night on patrol would do him good.

He had forgotten momentarily that he was short one car, but he had three more. Two of them were active frontline units, the third was a backup that had already put in its full life of service, but was held in reserve with its equipment still intact. He took the one remaining good unit, ran the usual check to be sure that all of the special police equipment was in working order, and noted that the gas tank was full, as it should have been. As he pulled out onto the street, it felt good just to be at the wheel, to be doing something out where the action was.

He made his radio check by reporting that he was in the field. The other active unit, driven by Ralph Hillman, would hear him and know that he was there in case he might be needed. Backup was a tremendously important factor in police work and in that category the Whitewater Police Department was weak. He simply didn't have enough men, or enough budget to hire any more, to keep two cars out at all times. The best that could be done usually was to have the watch commander respond from the station, but when that happened, as it very infrequently did, the phones were left uncovered until someone could get in to take over. It was a bad situation, but the only alternative was to call for sheriff's assistance and it was seldom that one of his patrolling units would be close enough to Whitewater to render any prompt help.

He drove first to the scene of the fire. Most of the people had left. The last of the fire equipment, the hoses that had been in use, were being collected. What had been the Landville home was a blackened ruin; two of the four walls were still standing like unburied skeletons, leaning on each other for the time being, avoiding the inevitable. To

Jack it was much more than a domestic fire: it was a major crime that had taken away not only the family's home—it had robbed them of all their possessions. A man, some gasoline, a match, and a getaway on a motorcycle had left this behind. Long years of police experience had taught Jack to keep his emotions under control, but every muscle in his body seemed to tighten when he saw the final result of the arson.

If there was any way in God's green earth he could lay that arsonist by the heels, he was going to do so.

He drove next to the place where the Dharmaville people had a contract to build six homes. One of them was fully framed in; the second had the first wood in place on top of the foundation. Tallon got out and for three or four minutes inspected the work. He was no expert in home construction, but he saw that the foundations were firm and solid, made of concrete that was good quality. The nails had been driven tightly and there was no evidence of sloppy toenailing that he had occasionally noted at other building sites. He concluded that the people who were doing the actual construction work were capable and conscientious; even the necessary warning signs were carefully and properly posted.

As he got back into his car, a new thought was turning over in his mind. The attack on the Landville house had been without any known reason. That left open three possibilities: Landville had been hit for some reason that had not yet come to light, he had been torched by a firebug who had wanted to start something and wasn't particular who his victim might be, or it was a cover-up—a fire started as the first of a series. The second hit might be against an equally innocent target. Then the third would be aimed at the new homes being built by the Dharmaville people. At the very least it would set them way back on their contract, and it could serve as a warning to the rest of Whitewater not to employ the community people for home-construction purposes.

He started up and then switched to the sheriff's number-one channel. He asked if there had been progress in locating the wanted motorcyclist.

The answer came back promptly: nothing yet.

Tallon drove up and down the main street a couple of times; it was also the main north-south highway through town. Somewhat to his disappointment, every motorist in sight was behaving himself and he had no real cause even to issue a traffic citation.

He realized that he was altogether too jumpy. To calm himself he pulled into a side street and stopped, facing the highway. A few minutes alone with his thoughts would bring things into better perspective, and if anyone should pick that time to highball down the main drag, then the patrol unit was in good position to put a stop to it.

Ten minutes did a lot to bring things into better focus. Jack accepted the fact that the motorcyclist had made a clean getaway, but as he so often had to in police work, he resorted to the knowledge that there would be another time. He had not completed his investigation of Landville, but even a single hour on the telephone had convinced him that the man was a good citizen who was very unlikely to be dealing dope or otherwise compromising himself to the point where he would be burned out as a warning. Of the three most likely motives for the fire, the second and third began to look much more important.

From somewhere to his right, he heard the explosive sound of breaking glass. He flipped the ignition key and shifted into gear the moment the engine caught. Within five seconds he was cutting around the corner toward the sound he had heard. It could be a perfectly innocent accident, but where a large piece of glass breaks people can be hurt. More to the point, he was only a block from the small downtown area where the storefronts were located.

Two blocks ahead of him he saw a van with a jacked-up rear end that was burning rubber as it raced north toward Spokane. It was equipped with oversized rear tires with double-width tread—the kind used to give maximum acceleration in hot-rod competition.

Tallon hit his lights and siren; he had not yet noted any broken glass, but the speed of the departing vehicle was a violation in itself. He was still accelerating when he saw that the large plate glass window in front of the library had been smashed. One quick glance gave him that; then he returned his full attention to the street and the normal traffic that it was carrying.

His siren cleared the way quickly; other vehicles pulled over as they should. One female pedestrian persisted in crossing the street at a slow pace; if she had stopped she would have remained on the left hand side and out of danger, but she was not to be diverted from her purpose. Light flashing and with his siren going full blast, Tallon passed her with a foot or two to spare. If it frightened her out of her wits, he reflected savagely that she didn't have much to lose.

The first moment that he could he unclipped his mike and put out a call. "This is Whitewater One. I'm in pursuit north on Main. Suspect vehicle is a dark maroon van, hopped up, no license number yet. Request backup and sheriff's interception on the highway. I'm running code three and the vehicle is going flat out."

Francie's voice came back quickly. "I copy, Whitewater One. I'll call the sheriff."

Francie didn't belong in the station at that hour, but Tallon had no time for that. The fleeing van was a serious hazard since it was doing sixty or better on an urban street. Granted that it was the through high-

way, but there were many intersections and pedestrian crosswalks
directly in its path.

Tallon picked up his mike once more and without bothering to identify himself, since his voice was well known, said, "The library front
window is broken. Send someone there and tell me ASAP what happened."

Francie came right back. "Mrs. Weintraub called us. Someone threw
a rock through it—a big one. The flying glass cut a little girl who was
checking out some books."

That piece of news had a strange effect on Tallon. He should have
decried it, but instead it gave him a far more serious charge against the
people in the van—when he caught them. But it wasn't going to be
easy; the fleeing vehicle had been souped up and it was practically a
high-performance racing machine. The patrol unit was, for all practical
purposes, a standard-model car with only limited modifications.

The intersections flew past. Tallon himself was traveling at a reckless
speed, but at least his lights and siren were adequate to warn cross
traffic and persons on foot to get out of the way.

"Whitewater One."

Tallon grabbed his mike. "Whitewater One, go ahead."

"Hillman. I'm behind you, also running code three."

"Be careful," Tallon warned. "We can't hear each other."

"Right. I have you in sight, about eight blocks ahead."

"Whitewater One." A different voice this time.

"Whitewater One—By."

"Sheriff unit Boy Seventeen. On the highway ten miles north of
your city. Will set up roadblock; backup coming."

Tallon held the wheel with his left hand as the car he was driving
reached past seventy miles an hour. "Suggest running roadblock," he
said. "Pursuit is now at seventy plus. Suspect car may turn off and attempt evasive action."

"Understand wanted vehicle is maroon van modified for speed."

"That is affirmative. Speed now reaching eighty."

"Whitewater One, we have six units closing in and helicopter airborne. We'll get him."

"Thanks for the help," Tallon reported. For a few seconds he lost
sight of his prey; a bend in the road was just enough to shut off the
view. As soon as he had rounded it, he saw that the highway ahead was
empty, but there was a cloud of dust at a side road that turned off at a
thirty-degree angle. Tallon eased off the gas until he was down to fifty,
then he spun his car onto the side road at the very edge of its top performance. The tires smoked, but despite the slide on the dry concrete,
he maintained control. The faculty that had taught him years before at

the Pomona High Performance Driving School would have been gratified to see the way he had handled that. When it came to pursuit driving, they had written the book.

On the paved, but considerably rougher, road, the patrol car swung and bounced so hard Tallon had to hang on to the wheel with both hands. To his delight, he heard Hillman behind him put out the change of direction. Seconds later the sheriff's unit had confirmed and was taking corrective action.

The rear door of the van opened and someone threw out a roll of bedding. It bounced crazily, but by the time Tallon reached the place where it was, he was able to dodge it handily. Grimly he added a charge: assault on a police officer. One thing was in his favor: he had an almost full tank of gas. The van might also be full, or it might be low. But wherever it went, he was determined to follow. He was not quite as fast as it was, but he sensed that he was the better driver. If only the Goddamned tires held out or something else didn't let go. He insisted that the patrol cars be in top condition at all times; now that policy was paying off.

Even as that thought was in his mind, the van ahead of him appeared to leap into the air. At its very high speed it was out of control in a fraction of a second. Tallon thought "pothole," but it was only a guess. The van came down very slightly sideways, but it was enough. It bounced into the air once more, higher this time, slowly turning over toward its side. It landed with a crash of metal against gravel and began to spin. There was a flash and Tallon saw a flame shoot upward.

He cut the gas instantly and fed in as much brake as he dared. At the speed he was going, any heavy pressure would burn out the surfaces in no time at all. When he was down to sixty, he pressed hard and, at fifty-five, shifted down. The mass-times-velocity squared energy of his vehicle was down enough so that at fifty he was able to brake hard; as it was he stopped less than a hundred and fifty feet from the burning van. Something was going out over the radio, but he had no time to listen. He leaped out and on the dead run made for the van; as he came closer he could hear screaming.

The front and the forward doors of the van were engulfed in flames. Tallon braced himself and, using all of his strength in one supreme effort, he yanked open one of the rear doors. A furnace blast of heat impacted against his body, but he dove forward, felt something like flesh, and pulled it out as fast as he possibly could. It was a girl and her hair was on fire. With his bare hands he beat it out while the strong odor of burning flesh hit him and with it a fresh awareness of the screaming still coming, at a terrible pitch, from inside the van.

Ralph Hillman rushed past him, went inside the burning wreck, and came out in a few seconds dragging a body—or a living person, Tallon could not tell which as he tried to go back himself into what was a sudden quiet. The whole inside of the van was in flames and he knew that it was impossible to get anyone else out of there. The metal when he touched it was red hot and burned his hands cruelly.

Because he could do nothing else, he ran to his car, seized the radio, and called for the fire department and ambulances. "Two possible survivors," he reported. As he put out the information, Ralph Hillman was making one more desperate attempt to get another victim out of the van, but the flames were almost ten feet high and seconds after Ralph backed away, defeated, the gasoline tank exploded.

It was the end and both men knew it. Although his hands flamed with agony, Tallon bent over the person that Hillman had somehow gotten out of the blazing van. It was a young man and he was whimpering like a small dog in agony, his vocal chords incapable of producing anything more.

Two sheriff's units, lights flashing came up from the opposite direction. One man jumped out, a fire extinguisher in his hands. He ran as close to the fire as he could endure and let loose with the extinguisher. It was hopeless and he knew it, but he still did his best. Tallon turned around and saw that Ralph Hillman was lying on the roadway, his limbs sprawled and as motionless as death.

Tallon knew that he should put something on the air; a message had to be sent. He looked and saw that one of the deputies was doing precisely that. When the man had finished he came over to Tallon. "A chopper is coming," he announced. "It can carry only one litter, so it will take the worst case."

The girl Tallon had pulled from the van began slowly to move. She managed to get her elbows under herself and then gave way to uncontrolled weeping.

Jack got slowly to his feet and walked to his car, in such pain that his actions were automatic. He heard Francie's voice coming from the car speaker. "We copied the sheriff. Backup is coming, the ambulance, and a doctor."

She had hardly finished when the sound of a helicopter drummed in the air. Within a minute it settled down on the roadway, its rotor barely clearing the wires that were strung along one side.

An observer jumped out and ran toward the three people who were lying on the roadway. Tallon pointed to the young man from the van. "He's probably the worst," he said.

By that time the pilot was out of the helicopter and taking a litter from the rear section. Without wasting any time on words, the two crewmen loaded the young man onto it. They took it to their machine, stowed it quickly, and took off within a matter of seconds.

Tallon heard a siren approaching, coming very fast. The ambulance. He thanked God for that, because he had no idea what condition Ralph Hillman was in; Ralph had gone inside the blazing van after Tallon himself had known that any further rescues were virtually impossible. His own hands were throbbing in agony; the thought hit him that he wouldn't be able to drive his patrol car to the station.

The ambulance rolled up rapidly, two fire department units directly behind it. Ralph Hillman got the first attention, which was what Jack wanted. The fire department units pulled past and went into action, pouring foam onto the burning van and stifling the flames. As soon as it was possible, a fireman in an asbestos suit went inside the van. Tallon felt a tap on his shoulder, looked up, and saw Dr. Lindholm. Mary Clancy was right behind him. "The girl," Jack said.

"She's being looked after," the doctor replied. He spotted Tallon's hands almost at once and gave a quick order. While a gurney was being brought, Mary expertly loaded a syringe. Tallon felt the prick of the needle, but his hands were burning so fiercely it was meaningless to him.

"Sit on the gurney," Lindholm ordered. Jack hesitated because it was his duty to stay on his feet, but Mary took charge and eased him down until his knees were almost under his chin.

He was quickly glad when he saw that Ed Wyncott and Jerry Quigley were on the scene; he had no idea when they had arrived, but they were certainly needed. He heard a hissing sound from the van as the foam hoses knocked down the last of the fire. Hillman was being loaded onto another gurney; the girl who had been crying was on her feet, being helped.

He watched as Ralph Hillman was put into the ambulance; he hoped to God that Ralph was all right. Apart from everything else, he was a damn valuable man and couldn't be spared.

For the first time, the acute agony in his hands began to ease off. The fire in the van was out; two of the fire crew were taking out a blackened body.

His eyelids began to feel heavy and he had trouble following all that was happening. The city wrecker drove up, he was aware of that, before the Demerol he had been given began to bring waves of respite. He knew that someone was shifting him onto the gurney, then he lost consciousness altogether.

CHAPTER 10

When he woke up, his first realization was that he was wearing boxing gloves. That didn't make any sense and he tried to reason it out. As the mists cleared he discovered that he was lying on his back in a hard bed and, finally, that he was in the hospital.

He lay still until his mind cleared. A quick inventory told him that both of his hands were heavily bandaged and that one shoulder, his left, was also covered with a dressing. Otherwise he seemed to be in good shape. With some effort he sat up and was grateful to discover that he was in no sense dizzy or doped. His hands had been burned, he remembered that vividly, but the daylight was bright outside his window and there was work to be done. He got to his feet clad in a hospital gown, when Mary Clancy came into the room. "Time for your bath," she announced cheerfully.

"What time is it?" Tallon asked. Even if he had had his watch on, he would not have been able to see it: the bandages covered both wrists and part of his forearms.

"About nine-thirty," Mary answered as she busied herself making preparations.

"Forget the bath; get me my clothes," Tallon said. "I've got to go to work."

Mary stopped and looked at him. "The police department is doing just fine this morning. Brad Oster has taken over your job and is carrying on well. Gary Mason is back on duty and is out on patrol. The murder investigation is continuing and Brad is following up on the arsonist."

Tallon was ahead of her. "How's Ralph, and the victims from the van?"

Mary continued her work as she answered. "Ralph is in the next room: he has some second-degree burns, fortunately not too extensive.

He's under sedation and won't be back at work for a few days. The girl you pulled from the van is a duster; she was on PCP and we've got her here, under guard and in restraints. The other live one is a nineteen-year-old from Spokane who apparently was along for the ride. No dope and no record; Brad's already checked. He was pretty badly burned, but we've got equipment for that and he's getting special care. Dr. Lindholm doesn't want him moved and his own doctor, who came in last night, agrees."

"There were others." He made it a statement.

Mary nodded. "Yes, two others. Both DOA. They're in the morgue. One has been IDed; neither of the survivors has been told as yet that their friends are dead."

"Families?"

"One notified, the other will be as soon as we have an ID and that won't be too long. The van's been towed to the police garage, but I hear it's a totally burned-out wreck, so if there was dope on board, it's long gone up in smoke."

"I don't need a bath," Tallon said.

"Yes, you do. You need one and you're going to get one—right now. If you remember, I gave you a bath once before when you had some busted ribs."

"I was unconscious then."

"Today you won't have to miss a thing."

"Can Jennifer do it?"

"No, she can't, and stop being childish. You're exactly like every other man, as I have reason to know. And as I recall, on that last stake-out we were on together, you had a pretty good view of me. So we're even and shut up."

Tallon had his bath. The warm soapy water did feel good and a considerable amount of grime he had acquired in and around the van was washed away. "The way this is done," Mary explained, "I start at your feet and wash up as far as possible. Then I begin again at your face and ears and wash down as far as possible. Then I wash possible." When she had completed the job, she had been as good as her word.

"Now," she announced. "Dr. Lindholm says that you can sit up and even walk around a little, but you must keep your hands up and don't under any circumstances try to move your fingers."

"All right," Tallon agreed. He realized again how extraordinarily attractive Mary was.

He could not wear a shirt, but she helped him with his trousers, his socks, and his shoes. In place of the hospital gown she supplied a cotton bathrobe of sorts with sleeves large enough to accommodate the dressings on his hands. When he at last stood up, dressed as much as he could be, he felt much better. His hands pained him only dully, so he knew some anesthetic was being used.

"Now that's very good," Mary announced. "You're ready for your breakfast. And you behaved very well."

"Reward me, then," Tallon said.

Mary kissed him in a sisterly manner, filtering out any real emotion. "Now go have your breakfast with Jennifer; she's waiting." With a tissue she wiped his lips and then steered him to the door.

By two-thirty in the afternoon Tallon was back at his desk. He felt singularly helpless with his heavily bandaged hands; he could not pick anything up, he could not sign his mail, and certainly he couldn't take out a patrol car. As a policeman he was, for the time being, a bust.

Sergeant Oster understood completely and supplied him backup. "You give the orders," Brad said. "I'll see that they're carried out."

"First of all, how's Ralph?" Tallon asked. They hadn't told him very much at the hospital, because he had been a patient himself.

"Ralph is OK, but he did get burned pretty badly in places. He'll have to stay off duty for a few days. I know that we can't spare him, but we don't have much choice."

"No, we don't," Tallon admitted.

"You know he was assigned to the swami's background. Gary took him the swami's autobiography and he's reading it in bed. He has a phone and I understand that he's made some calls."

Tallon had to admit his admiration for Hillman, carrying on like that when his burns had to be hurting like hell. But Ralph was never a man to call it quits.

"Gary is carrying on with the swami investigation," Oster added. "Hillman is calling the signals and Gary is carrying the ball."

"Any results to date?"

"Yes—they checked on those Harvard degrees and they're genuine. The guy in India he studied under is awfully damn hard to trace, even though we have his name. The Indian police apparently aren't too efficient."

"We only have to know one thing"—Tallon pointed out—"that is whether or not he is a recognized teacher of real stature. There are a lot of fakes—you know that."

"Gary's on it now; he's at the library in Spokane where they have some books on current religion in India. If it's there, he'll find it."

After Mason's performance in locating the murder weapon, Tallon was ready to accept that.

"One more thing," Oster said, a little carefully. "Mary Clancy has bought herself a uniform—so she can go out on patrol." He didn't need to point out that Mary was a sworn reservist—the only one the department had.

"She hasn't had the training," Tallon objected. "She could get her ass in a sling in a hurry."

Oster was not convinced. "Mary will hack it. We're going to give her OJT; that's already been arranged. Two weeks from now she'll be as good as any of us were before you came here." That was an exaggerated statement and Tallon knew it, but if Mary thought she could hack it in a patrol car, she had the right to try. Very little went down in Whitewater that had to be handled by patrol units, and he knew without asking that the men in his command would be backing her up every moment. She could get the necessary reservist training later if she still wanted it.

"Where's Walt Cooper?"

"He's out at Dharmaville. His subject is back from San Francisco and he's interviewing him."

Tallon very much wanted to be in on that interview, but he knew that it was impractical. He had appointed himself to work with Cooper on Narayan, but it was all he could do to stay in his office and keep up with things. Cooper had shown real resourcefulness and he might just do all right on his own.

Walt Cooper, however, was not interviewing the man to whom he had been assigned. He was, in fact, sitting in the reception center drinking a cup of tea, to which he was gradually becoming accustomed, and talking to the girl who chose to call herself Bhakti. Her hair was once more up in the severe style she seemed to prefer, and her granny glasses hid all hints of the attractive person she was. But, even as Bhakti, she had a rich warmth and Walt Cooper took her as she was.

"I need to ask you some more questions," Cooper said. "I hope that I'm not getting in your hair."

Bhakti regarded him evenly. "Are we still under suspicion?" she asked.

That was a tough one, but Cooper handled it. "I'm not here to do any suspecting. I'm after information that will help us to eliminate a lot of people and to zero in on the one, or ones, we want. When we catch him, and we will, then everyone else is permanently removed from suspicion."

"I guess that's fair enough," Bhakti said.

"Now, we know that when he was in police work himself Narayan was assigned to the Marsha Stone case." He spoke as though Marsha Stone was some person who neither of them had ever met.

Bhakti was right with him. "That's right," she confirmed.

"My impression of the man is that he is highly resourceful."

"And smart," the girl added.

"Do you happen to know if, at that time, he was interested in the kind of life you lead here?"

"As far as I know, he wasn't. He was simply a detective—and a very good one."

"Let me try a little deducing of my own," Walt said. He meant to go on, but Bhakti brightened with a sudden smile he hadn't expected.

"That might be fun," she said.

Walt Cooper tried his best to see past the disguise to the famous screen beauty hidden underneath. The complexion, yes, but the features that had reminded some columnists of Garbo at her finest eluded him.

"All right. Fact one: Detective MacNeil is now living here at Dharmaville. Fact two: the girl he was looking for for so long is here also. Deduction:—he can't help but know who you are."

Bhakti pursed her lips and pretended to think. "That seems logical," she agreed.

"But it certainly doesn't follow that everyone else here does."

"I'll give you an answer: Swamiji knows, Narayan knows, and that's all. If anyone else has guessed, I haven't heard a word about it."

"Yet you told me."

"Because I had to, Walt. I wanted to forestall any more investigation that would bring it all out in the open. So I decided to trust you."

She had not called him by his Christian name before and it hit him like an electric shock. "Let's go back to the deducting," he proposed. "Detective MacNeil eventually did find you. But he didn't report the fact. Instead he resigned unexpectedly from the Sheriff's Department, cutting short a very promising career."

Bhakti drank some of her own tea very slowly, obviously making up her mind. To prod her a little, Cooper added one more thing. "Detective MacNeil found you, but he's the only member of the task force that did. And you and he made a deal."

Bhakti had made her decision. "Not quite," she said. "In the first place, Narayan is a man of very high principle. While he was a policeman, he was all policeman. There should be more like him."

"I think that there are," Walt Cooper said quietly.

Bhakti drew breath and put her hand across her mouth. "Oh, I didn't mean it that way!" she protested. "Please . . ." She shook her head. "I'm very sorry."

"Are you saying that he did report finding you?" Cooper asked.

Bhakti nodded. "Yes, that's right. He told someone very high up and

. . . gave the reasons why I chose to . . . drop out of public view. I hadn't realized how much I had cost the taxpayers and how much work the police and sheriffs had put into trying to find me. I saw that man, by appointment, and made my apology. He accepted it."

"Then it was you who first thought of coming to Dharmaville."

Bhakti took off her glasses and her remarkable features were a little easier to see. "I wanted a place where I could be away from . . . a lot of things, but not all alone on some deserted island. I heard about this place somewhere, so I went to hear Swami talk. When he had finished, I knew I had found what I wanted, at least for a while. So I came here."

Walt Cooper finished his analysis. "MacNeil, or Narayan, is half Indian, so he knew something about Indian culture. You had met him, and he told you about Swami. He gave up his career and joined you here. Am I right, Mrs. MacNeil?"

"Will you walk a little with me?"

The request was so unexpected Walt did not know how to react. He saw quickly that he either had to accept or else break the rapport he had so carefully built up. "I'd like to," he answered.

Bhakti put her unflattering glasses back on. "I'm leaving my post," she confessed, "but if anyone comes, we'll see them drive up."

Walt noticed that she did not lock the door as they left. Then, quite naturally, she took his arm and began to walk at a slow pace. It was a magnificent day: not too warm, but with a clear sky and a still bright sun to cast rich shadows beside every tree and bush. It was very hard for Walt to remember that he was a policeman on duty, strolling through a lovely landscape with someone else's wife—someone, in fact, who was an active suspect in a murder case. He tried to block out of his mind the fact that she was Marsha Stone—whatever her true name might be.

"In the first place," she began, "I'm not Narayan's wife, or anyone else's. I think a great deal of him, but we both know it wouldn't be right—for us. You have to understand that he's a very deep person and I suspect that he has some ideals I couldn't supply. He's proud of his own heritage. Just don't ever call him black because he detests the idea of sorting people out by colors."

"Marsha, while you were in Hollywood, were you married then?"

"No. I came awfully close once, but at the very last minute I found out that I had picked one of the most notorious switch-hitters around. Later he was arrested for molesting young boys. That's the reason I came up here—to try and wash that out of my mind. It was pretty awful when I did find out."

Walt unconsciously tightened his arm muscles a little, holding her a bit more securely. "That must have been a helluva jolt," he said. It wasn't very apt or eloquent, but it was the best he could muster. At that moment he succeeded in forgetting who she was and thought of her only as a friend. Her long, old-fashioned dress was sweeping on the ground and her probably unnecessary glasses completed the illusion that she was just a girl. A rather nice one that he genuinely liked.

"Swamiji teaches us that we must learn to love all people, whatever their faults, but after I learned what some of my intended's other sexual habits were, I tried to just let it go away while I finished the picture I was in—I had to do that—but he began to spread stories that I was frigid. At that point I decided just to give it up. I already had enough money to be comfortable, and I get some residuals."

"How do they pay you?"

"Through my lawyer. He's keeping a trust account for me."

For the next several minutes Walt Cooper walked through the fields of Dharmaville with the girl who was called Bhakti, never very far from the reception office in case she should be needed there. He tried to visualize her as having been a conspirator in the death of Councilman Sullivan and the picture would not form. He was aware that she was intensely feminine, which told him that he had better break it up. Under normal circumstances he would have asked her for a date, but he knew he must not. Even if he could, he knew that his chances of actually taking her out somewhere were close to nil. He simply couldn't pitch in that league.

He left her soon after that. On the way back into the city, he considered what he had learned and reminded himself that under no circumstances must he allow himself to be conned. Whatever she chose to call herself, and no matter how she chose to dress, she was still the same girl who had so recently been a Hollywood sensation, and girls of that type don't go out of their way to be nice to small-time cops. Not unless they have a very particular reason, and what that reason could be caused him to hold his teeth close together and keep his mind on his driving, and his work.

It was a little after five when Tallon looked up from his desk to see Ed Wyncott and Jerry Quigley in the door of his office. They were both grinning like Cheshire cats, which told him immediately that they had something they very much wanted to tell him. "Come in," he invited.

Quigley wiped the smirk off his face when he noted the bandages on Tallon's hands. "How are you, Chief?" he asked.

"I could be a helluva lot worse. Ralph Hillman is still in the hospital because he made a hero of himself."

"We know," Wyncott said. "Everybody knows. He should be up for a medal. You too, from what we hear."

"It goes with the territory," Tallon said. "Sit down and tell me what's on your minds."

Quigley spoke for them both. "First of all, we got a court order to look into the financial status of Sullivan. You remember that his last forty-eight hours is our assignment."

"I remember very well," Tallon said.

"Once we showed up at the bank with the court order, there was no problem," Quigley continued. "We checked his expenditures for the past six months and everything appeared to be in order. Then we began to look into his charge accounts. He had both MasterCard and Visa with the bank; they made us copies of the last three bills, plus the most recent charges. Just the usual things you might expect."

Quigley looked at his partner who took the cue. "Then we asked ourselves another question," Wyncott continued. "Could he have had any other charge accounts, or credit cards, that didn't show? We learned that he had another account for his office funds. The court order didn't specifically cover that, but the bank stretched a point and we discovered that he was writing a check to the Diners' Club every month."

Quigley took over again. "It took us a little while to get the records of his Diners' Club purchases. As soon as we did, we paid a visit to a motel in Spokane and interviewed the manager. Councilman Wilson Sullivan, the great champion of the city's morals, had a girl friend. A mistress."

Tallon was genuinely surprised to hear that, and he let it show. "Have you IDed her?" he asked.

"Not yet," Wyncott answered. "But we've got a good description. And his secretary had to know because she paid all his bills. That could be why she's been so hairy with us."

Tallon looked at his temporarily useless hands that more or less forced him on to the sidelines for the next day or two. "Have you told anyone else about this?" he asked.

"No, sir," Quigley answered. He used the "sir" for emphasis.

"Then don't. I want this kept strictly in the dark. In particular, I don't want Mrs. Riley, Sullivan's secretary, to know what you've found out. The chances are good that Mrs. Sullivan doesn't know about this and it's not our job to tell her."

"Absolutely not," Wyncott agreed. "We'll write up our report and keep it to ourselves, or give it directly to you."

"How about Brad Oster?" Quigley asked.

It was a good question, because Oster was coordinating all of the data. The new information was vital to the investigation, or it well could be. "Do your report and give it to me," Tallon said. "I'll give it to Oster and tell him to keep his mouth shut."

"You haven't quite got it all," Wyncott said. "According to the motel manager we talked with, Sullivan was with his girl friend from about seven until ten on the night that he was killed. So what she may be able to tell us could be the key to the whole thing."

Tallon remained silent a moment before he spoke again. "We'd better find her pretty fast," he said, "because if a little theory I have happens to be right, she could be in serious danger."

CHAPTER 11

It was a long evening for Jack Tallon. After Jennifer had fed him his dinner, and had managed to do it without humiliating him in the process, he sat in the living room of his home, his bandaged hands resting on the arms of his chair, and resigned himself to doing nothing. The television program offered nothing that was of interest, he could not hold a book very well, and he was not in a frame of mind to try any parlor games. He wondered if people in institutions, some of whom he had helped to put there, felt the way that he did.

Jennifer tried to make conversation, but she read out his mood and after a short while left him alone. She knew, even before her husband did, that he just wanted to sit and think.

For more than an hour he kept his mind focused on the two principal problems that he faced: the murder of Councilman Sullivan and the unprovoked arson attack. As far as he had been able to find out, Herman Landville was an innocent victim; there was nothing whatever in the man's background to suggest any reason why his home had been burned. The only good thing about the whole problem was the fact that the children had been gotten out safe and sound.

In the Sullivan case a good deal of data had been dug up by his men, but in all of it he could not find any indications as to whom the attacker—the murderer—might be. As far as he was concerned, motive remained an open question. Sullivan's determined opposition to the Dharmaville operation was so widely known, he doubted that it, in itself, was the answer. It was too apparent and, while aggravating, it was not a sufficient provocation to incite deadly violence.

So something else had to have done so.

The quiet dull pain in his hands seemed to subside as he turned his mind to that one demanding question: *Why?* He went over everything that he knew about Sullivan, about his business, and about his conduct on the council. The fact that he had had a mistress was far too common a situation to incite murder, *unless* there was an irate husband in the picture. He was glad that he had told Wyncott and Quigley to check on the girl as quickly as possible.

Then he considered Dharmaville and reviewed all that he had learned about the community. He was satisfied that his own people were carrying out their assignments well where the spiritual colony was concerned. The fact that Marsha Stone was there was definitely interesting, but that single fact didn't seem to fit anywhere into the puzzle.

He thought about the swami, about Narayan the ex-policeman, and about the young woman who had first greeted him when he went there. The one who called herself Kumari. As a mental exercise, he tried to put himself in her place and attempted to analyze why she was choosing to spend her life there. Perhaps she felt that it gave her protection from the type of terrible experience that she had had. If that was her motive, it was probably valid.

Then, quite suddenly, a thought jumped into his mind from nowhere. It was something he had known all along, but had failed to consider fully when it had first come up.

For a long ten minutes he turned the idea over in his mind, because he wanted to be very sure that he did not blow a promising lead through an oversight. When he had thought it all out to his satisfaction, he called Jennifer.

She came quietly from her kitchen, aware that her husband had something on his mind. "Please, dear," Jack said, "would you go to the phone and make a call for me?"

"Of course. Who do you want?"

"Call Dharmaville and see if you can get the swami on the line. It's Swami Dharmayana, but if you just ask for the swami, that will be enough."

"I'll try," Jennifer said.

It took her only a minute to get the number. When it was answered, she was referred to another. She dialed that and when she had a connection she spoke briefly. "Just a moment, please; Chief Tallon is calling." She put down the phone and nodded.

Jack had to prop the instrument against his shoulder, but he managed to hold it in place. "Swami, this is Jack Tallon," he said. "Something has come up and I think it advisable that we should have a talk as soon as possible."

"If it's an emergency, I'll come to you at once," the swami offered.

"No, it's not that pressing; tomorrow morning will do if you'll be free."

"I'll arrange to be. I've been told that you were hurt in a traffic accident, but I don't have any details."

Experienced policeman that he was, Jack was touched by that bit of concern. "I wasn't hurt really, but two people were killed. Rather horribly, I'm afraid. All I got out of it was some burns on my hands, but for the moment I can't use them."

"Chief Tallon, if you wish I'll come in to see you at any time you say. Or, if you prefer, I'll send a car for you. It won't be a very elaborate one, but serviceable."

"Perhaps it would be best if we met at Dharmaville."

"What time shall we pick you up?"

"Ten o'clock."

"I'll have a car there for you, at the police station, I presume."

"Yes, that's right. And thank you."

After exchanging good-nights, Jack hung up. If all went well, by noon the next day some significant answers might be in his hands.

By eight the following morning he was at the hospital to see how Ralph Hillman was doing. It was not a normal time for visiting, but he was accorded special privileges. When he was admitted to Hillman's room, his first impression was that his sergeant did not look very well. There were a number of conspicuous dressings, but he was fully conscious and apparently in reasonably good spirits.

"I'm sorry to be laid up like this," Hillman said. "I'll be out and back on the job as soon as they'll spring me."

"Don't worry about that," Tallon told him. "In case you haven't been told, you saved a man's life. Right now you're the pride of the department."

"You went in and pulled a girl out," Hillman said. "I saw you."

A busy nurse came in with a breakfast tray and moved Tallon aside. She did not order him out of the room, considering who he was, but her wishes were evident. Ralph, too, would have to be fed.

"You take it easy," Jack said. "Don't worry about a thing except getting well. You're on full pay, injured in the line of duty, and your expenses here are all covered."

"That's nice to know, Chief," Hillman answered, "but we've got an arsonist to catch, and a murderer, and I want to be in at the kill."

"You will be," Tallon promised. That was as good an exit line as any, so he raised his hand in final greeting and went out, much to the nurse's relief.

At the emergency facility he checked in with Dr. Lindholm to have the dressings changed on his hands. The doctor removed the bulky bandages with delicate care and inspected the palms of Tallon's hands. There was a process of bathing that Tallon could have done without, then fresh salve was applied and new, much smaller dressings were put on. After that Dr. Lindholm produced a pair of over-sized thin rubber gloves that were perforated with ventilation holes and fitted them into place.

"That should be a lot better," he said. "You'll be able to feed yourself and do a lot of other simple things that don't put any strain on the damaged tissue."

"How about driving a car?" Jack asked.

"No way. Give it at least another day or two."

Jack thanked him and went back to where Jennifer was waiting for him in their car. When he walked into police headquarters, he discovered that Francie was on the air. Wayne Mudd, in the patrol unit, had spotted a large, hairy motorcyclist whose driving pattern hadn't looked quite right. Jack had a strong urge to hop into the spare unit that was waiting outside at the curb, but he knew that he must not. Instead Brad Oster burst out of the station on the run, took the wheel of the waiting car, and was gone in seconds.

There had been a time when the Whitewater Police Department had not been that responsive; he gave silent thanks that his training program was paying off so well.

In his office he listened to the monitor that carried the police communications. Even though there was very little, if any probable cause, the motorcyclist was stopped and briefly questioned. He identified himself as a student at the college and, when asked, provided what sounded like a solid alibi for the time of the arson attack. He was thanked for his cooperation and asked to keep an eye open for any other motorcyclist who might be the man who was wanted. The student agreed to do that and added that burning down a man's house was an inexcusable act. Mudd, Tallon noted with satisfaction, carefully took the license number and ran it for wants or warrants. It came back clean.

The incident over, Tallon called Hillman's wife and told her that

her husband seemed much better and was in good spirits. She would be at the hospital as soon as the regular visiting hours began, but a word of encouragement was always welcome.

Nancy Snodgrass, the new reporter, appeared to interview him. He told her how Ralph Hillman had gone back into the burning van after Tallon himself had decided that any further rescue attempts would be hopeless. That enlarged lightly on the truth, but it was in a good cause: there was no question of Ralph's heroism.

Francie fluttered her hands in the doorway and told him that a car had arrived from Dharmaville. She carefully pronounced the "h" to make sure he understood.

The announcement that the car was waiting brought back into sharp focus his thinking of the night before. As he went outside, he wondered how anything so obvious had escaped him for so long, but that was how it was sometimes.

The driver from Dharmaville was Santosh, the young man who normally worked in the office. He introduced himself and then drove back to the center while he conversed, for his own benefit, about the excitement, and the trials, of police work. Tallon led him on a little, probing to find out the young man's real viewpoint toward law enforcement. By the time they turned into the driveway the topic had been well aired, but Santosh had made no mention of the fact that an ex-policeman was second in command of the Dharmaville operation.

During the drive up the hill toward the swami's residence, he supplied a commentary on the layout of the premises and explained why the geodesic dome had been found to be the most practical type of structure, both for individual homes and for the temple that was the center of the community's spiritual life. "You know that we don't just sit around all day and mutter incantations," Santosh explained with the enthusiasm of the new convert. "There's a lot of work to be done; we have our industries as well as the farming. We publish books and distribute them, and we do a lot of teaching. I'm in line for the next opening in the editorial department."

He was fully prepared to say a lot more, but they had arrived at the plateau where the swami's residential dome was located. When the car pulled up in front, the door was opened immediately by Kumari who greeted Tallon as a friend. As she held out her hands, partly extended, to him, she seemed indeed a happy young woman; one who had overcome the terrible experience in her background.

"How's Jon?" Tallon asked as he held out his bandaged hands to her.

She touched them very lightly, so as to cause him no pain. "He's just fine, thank you. Right now he's in school, but he asked me to say hello to you."

She led him inside where the swami was waiting to receive him. He was wearing a set of robes and to Tallon's eye, the rather dramatic change of dress had the effect of making him look really like a swami for the first time.

"Kumari is going to serve some coffee," the swami said. "We have an Indian blend you might find interesting. After that we can be alone."

Since the ambience was for the moment a social one, Jack responded to it as was clearly expected. There were some very serious matters on his mind, but he took a page from the book of Inspector Bucket and made himself the good guest.

"I hope you will excuse my attire," the swami said, "but later today I have a wedding to perform. Two of our young people are getting married."

In trying to be agreeable, Tallon spoke without thinking. "I didn't realize that you officiated . . ." he began, and then stopped abruptly.

"I quite understand," the swami said, "but I am the spiritual leader of this community, and I have been formally ordained—in India."

"Of course," Tallon said, hoping that would cover it.

The swami motioned him to a seat and then sat down himself on the opposite side of a brass coffee table that stood on six wooden legs. "People often have interesting ideas about a yoga community," he said as he settled himself. "This is not the only one, you know. The Ananda Cooperative Community in central California is very well known, and deserves to be. Swami Kriyananda has accomplished some wonderful things there. We enjoy a tax-free status as a religious institution except for that part of our property that is used for our publication work and other commercial ventures. Of course all of our profits are plowed directly back into the maintenance of our principal facilities."

"I hope things are going well for you," Tallon said politely.

"We are managing, and we are laying aside for some quite ambitious building plans we have."

That remark interested Tallon very much, but he did not reveal his thoughts in any way.

The swami looked about him for a moment. "From a purely legal standpoint," he went on, "if you have a storefront operation that calls itself The First Church of the Holy Spirit in Ecstasy, the spiritual head, trained or otherwise, can perform weddings, conduct funerals, and carry out other religious duties."

"That's absolutely right," Tallon agreed. "The fact that we keep church and state strictly apart is one of the major strengths of this country."

"How right you are, Chief Tallon, and let me add that religious freedom is also an immense blessing."

Kumari appeared carrying a large tray. She set it down on the brass table and poured coffee. Cream and sugar were also on the tray as well as some attractive-looking streusel. Functioning as the perfect hostess, she passed out the cups and saucers and then offered the cake with just the right touch of elegance. Tallon noted again that she was not a conventionally attractive girl, but she had a charm that was in itself quite magnetic. Someday, he surmised, someone would want her very much and perhaps become a good father to Jon. Then he remembered that she was a nun.

When Kumari had finished, she said, "May I be excused?"

"Of course, my dear," the swami answered. In response Kumari offered Tallon a parting smile, then went to the door and let herself out. Tallon tried his coffee and found it excellent; in fact it was the best he could remember having for some time. Police station coffee was notorious all over the world, and usually for good reason.

"Now," the swami began, "we are quite alone and we won't be interrupted—I saw to that. Please tell me how I can help you."

Tallon deliberately was not too quick to answer. He sipped a little more coffee and had a bite of the cake. Then he began. "Swami, I would like to ask you, in confidence, of course, if anyone has approached you recently about selling your property here."

The swami did not hurry his answer. He too ate a small piece of cake before he responded. "For the past several months, Chief Tallon, I have been under the heaviest kind of pressure to do just that. I was virtually offered the opportunity to become a millionaire."

"Have you had one offer, or several?"

"Basically one offer, but that has been turned into almost a demand. I have been enticed on one hand and threatened on the other to a degree you might find it hard to believe."

"Was the late Councilman Sullivan the man who wanted to buy?"

The swami sipped his coffee and set the cup down carefully. "Now I see the genesis of your question, Chief Tallon. No, Councilman Sullivan never approached me except on one occasion several months ago. Because he did not have very much financial backing, he virtually offered me a partnership."

"A partnership?" Tallon was stunned.

"That was substantially it. I thanked him for his interest but told him that we had no intention of moving. I explained how long it had taken us to find this location and how happy we have been since we moved in."

"Was Mr. Sullivan abrasive when he was turned down?"

"No, not precisely. He did say something about my not having heard the last of his suggestion, but otherwise he was entirely reasonable."

Tallon was thinking very hard. "Swami, am I right in guessing that Mr. Sullivan's offer preceded the one you've been discussing?"

"Yes, that's correct. How did you deduce that?"

"I'd rather not say for the moment, Swami, not until I get some more information first."

"As you wish. I might add that it's very fortunate for us that the deed to our property is in good order and that we have kept up the payments on schedule because the pressure has been relentless."

"As I see it, Swami, your position in refusing to sell is legally secure."

"It is now, Chief Tallon, but ever since the tragedy at Jonestown, the good name of institutions such as ours has been suspect. I was told flat out that if I didn't consent to sell our property, steps would be taken to make our kind of community illegal in the state of Washington."

Tallon shook his head. "I doubt very much if they can do that. Religious freedom is guaranteed by the Constitution."

"I know that well, Chief Tallon. Here, let me pour you some more coffee." The swami reached over and refilled Jack's cup. "However, if a powerful enough force wants us out of business, all kind of difficulties can be put in our way. You know how Mr. Sullivan tried to force us out by ordinance. The health department received complaints that our sanitation isn't up to the required standards. Fortunately it is, but we had to go through a troublesome period. Then we were accused of being a brothel in disguise. Mr. Sullivan referred to us several times as a 'sex colony.'"

Tallon made a swift decision; by giving a little he could fuel the conversation, and the swami was not a man likely to gossip. "We've naturally been looking into Mr. Sullivan's background," he said. "He was not precisely in a position to throw stones."

The swami lifted an eyebrow. "That doesn't surprise me too much; he was so conspicuous as an upholder of the community's morals. Obviously I'll consider your information a confidence."

Both men returned to their coffee. It was the swami who broke the silence. "You are aware that we were permitted to buy this property at a low price and on generous terms. The lady who was the seller has been a member of our yoga fellowship for some time, but for personal reasons, she doesn't wish that fact known."

"Understood," Tallon said.

"One provision of the sale was that she could come here to live at any time for the rest of her life. That alone would prevent me from accepting any offer for the property."

Tallon remained silent.

"Do you know the name Mortimer Brown?" the swami asked suddenly.

It did have a faintly familiar ring, but Tallon could not bring anything to the front of his mind. "You'd better tell me," he advised.

"Mr. Brown is a land developer. It is my opinion that he was sired by a shark out of a cobra. He is a totally ruthless individual. Our teachings tell us that we must love and speak well of everyone. In the case of Mr. Brown, I'm forced to make an exception."

Tallon had it then. "Now I remember him. He got into the papers when he tried to override the Coastal Commission in California. There was some litigation."

The swami nodded. "That's the man. He wanted to build some very expensive condominiums that would have ocean views. To do that he needed some land the Commission controlled. Eventually he was indicted for attempted bribery."

"And beat the rap," Tallon added.

"I believe he did. At any rate, he seems not only anxious, but desperate, to acquire our property here. This is a very nice location, but his insistence on trying to take it away from us is beyond my understanding."

The fact that he had a piece of cake to eat gave Tallon the excuse he needed to remain quiet while he thought. He felt that he could trust the swami, but the information he held was very highly restricted. Somehow, he realized, Mortimer Brown had gotten hold of it. That made it an unequal fight. If Brown knew it, then somehow, some way, it had leaked. "Do you happen to know what Brown proposes for this property if he could acquire it?"

The moment he spoke he realized he had touched a sensitive spot. The swami might be a peaceful man of God, but he did not look it as he considered the question.

"I know in appalling detail, Chief Tallon, because he had the effrontery to show me the detailed plans he had drawn up *after* I had told him that my decision not to sell was final. He proposes to convert this whole area into a huge recreational area with condominiums on the hill, a large motel, restaurants, a disco, winter sports facilities, and you name it."

"I think I can," Tallon said.

The swami drew breath to speak and then decided not to. Instead he looked calmly at his guest, waiting for Tallon to go on.

Jack began very carefully. "Swami, for some time the subject of legalized gambling has been under discussion in the state of Washington. Naturally there is divided opinion and, like so many things in the legislative area, a tentative compromise was agreed upon."

"I know that," the swami said. "It was finally decided that certain limited places . . ." He stopped as the full realization came to him. "This site could possibly be one of them," he concluded.

"Possibly," Tallon agreed.

The swami shifted in his chair and then sat forward. "Chief Tallon, I should have thought of that myself, but the idea never crossed my mind. Those renderings that Mr. Brown showed me were expensive, ten thousand dollars at least, and I had already firmly refused. *If* he has some inside information, that would account for his ruthless determination to have this place. He wants to build a casino."

"Is Mr. Brown the reason why you sent MacNeil to San Francisco?"

"Yes, that's right. Narayan is a very skillful corporate attorney."

Tallon got to his feet. "Swami, I have work to do and you have a wedding to perform. Give my best wishes to the young couple."

Santosh was waiting patiently outside in the car. Tallon spoke his thanks for the swami's time and hospitality, then he got in to be driven back to his office. As the car started up, his hands began to burn again or perhaps he was just more conscious of the pain. He had not taken anything for it; it was a bearable discomfort and he wanted to keep his wits about him as a matter of principle. He was still the chief of police and he could not afford to make any avoidable mistakes.

"Did you have a good talk with the boss?" Santosh asked.

"Yes, I did," Tallon answered. "He's quite a remarkable man."

"You don't have to tell any of us that. May I ask what it was all about, or is that confidential?"

Tallon observed his usual caution. "Basically it was about the murder of Mr. Sullivan; that's still under intense investigation. Then we had an arson fire recently that destroyed a home."

"You don't suspect any of us, I hope!" Santosh spoke with quick intensity.

"I have no reason to," Tallon answered truthfully. "And we discussed some other matters."

"That's all Swamiji needs—something else to worry about."

"He strikes me as a very capable man," Tallon said. "And if he feels the need of any help, you have a council, I understand."

"Yes, we do. I hope to be on it some day."

"Then you plan to stay here a while."

"Damn right. Man, this is the place."

The rest of the short trip back passed largely in silence. Santosh drove well but carefully; he was very much aware that his passenger was the police chief. When he pulled up in front of the municipal building that housed the police department, he thanked Tallon for taking the time to come out to the yoga community. It was a nice touch. Jack thanked him for the transportation and went inside.

Despite the fact that one of his key men was in the hospital, the department was running smoothly. Brad Oster was serving both as data coordinator and watch commander. One car was on patrol, being driven by Sergeant Mudd; the rest of the sworn personnel were working on their assignments.

As soon as he was in his office, Tallon called the Spokane Police Department to ask if there was anything new on his arson suspect. There was nothing, but every car on patrol had been alerted. Captain Long of the sheriff's department reported almost exactly the same thing. Partly because of the college, and partly because of the size of the city of Spokane, there were a great many motorbikes on the road and many of the riders were bearded.

The garage that did the city's work reported that the damaged patrol car would be repaired and back on the line that afternoon. The frame had not been bent and the front-end replacement parts had been on hand. The garage owner did not add that they had been on hand since the cars had been purchased with the expectation that sooner or later they would be needed.

There was no fresh word from the hospital, so presumably Ralph Hillman was doing as well as could be expected. Tallon settled down to go through the accumulated paper work on his desk before he began to check into a new angle he had in mind concerning the arsonist.

Although he hated to admit it even to himself, the motorcyclist was worried; he had been seen by the cop who had chased him across the field in his patrol car. The cop had been a fool to try that against a high-powered bike in the hands of an expert rider, but he *had* tried it and he had seen too much.

Normally the motorcyclist didn't let anything bug him; but he didn't know exactly how well he had been seen, or from what distance. He had barely gotten the fire started when, by foul luck, the police car had happened to come by and he had had to take off. He had been smart enough to keep his driving gloves on, so there wouldn't be any prints on the gas can he had been forced to leave behind.

The thought of being caught and sent to the joint was so devastating that he tried to block it completely out of his mind. But he had a fresh problem: it was time for him to go back to Whitewater and he was being paid so generously he had to take the risk. He could have minimized it by changing his appearance, but he resisted that. He had discovered that his very long hair and unkempt beard offended people, consequently he refused to alter them in any way.

But the time he had been ten, he had already discovered the intoxicating sense of power that went with being bigger and stronger than others of his age. Just a threat had always been enough to intimidate his classmates and force them to do what he wanted. When he had gone on to high school, he had played some football for the savage satis-faction of powering his opponents to the ground as murderously as pos-sible. At the cost of a few penalties he had forced a lot of fumbles that way, and he had seen many who had challenged him carried off the field with smashed knees or other injuries. His football successes had brought him all of the girls he wanted, and he had made the most of that opportunity.

As soon as the football season was over in his senior year he had dropped out; the offerings of the collegiate scouts had not interested him. From that moment forward, he had resolved never to do anything except what he chose. He turned on to narcotics, loved them, and sold them. He was busted, but a well-rehearsed contrition act got him a sus-pended sentence. He was apparently deeply humble when he left the courtroom. On his way out, he found an empty office and made up for his humiliation by urinating generously on the floor.

When he rode his bike he always wore the same outfit. On his sec-ond trip into Whitewater he knew that he would have to make an ex-ception. For one thing, he would conceal his appearance by wearing a full visor helmet. He didn't like them because he preferred to yell ob-scene insults at drivers who got in his way. He was uncatchable, so he could do exactly as he pleased. He could turn off the road at almost any time, or turn down narrow, seldom-used trails where angry motorists could not follow. His license plate was small and he kept it nicely dirty so that it would be almost impossible to read from any distance. He weighed two hundred and eighty-nine pounds, and that much beef in-timidated almost everyone.

Because he was being paid plenty for the job, he bought himself a full visor helmet that completely covered his face. Then from his assorted possessions he extracted a backpack, filled it up, and mounted it on his motor. With it he mounted a two-gallon can of gas. If he were to be stopped for any reason, everything was legal: the helmet, the backpack, and the gas. He could state that he was going off-road and al-ways carried some spare gas when he did so. No one could prove other-wise.

With rich satisfaction he rode into Whitewater in full daylight, his beard rolled up under the visor, his long hair concealed in the top. He rode very properly, so that when he started up and down the streets of the city in the vicinity of the college, he would attract almost no notice. He found his target with no trouble at all. Thanks to his careful schooling in what he was to do, one pass down the street told him that he was really in luck; the house to the left of his target was empty; the garage was wide open and both cars were out. Nothing was parked in the street in front.

To be sure, he went up and rang the bell. If anyone answered, he would raise his visor and ask where the Millers lived. That ploy never failed. When no one answered, he got back on his bike and rode into the driveway behind his target house. The garage was directly behind the back so the driveway bent enough to conceal him from the street.

Quickly and efficiently he poured the gasoline where his experience told him it would be most effective. A dog was barking inside the house, so what it was about to get would serve it right. When he was almost finished, he kicked the rear door open, sloshed the rest of the gasoline inside the kitchen, and lit a birthday cake candle—one of the trick kind that couldn't be blown out. That gave him a good three minutes. He rode sedately away until he was clear of the area, in that way he would attract little if any attention. No one was visible who could possibly read his license plate.

He got cleanly away. Since the house had been empty, no one noticed the flames at first. A woman across the street was the first to see smoke and to phone in an alarm. The fire department came very quickly, but the blaze was roaring before the first hose could be uncoiled.

Jack Tallon heard about the fire when his patrol unit was sent to the scene. Asher left the station on the run to provide backup, but before he could pull the spare car away from the curb, Jack jumped into the front seat beside him. "Let's go," he ordered.

The fire department was both efficient and courageous; two men broke down the front door and went inside to be sure that no one was trapped. A German shepherd burst out, barking wildly. It was hell inside the house, but the firemen checked it out within sixty seconds, working away from the burning section as they cleared the bedrooms.

His roof lights on, Ned Asher almost whipped the patrol car up to the curb. The regular patrol unit was already on the scene and Mudd was doing his job, keeping the people away. As Asher joined him, Jack literally ran to where the fire chief had stationed himself. "What about it?" he asked.

The fire chief was extremely busy, but he knew the importance of Jack's question. "Arson," he answered. "No possible doubt. Gasoline or some similar liquid. The back door was forced and the kitchen floor soaked with the fuel."

Tallon considered that very quickly and then asked a second, very important question. "Any attempt made to conceal the arson?"

"No, Jack. It's the other way. It was done so that we would know it was arson."

Jack stayed on the scene while he put in a radio call to Francie. She answered back within two minutes, which was a fair performance. But by the time she replied, Jack already had the answer. One of the neighbors who was watching knew who he was and answered his swift question. "The house belongs to Professor Weintraub at the college. It's usually empty, because Mrs. Weintraub, Sarah, is the city librarian. She's probably at work right now."

CHAPTER 12

Before the fire department had finished cleaning up the site, Jack was back in his office mustering his full forces. He did not want to call in the one patrol unit, but he needed every possible man with Ralph Hillman out of the picture. Francie rang every member of the department who was not already on duty and every one of them responded. Some had very recently come off shift, but they returned despite the twelve hours they had already put in. For a long moment Tallon considered calling in the sheriff, but he was not ready to do that until he and his men had done all they reasonably could first.

He picked up his private line, told Jennifer about the fire, and added that he wouldn't be home until God knew when. Jennifer was hit too by the news; when they had first come to Whitewater, the Weintraubs had given a party for them to meet some of the people from the university. Since then they had been friends and had exchanged frequent visits.

Jack gathered his people in the courtroom, which did double duty as an all-purpose meeting room, and was ready to begin his briefing when Mary Clancy hurried in. She was wearing her new uniform for the first time. Jack thought very quickly, but as a reservist she was entitled to do so, and she was reporting for duty. He could use her.

"Professor Weintraub's house has been torched," he said for the benefit of the few, if any, who didn't already know it. "The MO looks similar to the last arson fire we had. That was a big, hairy man on a mo-

torcycle—one that we know is high powered and has at least some
off-road capability. I want to work this in teams because I think we'll
get better results that way. Two officers carry a lot more weight than
one; it's too easy to say 'no' to a single person.

"Starting immediately, I want every home contacted and the occupants interviewed within two blocks of the Weintraub home. Don't say
'motorcycle' to anyone, but try to see if anyone saw such a machine and
volunteers the information. If you draw blank, then mention the motorbike and see if it gets a response. Don't waste time, but don't overlook
anyone, ten years or older, who might be a possible witness."

"And after that?" Wayne Mudd asked.

"Widen the field and keep on going. *Someone* got to that house and
he didn't walk away."

"Shall we work with our regular partners?" Walt Cooper asked.

"Partly," Tallon answered. "Wyncott and Quigley, Asher and Mudd
will make up two teams. Since Ralph is in the hospital, Cooper and
Mason will make up a third team. I'll work with Mary, because she has
the least experience and I have the most.

"One more thing," Tallon added. "I want Brad to double in brass by
coordinating and making sure that every house is covered."

Sergeant Oster for once was ahead of the boss. "I've got the assignments ready," he said. Swiftly he named streets and specified the ones
that each team was to cover. Since everyone present with the exception
of Mary knew the city with an intimacy that only a policeman has, no
map was needed. He knew without being told that he was to cover the
station, serve as watch commander, and respond himself if anything important went down. In a real emergency, he would have radio contact
with the people in the field.

As the office cleared, Oster took his place at the front desk where the
radio equipment was and where he could interview anyone who came
in. Tallon took his own car since there were not enough patrol units to
go around. Mary got in beside him and they started out. A small procession made its way to the site of the arson attack, then the cars were
parked and the teams set out on foot.

As they started out together, Tallon realized that Mary was both
proud and a little tense. He could not have her uptight during the first
interview, so he asked, "Where did you get that hat?"

"At the uniform shop. They told me it was the approved one for female officers."

"Get yourself a regulation cap. In this department everyone wears
the same uniform."

Mary looked at him. "I can't help filling it differently."

"Nobody is going to hold that against you," Jack reassured her. "In fact . . ." He stopped because they had reached the first house in their assigned area.

When the doorbell was answered, he did the talking. "Good evening," he said to the woman in the doorway. "I'm Chief Tallon of the Whitewater Police Department. This is Officer Clancy. We'd like to talk with you about the fire."

"Please come in," the woman invited, "although I don't think we have anything to tell you."

In the living room of the very nice home, Tallon swiftly interviewed the woman, then her husband. Both were fully cooperative. During this time Mary remained completely silent. "Who else lives here besides yourselves," was Jack's final question.

"Our daughter, Cindy," the man answered. "She's upstairs if you want to see her."

As the girl was being called, Tallon looked at Mary and nodded. When Cindy appeared, Mary conducted the interview. She had just seen twice how it should be done, so she handled the teenaged girl quite well. None of the three people had contributed a thing, and when a motorcycle was finally mentioned, they had not seen one or heard one. Tallon thanked them for their time and with Mary went to the next house.

At the seventh house he let Mary conduct the interviews. She followed well what she had seen him do, but when they were once more outside, he sat with her in the car for a few minutes. "You want to watch something," he pointed out. "I think that those people were being candid with us, but they may have left something out. When the husband was speaking toward the end, the wife drew breath to say something and then stopped because she didn't want to interrupt. Did you notice that?"

"No," Mary confessed, "I didn't."

"When you're interviewing someone with other witnesses present, keep your eyes open. If you had, you would have noted that and later asked the wife what she was about to say. It could have been meaningless, or it could possibly be of value. You've heard about making bricks without straw. What we're doing is possibly building a whole structure of evidence *just* from straws."

"Let's go back and ask her," Mary said.

"I did that on the way out," Tallon told her. "It wasn't important, but it could have been." He clicked on the radio and in a few seconds spoke with Brad Oster. Things were quiet at the station; nothing at all had happened since the investigation teams had gone out. Some had phoned in reports and, as of that moment, no one had dug up a single lead.

After the eleventh interview he took Mary downtown and together they got a quick portable meal in a fast-food stand. As they ate, Jack drove back to their area. Another radio check came up empty, but the troops were trying. As long as they kept it up, it was all he could ask.

At the sixteenth house it was Tallon's turn to do the interviews. The door was opened by a twelve-year-old boy who looked at his two unexpected visitors and asked very quickly, "What in hell did I do?"

Jack picked him up immediately. "Nothing that I know of, but we'd like to talk to you for a few minutes anyway."

"My favorite TV program is on."

"Stand by, then, for a special episode of 'Police Story.' You're going to be the star."

"Come on in," the boy said. "It was written by a cretin anyway." Jack glanced at Mary who had not missed the boy's scope of language. Obviously he was intelligent. Once in the living room, he introduced himself and Mary. "And who are you?" he asked.

"Marvin Bettman. Actually it's Marv Bettman the Third, if you want to get technical about it."

"And I'd say you're about twelve."

"You win the cigar."

"May we sit down?"

"I forgot," Marvin said. "You have to be invited, like Count Dracula." He waved them toward the expensive long davenport that filled one wall of the room. "Let me guess," the boy continued. It's about the fire. Only you're quite a ways from where it happened."

"That's right, Marvin. Now, where are your parents?"

"Out. They won't be back until late."

"Is there a sitter?"

"You're looking at him."

Mary took over. "Your parents trust you a lot, don't they?"

"Up to a point. And I don't let them down either."

Since she had stepped in, Tallon let Mary do the interview. By then she was becoming much more proficient and she ran down the standard questions without a slip. To each of them the boy gave a clear, but negative answer. He had been at home since returning from school. He had eaten the dinner his mother had left for him, he had done a little homework, then he had turned on the TV.

He had not seen anyone hanging around, nothing unusual whatever. He had not spotted any cars that did not normally belong in the neighborhood. Yes, if he did see or hear of something, he would call police headquarters.

Mary stood up. At that point, as agreed, Tallon put one more question. "Someone told us that the firebug might be on a motorcycle," he said. "It's a long shot, but did you happen to see a motorbike at all?"

Marvin turned his attention from Mary to him. "How does a dark blue Kawasaki KDX-400 grab you?" he asked.

"It grabs me good," Tallon answered as a sudden sense of warmth flooded him.

Mary was equally quick to react. "Tell me about the KEX-400."

"That's K D X," Marvin retorted, separating the letters to make them clearer. "It's a great bike. She's powerful with a top speed around ninety-five, and that's all you'll want to do on it. And it has good off-the-road capability. You can take that bike almost anywhere."

"How come you know so much about it?" she asked.

"Because motorbikes are a hobby of mine. I can't have one yet; I'm too young for a license. But I'm working on that every day. If you want to see a picture of it, I can show you several."

"Yes," Mary said.

In response Marvin led his guests into his room which was cyclonic, but stacked in one corner there was an impressive pile of motorcycle magazines. Marvin knew what he was looking for; he ran through the pages of the fourth magazine from the top and then held up a full-page ad. "That's the   achine," he said, "and before you ask me, yes I'm certain that's the one I saw. I know my bikes. You can try me out if you want to."

Tallon did exactly that. From the center of the pile he took out two magazines, selected pictures that illustrated the editorial copy, and flashed them with the captions covered up. Marvin made correct identifications without the least hesitation. Tallon knew that he could have memorized the contents of the magazines, but the boy was impressive nevertheless. "May I use your phone?" he asked.

"Be my guest," Marvin answered.

Tallon dialed the police station and then let Marvin hear him as a partial reward for his cooperation. "I have a lead," he reported. "A young witness who is an expert on motorcycles saw and identified a dark blue Kawasaki KDX-400 going past his house about the time of the fire, or a little before." He looked at Marvin who nodded. "Get on that right away."

"Will do!" Oster replied.

Tallon hung up and then turned to his young host. "If this pans out, how would you like to become the motorcycle expert for the White-water Police Department? We need one."

That got a reaction: the semisophistication dropped away. "Hey, man, that would be great! Do I get to ride in a patrol car sometimes?"

"That's part of the job," Tallon answered. "Your dad will have to sign a waiver."

"He will, no sweat."

Mary spoke up. "Would you be willing to loan us a picture of that bike?" she asked.

"Sure, let me get a good one for you."

While Marvin was excavating his pile of magazines, Tallon led Mary back into the living room. "The fact that our Marvin has such a collection of motorbike magazines, though he can't even ride one yet, leads me to believe that he does know his stuff."

"Me too," Mary agreed. "My money is on Marvin to be right."

Marvin came back with the picture and more information. "This is the bike, but the picture's the wrong color. I told you the one I saw was dark blue, and there isn't any bike like that around here that I know. It had a backpack fastened on, or some kind of gear. It was a great big dude riding it, and I can give you a clue if you want one."

"I want it," Tallon said, giving the boy as much play as he could.

"He was riding with a full visor helmet: you know, the kind that covers your whole face so that you look like an astronaut."

"That helps," Tallon said.

"That isn't the clue. The clue is that he was riding with the visor *down*. That's the way you ride on the open highway, or off-the-road when there's a lot of dust. Or in a race. But slow in the city, he'd ride with the visor *up*, that is, unless he didn't want to have somebody see his face."

That added bit of information did it for Tallon. Up to that point, he had kept in reserve the suspicion that Marvin had been laying it on because he had a chance to show off before the police chief himself. But the helmet information sounded genuine.

Eleven minutes later Ed Wyncott radioed in that he and his partner had found a witness who was sure she had seen a very big man riding on a blue motorcycle. She had noticed him because the city had had a bad series of rapes not too long before and she was concerned. Wyncott and Quigley had not gotten the word on Tallon's call in about the Kawasaki. With that semiconfirmation, Tallon called in his people in the field and, when they were all back at the station, gave them the new information. Those who were normally off duty he sent home to get some rest. He stayed on himself to get the results of the computer readouts on owners of blue KDX-400s. He presumed that Mary had left, when she came in with a cup of coffee for him. He tried it and it was nothing like the blend he had been served by the swami, but neither was anything else he could at that moment remember.

It was the Spokane Sheriff's Department that came back with some definite information. A Sergeant Kosterman had apparently been on it since the new information had been phoned in by Oster. "Here's what we've got," he reported. "There are fifty-six blue KDX-400s in the area. I checked with our motorcycle unit. We don't advertise it, but we keep a pretty close track on bikers. Most of them are OK, but we get a lot that aren't. All but fourteen of the Kawasakis belong to good citizens as far as we know, at least they've never come to our attention in any other way. Of the fourteen left, we've had most of the owners in here at one time or another, some of them pretty often. Only two are really big men."

Tallon's blood was pounding; the chase was narrowing fast.

"Of the two, one seems to have an alibi; we know him well and we checked him out. He's been stoned most of the day; he's a duster. The other possible suspect lives in River Falls. He's a hired-muscle type known to be violent. There's a file on him. His name is Wesley no middle name Obermann, with two n's. Description: male Cauc. six four two hundred and seventy-five to three hundred pounds. Very long hair, full beard."

"It fits," Tallon said, "and Chief Smallins in River Falls is a close friend of mine; he used to be a sergeant in this department. I'll give him a call." He didn't add that he had gotten Smallins the job.

As soon as he had thanked Sergeant Kosterman for his help, he hung up and then put in an immediate call to Chief Smallins. It was late in the evening, so he called the other chief's home number and within a minute had Smallins on the line. "Frank," he said after the greetings had been exchanged, "I've got one for you. We've had two houses torched down here by an arsonist described as a very big man with long hair and a full beard who rides an off-the-road motorcycle."

"Wesley Obermann," Smallins said promptly, "and since you're calling me, I take it that you have a lead on him."

"Right—we do. Can you have your watch commander check the files and see if Obermann rides a blue motorbike and, if so, the make and model number. Also I'd like to know his rap sheet."

"No problem," Smallins said. "Anything else?"

"First, since you know him, what's your personal evaluation?"

"Five will get you ten that he's in the joint within the next five years. Offhand I know that he's been arrested twice on suspicion of rape, but the victims were afraid to testify. Spokane has had him on suspicion of armed robbery, but it didn't stick. He lives out of town about four miles, by himself. No one goes near him if they can help it."

"He could be my boy," Tallon said. "Let me know about his motor."

"I'll call you back," Smallins promised. "Are you at home?"

"No, at work."

"Fifteen minutes," Smallins said, and hung up.

He was back in nine. "I have the info on Obermann's motor," he reported. "He got a new one a short while ago. It's a Kawasaki Kate David X-ray dash four hundred, dark blue. And get this: he went into the bank a short while ago and paid off the balance due on it in cash."

"What's his normal means of support?"

"None that we have on file. He listed his occupation as 'mechanic,' but I've never known him to be employed. He's pretty much a recluse and has been suspected of dope dealing. He disappears from time to time and then comes back; we don't know about his movements when he's away."

"He sounds to me like muscle for hire," Tallon said.

"Right, but as you know, Jack, we can't bust him on suspicion or even search his place in his absence without court authority. But he'll stub his toe sometime when he's visible and that will be it. From what you tell me, that time may have come."

"That's possible, Frank, and thank you. Can I have a copy of your file on him?"

"I've already ordered it; you'll get it ASAP."

Jack hung up with a deep sense of satisfaction. In his professional judgment, Obermann was about a 90 percent likely suspect. He fitted exactly all that was known in Whitewater concerning the arsonist, and he rode precisely the motorcycle that young Marvin had described. However, there was no known witness who had actually seen him start the fire or who could even place him at the scene. He had an absolute right to ride his motorcycle through the streets of Whitewater, assuming he was the man who had been seen by at least two witnesses. If Gary Mason could make a positive ID of him as the man he had chased across the field in his patrol car, that could do it, but Gary had already said that he had only seen the man from the rear.

The tentative identification of Obermann was a major step forward, but proof was a long way away.

Abruptly Tallon found himself exhausted; he wondered seriously if he had enough energy left to drive his own car home. There was only one way to find out. He got to his feet with a real effort, dug out his keys, and headed for the front door.

CHAPTER 13

In the morning, Tallon felt much better. He didn't care what day of the week it was, he had work to do and lots of it. He ate a good breakfast, because Jennifer insisted on it, and then drove to his office. He had already thought out his plans for the day with the certain knowledge that he could not possibly complete them all.

Surprisingly, the mood he was in was apparently infectious, for most of his people were in. Many of them were technically not on duty, but even Mary was there—in uniform. "I didn't have time to get a new hat," she informed him.

He should have thought of something bright to say in response to that, but his mind was too full of other things. Brad Oster was taking his turn on patrol, otherwise only Ralph Hillman was not there.

He made a quick call to the hospital to learn that Sergeant Hillman had been discharged. When he returned to the meeting room he found that Hillman had arrived, still well bandaged, but ready for whatever he could do.

Tallon took a second to congratulate himself on having one hell of a good department to command, then he got down to business. "Welcome back, Ralph," he said. "How do you feel?"

"I'll make it," Hillman answered. "I'm under orders to take it a little easy for the next day or two."

"All right, you're the watch commander. You stay in the station and cover all calls. Don't respond yourself, no matter what; and that's an order, clear?"

"Clear."

For the benefit of his people, whose trustworthiness he knew, he told them about Wesley Obermann. "I'm almost certain he's our man," he concluded, "but I have no way of proving it. Chief Smallins is going to have an eye kept on him and if he starts out in our direction, we'll be called immediately. Don't forget that he is one rough, tough dude, and there's no way he'll submit to peaceful arrest. So watch your step if he comes in range."

Ned Asher, his regular detective, spoke up. "I'd like to go back to the scene of the fire and see if there's anything at all I can find. I know that the whole place is trampled, but there might be something."

"Do that," Tallon said. "You know what to look for. Take Mudd with you if you like and come back when you're satisfied that you've done all you can."

Tallon turned to Wyncott and Quigley. "I want you two to drop everything else and get after locating Sullivan's mistress. She may be in some real danger if my theory is correct. I want to interview her at the earliest possible moment."

"Got it," Quigley said. He was flattered that Tallon had not spelled out just how he and Wyncott were to go about the job. Between them, they'd find a way.

"Call in the patrol unit," Tallon continued. "I want Mary to go out with Brad for some OJT. I hadn't thought of her that way before, but if things get really tight, we may have to ask her to handle some patrol shifts. She hasn't had a crack at any academy yet, but that can come later."

Mary nodded her willingness to accept the assignment.

"Mason and Cooper, I'm going to put you together for the time being. Come into my office for your assignment. That does it, I think; let's go to work."

As soon as he was back in his office, with Gary Mason and Walt Cooper on hand, Tallon shut the door and waved them to chairs. "I have a job for you that's very important, and very urgent. I'm using you two because I know Walt has sound experience and you, Gary, have shown me a lot of good stuff during the past few days."

Mason wanted to say "Thank you," but wisely chose to remain silent.

Tallon went on. "In San Francisco there is a land developer called Mortimer Brown. He's apparently a pretty hard type and he's been involved in a major flap with the California Coastal Commission. I have reason to believe that he's trying to get hold of a large piece of property in this vicinity."

"Dharmaville?" Cooper asked.

"You've got it," Tallon acknowledged. "Now who buys or sells real estate in our jurisdiction normally isn't of interest, but the swami doesn't want to sell. According to him, Brown pushed him to the wall on it and then threatened him."

"Do you know why Brown wants the land?" Gary Mason asked. "It's a very nice place, but there are a lot of others."

"For confidential reasons, I happen to know that Brown wants that particular piece of property and he's apparently willing to go to illegal lengths to acquire it."

Cooper was thinking. "Chief, that deal, or lack of a deal, might just be part of the motive for Sullivan's death."

"Go to the head of the class," Tallon said.

"We'll get on it right now," Gary declared. He was fully charged and ready to go.

"Don't let me keep you," Tallon concluded.

Officer Jerry Quigley had a string-bean build, he was tall, and he wore glasses, but he also had an innate sense of diplomacy. His partner, Officer Ed Wyncott, had light blue eyes that could be baby innocent or rock hard as the circumstances required. Between them there was a good understanding of how to work together. They knew they were going to need it.

After a brief consultation they decided where they should begin their investigation into the identity of the late Councilman Sullivan's accommodating lady friend. It wouldn't be easy, but they were fully prepared.

Mrs. Harriet Riley received them at what had been Sullivan's office. She was still very much on the job, and judging by the amount of paper work visible on her desk, Wyncott decided that she would be needed for some time more at least. Mrs. Riley was civil, but her greeting was just over the borderline from hostility. "I have already talked with Chief Tallon," she said, as though that ought to cover everything they might wish to ask.

Jerry Quigley took her on for the first round. "Mrs. Riley," he began, "we are aware that you talked with the chief and you were of considerable help to us. We also are very keenly aware of something else: that you are a very discreet person."

"That is part of my job," Harriet Riley replied evenly.

Quigley nodded his approval of her statement. "Quite frankly," he continued, "if that were not the case, we would not be calling on you."

"I don't quite understand." The air grew a little thicker.

"In police work, Mrs. Riley, we are frequently called upon to guard private and personal matters even to the point of refusing to testify in court."

"I wasn't aware of that."

Quigley could not recall ever having heard of a sworn police officer refusing to answer a question in court, but he did know that sometimes, by agreement, certain avenues of questioning were not opened up. His statement was close enough to the truth to satisfy his conscience.

"Mrs. Riley," he continued. "We are here to take you into our confidence because we feel two things: first, that it is necessary and, second, that we can rely on your total discretion."

Harriet Riley pushed back from her desk a little way, put down her arms, and looked at him without speaking. Quigley, with rare insight, said nothing at all himself as the silence continued to grow. Finally Mrs. Riley broke the impasse. "Is the matter important?" she asked.

Ed Wyncott nodded very gravely and inserted one remark. "In literal terms, Mrs. Riley, it is a matter of life and death."

Wyncott picked up smoothly. "I know that you have heard that expression before," he said. "This time it happens to be all too true. Furthermore, time is very much of the essence."

Harriet Riley picked up a pencil and began to push it through her fingers by putting first the point then the eraser end against the top of her desk. "Are you trying to tell me that I am in personal danger?" she asked.

"Fortunately, no," Quigley answered. "But another young woman is. It is quite possible that she may be murdered."

For the first time Mrs. Riley's composure broke, but only a trifle. "Could you be exaggerating that just a little?" she asked.

Again Ed Wyncott saw the right moment to speak his own piece. "Mr. Sullivan's death, to our deep regret, was not exaggerated."

There was another long moment of silence until Harriet Riley spoke again. "You believe, then, that the same people responsible for Mr. Sullivan's death may be planning another . . . attack?"

"Very definitely. You understand that we cannot say more."

"It is at least encouraging," the secretary said slowly, "that the police department is at last showing such a gratifying sense of responsibility."

"The reason why you didn't credit it to us before," Ed Wyncott replied, just as slowly, "is because we never permit anyone who is not directly concerned to know about it."

The tapping of the pencil became a tiny fraction firmer. "You have never taken action against the sex colony," she said.

Jerry Quigley suddenly became quite a bit firmer. "We are not here to discuss that matter, Mrs. Riley. I'd like to impress on you that time is a very essential element in what we *are* investigating. Had we known some things in time, we might have been able to save Mr. Sullivan's life. We can no longer do that, but we may be able to keep a young woman alive—with your cooperation."

"Who is she?" Harriet Riley asked.

"That's our problem, Mrs. Riley; we don't know her name. We do know, very definitely, that she was a close friend of Mr. Sullivan's."

"Mr. Sullivan had many friends."

"Of course, Mrs. Riley, but here is where your unquestioned discretion becomes essential. We are aware that she was an intimate friend. We have to locate her in minimum time. She is under a death threat right now, and she doesn't know it."

"We believe," Ed Wyncott contributed, "that Mr. Sullivan, were he here, would want to do everything possible to protect her."

Mrs. Riley sat very still, apart from the continuing tapping of her pencil. She drew a meaningless jagged line on a piece of paper, her brows knit. She took a small slip of paper and made marks on it. Then she looked up. "I've listened to what you have to say," she said, "and I will credit you with being well intentioned. But I want to inform you that Mr. Sullivan never, at any time in his life, I am sure, had what you described as an intimate lady friend. Since she does not exist, obviously she cannot be in any danger. That is all I have to say on the subject, and you may put it in your report."

Her decision made, she put down the pencil she had used to focus her thoughts. As she laid her arms on the top of her desk, her face firm and unyielding, the last bit of paper she had marked fell to the floor. Inwardly boiling, Ed Wyncott bent over and picked it up for her. "You may keep it," she said, almost disdainfully.

Ed glanced at the slip in his hand. Penciled on it was a telephone number.

By eleven o'clock Ned Asher and Wayne Mudd were back. Sergeant Mudd gave a verbal report to his chief. "Ned and I did all we could, which was nothing. By the time the fire department got through, the place was completely trampled. There was no hope of tire prints, paint chips, or anything else we could think of."

"That's what I expected," Tallon told him, "but we had to check it out."

"Of course," Mudd agreed. "What's next?"

"I want you to bring me up to date on the Dharmaville people," Tallon told him. "I'd like to know just how far you've gotten and how much more there is to do."

Five minutes later Asher and Mudd were seated in Tallon's office with some large work sheets spread on the desk. "To review," Asher began, "we got a full list of the membership from Mr. Santosh and everything we've checked on so far indicates that the list is complete and accurate. Every name on it has turned up as a person and we haven't found anyone who isn't listed."

Tallon studied the work sheet carefully as Asher continued. "As you know, on the night that Sullivan was killed, they had a meeting at

Dharmaville where they showed some movies of India. The films were very popular, since they dealt with ashrams in that country. Incidentally, Mr. Santosh has arranged for us to see the films if we want to."

"The answer to that is yes," Tallon said. "We might just get a line on the place where the swami reportedly trained."

"I didn't think of that," Asher admitted. "We'll let him know right away. Now, at the same time that Santosh gave us the list, he supplied the names of twenty-four people he remembered having been at the meeting. We interviewed them all and got some more names. Look." He took a pen out of his pocket to serve as a pointer. "As soon as someone was alibied by someone else, we put a check mark opposite his name. If someone else subsequently gave us the same name, we ticked it again. We kept on doing that until we reached five ticks; there was no need for more after that. By keeping on with it, we established that a hundred and thirty-four people are accounted for at the meeting—unless someone is lying."

Wayne Mudd added to that. "We conferred frequently, and we're both convinced that there was no evidence of lying. Everyone seemed to us more than willing to help. They don't want their community suspected."

Tallon was still studying the work sheets. "So as of this moment there are six people not accounted for. Have you interviewed those six?"

"Yes. They have a thing called being in seclusion. Members drop out of the community life sometimes and spend from a day to a week or more by themselves, meditating and praying or whatever else they do. Three of those people were in seclusion, but we were told several times that there was no way they could come out of seclusion without others seeing them. We interviewed all three and they told us that they had not left their quarters at any time on the day that Sullivan was killed. Those statements are partially supported by the fact that they weren't seen by anyone else. One more point: there isn't any back way out, or anything like that, so that they could come and go without being seen. At least not that we could discover."

Asher came in once more. "Of the people who were in seclusion, two were women and the third is a man in his seventies."

"I didn't know they had members that old," Tallon commented. "Most of the people I've seen are young."

"They predominate, but there are quite a few older people out there."

Tallon had been listening carefully. "So your conclusion is that the three people reported to have been in seclusion are out of it."

"For the reasons given, yes," Asher answered. "Now about the other three. One of them is Narayan, or MacNeil, who has been out of state and we haven't had a chance to talk with him yet. A second is the community receptionist who goes by the name of Bhakti, a female. We interviewed her and found her quite civil, but she told us that if any more information was needed, we should send Walt Cooper to talk to her."

"Can you describe her?" Tallon asked for reasons of his own.

Mudd gave it a shot. "About twenty-five, or maybe a little more, average figure. Not very pretty; she pulls her hair back in a severe bun and she wears granny glasses. Also she had on an antique-type dress. A kook, I'd say, who goes out of the way not to be attractive."

"And the last person of the six?"

"The last person," Mudd added, "is the swami himself. We talked with him briefly. He was courteous and all that, but he absolutely refused to tell us where he was that evening."

At least, Tallon consoled himself, the field was narrowing. The great majority of the Dharmaville people could be written off as likely suspects. Remembering something, he picked up his phone and put in another call to Chief Smallins at River Falls. When he had him on the line, he asked if a check could be made of the whereabouts of Wesley Obermann on the evening of Sullivan's murder. Smallins promised to call back as soon as there was any information.

He decided that he knew enough for the time being about Narayan and that he would take Cooper permanently off that assignment. Also Asher and Mudd had effectively finished up their job of checking out the Dharmaville population. The background investigation of the swami himself was reasonably conclusive; Tallon had himself verified the fact that Van der Water had never been arrested, at least not under his own name or as Swami Dharmayana.

Francie appeared in the doorway to tell him that a Mr. Upchurch was in the lobby and wanted to see him. Tallon couldn't place the name, but he motioned with his arm to let him come in.

Upchurch proved to be a clean-shaven, middle-aged man who took care of himself. He wore a sports outfit in very good taste: a dark brown blazer with a pair of lighter slacks and good quality shoes. He was an open-faced man who was clearly not uncomfortable in a police environment. On invitation he sat down and dropped a card on Tallon's desk. "Don Upchurch, Chief Tallon. I'm in real estate."

Tallon remembered then. "I've seen your name on signs around town, Mr. Upchurch," he said. "What can I do for you?"

Upchurch knew how to come to the point. "Mr. Landville has commissioned me to find a new home for him and his family. I've located a nice piece of property that should do well for him and his children. It's three or four notches better than what he had. His original lot was a full acre and with the increase in land values, it and the insurance settlement should put him into his new home on an even-Stephen basis."

"Has Mr. Landville seen the house you are proposing?"

"Yes, and he's more than pleased with it. There's only one thing that's holding up the insurance settlement and that's the question of the loss of his home."

Tallon knew that Upchurch wanted to make a deal; it was his legitimate business, so his statement was a little surprising. "There is a police report on file," he said, "that establishes arson as the cause of the fire. In case you haven't heard, the arsonist was seen by one of my men who chased him across some open fields in his patrol car. Unfortunately, the man was on a motorbike and got away."

Upchurch listened, but he was anxious to be heard himself. "I'm fully aware of all that, Chief Tallon, but the insurance company has raised the question as to whether or not Landville may have hired the man who burned his old house down. It was in need of repairs and the contents, I understand, were in poor condition. It could have been what they call in the East a successful fire."

"You can forget that," Tallon told his visitor. "First, there were two children in the house at the time that it was torched. If he had arranged the hit himself, he would have been careful to specify a time when his kids wouldn't be endangered. Second, we checked Mr. Landville out, as we always do in such cases, and he came up Mister Clean. There's nothing whatever in his background or recent conduct to suggest that he would have an arson attack made on his own house. I'd say that there is no basis for denying the claim on that suspicion."

"Would it trouble you too much, Chief Tallon, to give me a written memo to that effect? It might speed up the settlement and help the Landvilles to move into their new home. The property is vacant and ready for them."

Tallon called in Francie and dictated a short letter clearing Landville of any police suspicion that he might have in any way contributed to the loss of his home. While it was being typed, he asked two questions. "Was the insurance adequate at the time of the fire?"

"Yes, it was. The mortgage holder had arranged for the policy, so it was close to maximum limits. That's Mr. Landville's good fortune, of course."

"Since the policy was in good order, why is the insurance company making waves?"

"I guess because any time they can they do, Chief Tallon. They don't like to pay out. However, in fairness I have to point out that they

have been defrauded many times and so they usually look at every possible out before they pay."

When Francie came back with the letter, Tallon signed it and passed
it across the desk. "How is your client doing at Dharmaville?" he asked.

Upchurch stood up before he answered. "It was a Godsend for them,
Chief Tallon. They were really out on the street without too much in
the way of cash reserves. They've been made welcome and while the
kids are complaining about the lack of hamburgers, they seem to be
doing very well. They're even in the school that the people out there
run."

When Upchurch had left, Tallon continued with the paper work he
had to have in order for the end of the month. Francie had everything
prepared, but he went over it in detail, making sure that there were no
visible mistakes. Because he was running behind, he made do with a
milkshake at his desk and a not too tasty grilled cheese sandwich.

Early in the afternoon his private phone rang. He picked it up immediately knowing that very few people had the number. "Yes?" he asked.

"Jerry Quigley, Chief. Ed Wyncott and I would appreciate it very
much if you could come down to the Hawaiian Gardens right away."

Tallon got it immediately. "You have someone for me to meet?"

"That's it."

"On the way," Tallon said, and hung up.

Eight minutes later he parked his personal car outside the restaurant
and went in. As usual, the place was all but deserted, which was
desirable under the circumstances. He spotted Quigley in one of the
booths and walked over, wearing a pleasant smile and his most relaxed
manner. When he reached the front of the booth he saw Wyncott sitting with a quite ordinary-looking woman beside him. She was dressed
in an inexpensive suit and wore her hair in a very conventional manner. There was nothing whatever about her to mark her as distinctive
or outstanding. She was, visibly at least, another housewife dressed for
some routine occasion.

Quigley stood up. "This is Chief Tallon," he said. "Chief, this is
Mrs. Louise Hunicutt."

"How do you do," Tallon said in his most disarming manner. He sat
down and looked at the three cups of coffee that were on the table top.
When the single waitress who was on duty came up, he ordered coffee
himself.

"I very much appreciate your taking time to help us, Mrs. Hunicutt,"
Tallon began. "We have quite a serious problem here, as you know."

The woman looked at him and spoke in a very ordinary voice. "Yes,
I know."

"What is Mr. Hunicutt's line of work?" He made it an innocent expression of interest, which it was not.

"I'm a widow, Chief Tallon. I live by myself."

"In Spokane?"

"Yes."

"You work, then, I take it."

"I have a part-time job as a bookkeeper. That and what my husband left me is enough for me to get by."

"But it's not easy with costs going up every month."

"No, it isn't."

The waitress brought Tallon's coffee and refilled the other cups. Then, very quickly, she absented herself.

On the walls the dust-covered plastic decorations hung in complete defeat. Even when new they had been inadequate to convey the tropical atmosphere that someone had dreamed of at some time in the past. Now the depressed spirit of the place seemed to be tinging the conversation. Because of that, Tallon decided to get down to cases before he lost his witness altogether.

"Mrs. Hunicutt . . ." he began.

"Louise is easier."

"Thank you, Louise, it is. I take it that you knew Mr. Sullivan."

The woman looked at her coffee cup, but did not pick it up. "Yes, I did. We were friends for some time."

"Was he considerate toward you?"

She looked up from the table toward Tallon. "If you mean did he pay me for our companionship, the answer is no. I'm not coy, we spent the night together, or a few hours when he could get away, when it was mutually convenient. We were that kind of friends."

Tallon drank a little coffee and found it worse than what the station had to offer. "Louise," he said, "let me clarify something for you. The day is past when the police take any notice of what consenting adults do in private. So please understand that your relationship with Mr. Sullivan is your affair and, speaking for these gentlemen and myself, we're not going to make it public unless it can't be avoided. Usually it can."

"That's comforting," Louise said. "They told me the same thing, and I believed them."

"It's true. It's also my personal opinion that law enforcement has no place in the bedroom unless a crime is being committed, like rape. Now, I presume that Mr. Sullivan confided in you from time to time."

"Yes, he did."

"About his business?"

"Sometimes. Wilson was uptight much of the time and he needed me to help him. He didn't get that kind of help at home. His wife believes that sex is just for one purpose—to have children, and that it's a sin to use it for any other reason. So when she reached the point where she couldn't have any more, she . . ."

"I understand," Tallon said. "Louise, the reason we looked you up is twofold, if you'll excuse that old-fashioned word. First, we're making an intense investigation to find Mr. Sullivan's killer. Also, we want to protect you. I have a rather far-fetched theory, but if it's right, you could be in some personal danger."

"I don't see why; we were just friends."

"Louise, it's just possible that Mr. Sullivan may have been killed to keep his mouth shut, and someone might assume that he had shared his knowledge with you."

"Oh—I see."

"Is there any convenient place where you could go for, say, a week?"

"Yes, I could visit my sister. She and her husband are always inviting me. They live on a large ranch in Wyoming; there are no close neighbors."

"Then that might be a good idea. I'd suggest that you call her, use a public phone booth, and go as soon as you can. We'll keep in touch with you."

"That's very kind," Louise said. "What will I tell my sister?"

"Tell her that you were an accidental witness that the police want to protect. That's close to the truth and will explain any calls we may put in to you."

"Yes, that's good. I can tie it in with my bookkeeping work."

"That's an excellent idea. Do you have a car?"

"Yes, I'll probably drive."

"Then I'd suggest that you get going today, even if it means driving a while at night."

"I'll do it," she agreed. "I'm glad that you're telling me all this. I had no idea . . ."

"Of course not. Before we break up, Louise, I'd like to ask one or two questions. Did Mr. Sullivan tell you how his business was doing lately?"

"He didn't have to; I was his bookkeeper. If you want to see his records, I'll show them to you."

"That will help a lot. Ed and Jerry will drive you home; perhaps you could give the records to them."

"All right."

"Do you happen to know if Mr. Sullivan knew or dealt with a developer called Mortimer Brown? He's in San Francisco."

Louise's mouth visibly tightened, giving Tallon his answer before she spoke. When she did, he got more than he had expected. "If it weren't for Mr. Brown," she said with quiet intensity, "Wilson would be alive and happy right now. Because Brown is the man who killed him."

CHAPTER 14

Officer Walt Cooper slept until past eight-thirty, luxuriating in the rare treat of a day off. The whole department had been working so hard for the past several days, he had automatically dismissed from his mind the thought that there was something known as leisure. He took his time shaving, had a long, soul-satisfying shower, and let his thoughts run as they would.

They ran to Dharmaville.

He tried to tell himself that he was only intrigued by the secret that he knew, but the thought wouldn't jell. As he ate his breakfast he considered things soberly. His decision took him to the telephone where he called a number that he was surprised to discover he knew from memory.

"Good morning; this is Dharmaville."

"Could I have the reception center, please?"

"Who would you like to speak to?"

"Bhakti."

"I don't know if she's there or not. Hang on a minute, please."

Almost half a minute elapsed until a mature male voice came on the line. "Good morning. May I ask who's calling?"

"Officer Walter Cooper of the Whitewater Police Department. And who is this?"

"I'm Swami Dharmayana. Is there any way I can help you, sir?"

"This isn't an official call, Swami. I'd like to speak to Bhakti if I may." At that moment he began to regret that he had made the call at all. He should have known that he would run into complications.

"This is a social call, then?"

There was no way Walt could retreat with dignity. "That's right." He decided to take the whole plunge. "I have a day off, which is something of a novelty lately. I plan to ask Bhakti if she would care to spend part of it with me."

"How very nice of you, Mr. Cooper. She has spoken to me about you. You are aware that she has another identity."

"Yes," Walt answered, "but I'm willing to overlook it."

The swami laughed lightly over the phone. "As it happens, Bhakti is taking a day of seclusion, but I'll see what I can do for you. May I have your number?"

Walt gave it to him and then hung up. He had the feeling that he had committed himself too far, but it was his understanding that practically all of the Dharmaville people had been cleared of suspicion by Ned Asher and Wayne Mudd. He didn't know that there were still six open names and that he proposed to take out one of them.

He realized that he was a fool to think that he could date a girl who had chosen to live in the swami's stable. Particularly *that* girl. He saw, clearly and starkly, how far out of line he had been. Idiot!

When the phone rang, almost three quarters of an hour later, the sound of the bell created an actual physical reaction in him. The adrenalin in his bloodstream jumped, but he carefully waited until after the second ring before he answered. "Hello," he said.

This time the voice was feminine. "This is Bhakti. Swamiji told me that you called."

"Yes, I did," Walt admitted. "Chief Tallon gave me the day off. I haven't had one for some time. I don't know what the rules are out there, but I thought I'd call and see if you'd care to go out to dinner with me. If it's allowed; I don't know."

"Oh, it's allowed, of course. We aren't prisoners here." She stopped. "I haven't had an invitation like that for a long time."

"If you'd rather not . . ."

"No, I didn't say that. Actually, I think it would be nice."

Walt could hardly believe it. "Is there any particular place you'd like to go?" he asked.

"No, I don't know too many places."

Walt was gaining confidence. "There's a very nice place in Spokane. Actually it's connected with a motel, but it's a class dining room. Not too crowded, and the food is great."

"Do you know where Swami's dome is?"

"No, but I can find it."

"If we're going into Spokane, suppose you pick me up at six-thirty. At Swami's. My home is just a little cabin and, well . . ."

"At Swami's at six-thirty. I hope I get to meet him."

"Oh, you will. I'm sure of that." She hung up.

Walt looked at the clock and made a swift mental calculation that was divided into hours and minutes. Then he picked up the phone once more and made a reservation.

"A table for two at seven-thirty. Thank you, Mr. Cooper, it will be ready for you."

That was all he could do. He sat down and told himself that he had a dinner date for the evening with a girl that he liked. In a sense he would be taking part in a small conspiracy because he knew who she really was. However, he told himself once more, that didn't matter.

The hours marched slowly by in leaden shoes. He washed his car and cleaned out the interior. He went to the tailor shop and had his best suit pressed while he waited. He went to the men's shop and bought a new shirt. He carefully shined his own shoes, because any policeman could do that better than the usual professional bootblack.

With a sudden inspiration he went to the library and spoke with Sarah Weintraub. He offered his sincere sympathy over the loss of her home and all of her possessions.

"The worst part of it was my husband's stamp collection," she told him. "It was insured, but it can never really be replaced. He had spent hundreds of hours working on it, and it was his only real interest outside of the college. He had had it for more than twenty-five years."

Once again Walt Cooper was glad that he was a cop. When outrages like that were taking place, he wanted to help stop them and to catch the people responsible. To testify against them and to see them sent to prison, where they could no longer harm innocent people.

Sarah Weintraub was not one to visit her misfortunes on to others. She closed the subject and then asked, "What would you like, Walt?"

"I hear that you have some material on Dharmaville."

"That's right, we do. Some of it is out; the swami's autobiography is already at your department. We have a brief history of Dharmaville and how it was established."

"I'd like that," Walt said.

"I'll get it for you. Come along, and see what else we have."

Walt Cooper drove home with three books. The one about the history of the Dharmaville community interested him the most. He found it well-illustrated and written. It was actually a brochure rather than a book, but it ran more than fifty pages. Toward the back, in a group picture, he spotted the girl who was to be his date that evening. Even though he knew who she really was, he was unable to recognize her as anyone but Bhakti. He had always laughed a little at the idea of disguise, but she had it down to a science.

The clock's weary hands at last dragged themselves into position where they indicated 5 P.M. Walt had already decided that when that time came, he would begin to get ready. He was looking forward to the evening with a nice girl from Dharmaville, but he could not forget that she was also the most sensational screen beauty of his generation, or that she was the same person who had so mysteriously disappeared.

Bhakti was Marsha Stone and there was no way he could erase that knowledge. As he took a long and careful shower, he tried to ask himself if he would be this uptight if it were only Bhakti he would be taking out: the rather nice person who had served him tea and made him like it. He remembered, very carefully, how he had been attracted to her despite her outlandish getup, and before her sudden revelation of her identity. And why in hell had she chosen to tell him that presumably closely guarded piece of information? He, who was a cop, who was more or less committed to putting everything that he learned into his reports.

As he toweled down vigorously, he was grateful that he had a trim, well-muscled body.

He spent almost five minutes taking all of the pins and fasteners out of his new shirt, along with the piece of plastic that held the collar in display position. His freshly pressed suit fitted him nicely, especially since he had knocked off the extra five pounds that had been plaguing him. His tie and coat could wait.

It was only five-twenty when he finished, and he had an hour to spend before he left his apartment. He picked up the Dharmaville books once more and forced himself to read. He had never been a clock watcher, but it was hard for him to concentrate on the text that spoke about brotherhood and love for everyone. Somehow, he had heard it all before.

At a quarter to six he began to fear that the phone would ring. Either Bhakti would beg off or he would be called in to help cover a police emergency. In either event he was dead in the water and there would be nothing he could do.

At five minutes to six he put on his tie and coat, checked his pockets, and left. He was much too early, but if he were out, then the station would not be able to reach him; he did not have a police radio in his car. He asked himself once, quickly, if he was copping out on his duty and convinced himself that he was not. If Bhakti had said six instead of six-thirty, he would have been long gone anyway.

He killed fifteen minutes sitting in his car before he started the engine. When he finally took that affirmative step, he knew that he was on his way, come hell or high water. He turned onto the highway and headed toward Dharmaville.

At the main office, someone who was working late gave him directions to the swami's home. He drove up the hill, conscious of the fact that he was on time to the minute, and parked when he reached the plateau that had been described to him.

As he got out of his car he wondered too late if he should have brought her something. He usually did when he was coming to dinner, but this time it was the other way around. He walked up to the entrance of the large blue dome and knocked.

The man who opened the door was the swami himself. Walt had seen several pictures of him in the Dharmaville literature and there was no possible mistake. "Good evening, Swami," he said. "I'm Walt Cooper."

"Come in, Mr. Cooper, delighted to meet you. Please sit down." The swami waved a hospitable arm toward a large sofa. "Bhakti will be out shortly."

Cooper looked about him, taking in the unusual interior of the dome and noting that there was a second story that covered about a third of the interior area. Then he sat down and prepared himself for whatever inquisition was coming. He had frequently testified in court, so the experience would not be entirely new.

"It was so very nice of you to invite Bhakti to dinner," the swami continued. "As I told you on the phone, or I believe she did, she doesn't go out very much."

"She should," Walt answered. "She's a very nice person."

"Your judgment is sound there, Walt. You don't mind if I use your first name, do you?"

"Of course not."

"Also, if I may add this, it's reassuring to know that Bhakti isn't under any suspicion. If she were, you obviously wouldn't be taking her out on a social engagement."

Walt was right with him on that one. "This has nothing to do with the police department, and they don't know about it," he said. "But if you had it in mind that I asked her out to pump her, dismiss it."

"That's very good," the swami responded.

"What time does she have to be back?"

"Whenever she chooses. We have no rules here, only traditions."

A sound behind him told Walt that his date had come into the room. He got to his feet and turned to greet her.

Bhakti was not there. Instead there was a girl in a long dinner dress —a white one that was exquisitely molded to her figure. Her hair was down to where it fell almost to her shoulders. And her face, with its perfect nose and wide-apart dark green eyes with their slight suggestion of an oriental slant, was the face of Marsha Stone.

It was a face known to millions, and it took his breath away.

She had shaken down her hair the first time he had met her, but he hadn't realized—hadn't truly seen what had been before him. Now, as he looked at Marsha Stone, he understood why she had been a sensation.

He knew that he should say, "Good evening," but for the moment he was incapable of it. Instead he let his mind form its own words. "I can't believe it!"

The girl he had known best as Bhakti came forward and offered him her hand. Closer, her startling beauty was almost more than he could endure. "I decided that it was time for my coming-out party," she said. "Swami convinced me that you wouldn't mind too much if I dressed this way."

Walt said, "'Then did brave Odysseus' knees grow feeble.'"

Behind him the swami laughed pleasantly. When Walt turned toward him, he spoke. "I convinced Bhakti that she couldn't run away from herself forever and that the problems that had beset her are all in the past. So I persuaded her to be herself once more."

Walt was still stunned. "Do I call you Bhakti—or Marsha?" he asked.

She countered without answering. "Do I look all right?"

"Oh, God," Walt said.

"Then why don't we go. One thing more: Marsha is my real name. Marsha Ellenbach."

In somewhat of a daze Walt escorted her to his car.

He was glad to drive, because it gave him something rational to do. As he approached Whitewater, he contemplated running a red light so that he would be stopped, but they all knew his car. And the chief did not take kindly to things like that; policemen had to set an example. He drove through the city and not a soul seemed to notice him or who he had with him in his car.

It surprised him how well Marsha, for he could not think of her any other way now, kept up a pleasant flow of small talk, putting him at his ease and behaving as though she were just another girl who had been lucky enough to receive a nice dinner invitation. All the way into Spokane she was an ideal companion. Once or twice, when he turned to look at her, he felt a bomb go off, but she smiled away his tension.

When they reached the outskirts of the city, he offered silent thanks that he had chosen the very best place he knew to take her. Marsha Stone in the Hawaiian Gardens was a concept that defied possibility. When he had made his reservation, he had assumed that she would gather him a few pitying looks, but he had picked the top spot anyway.

He parked the car and helped her out. At that moment she seemed

as excited to be with him as he was with her, except in his case he was
a bit off balance. But he still knew how to conduct himself. He opened
the door for her, guided her up a few steps, and down the short corridor flanked with celebrity photographs that led to the dining room.

The maître d' wore a formal outfit, part of which was a red-striped
vest that apparently had some meaning. He was bent over his reservations desk, attending to a party of four, so Walt waited patiently, his
date on his arm, until he was finished. The headwaiter took the people
in. Then, automatically, he plucked two menus out of a bin and
straightened up to face his next guests.

"The name is Cooper," Walt said. "I have a reservation for two."

The headwaiter appeared to ignore him. "I beg your pardon," he
said, his voice on the lowest rung of humility, "but I was totally un-
prepared." He recovered himself. "We have your reservation, of course,
Mr. Cooper. It's just that we didn't know . . ." He turned and con-
sulted the table chart; Walt deduced correctly that he was about to
make a drastic change.

The maître d', a good product of his training, completed his recovery.
"This way please, Mr. Cooper. And Miss Stone. It is Miss Stone, isn't
it?" His voice vibrated with eagerness.

Walt answered for her. "We would like something a little private, if
you have it."

The headwaiter misunderstood. "A private dining room? It can be arranged in a few minutes. Perhaps until then . . ."

Walt shook his head. "We just don't want to be seated near the doorway," he said.

The headwaiter, his sensational discovery confirmed, led them to the
table he had been saving for a very rich patron of the premises. "Enjoy
your dinner," he said as he put down the menus. Then he retreated,
slipped at once into his office, and made an urgent phone call.

The manager of the hotel exercised his best judgment. First of all, he
wanted it positively confirmed that the unexpected guest in the dining
room was actually Marsha Stone. If it were not, then any news leak
from his establishment could turn into a serious embarrassment. Second, he specified that Miss Stone, if it was indeed she, and her escort,
were not to be subject to any annoyance during or after their dinner.
Maximum discretion was imperative.

By the time that Walt Cooper had ordered drinks for them, the entire small room was filled with an electric undercurrent. Heads turned,
most of them politely, and diners in disadvantaged places found excuses
to get up and try to secure a better view.

The maître d' had put them in the corner booth at the end, the most
comfortable seat he had to offer. Marsha sat with her back to most of

the rest of the dining area, but several women hurried out and rushed to the telephones.

When the drinks had been served, the cocktail waitress followed her instructions. "Miss Stone," she said. "I don't want to be forward, but I have a fifteen-year-old son who is a great movie buff. Would you possibly be willing to give him your autograph?"

Marsha smiled, a little mechanically Walt thought and accepted the offered pen and pad of paper. She signed quickly and then handed it back. "I'm glad to do it for you," she said, "but I want to have a private dinner."

"I understand, Miss Stone. I'll pass the word."

When she had gone, Walt measured up to the unexpected requirements that had been laid on him. "Now we come to dinner," he said. "I know that the food at Dharmaville is all vegetarian. What are your preferences?"

When Marsha smiled at him, it was warm and cordial, nothing like the professional smile she had given the cocktail waitress. "I see they have prime rib," she said. "I haven't had any for a long time."

"Good, we'll have some. How do you like it?"

"Medium rare, and English cut if they have it. I used to get it at Lawry's in Beverly Hills."

"Salad?"

"Thousand island."

"Potato?"

"Baked, with sour cream and chives. Oh, I've waited for this for so long!"

"I don't want to spoil you for Dharmaville," he said, very carefully.

She picked up her cocktail glass and looked at him over the rim. "You won't. But you can always ask me out again—if you want to."

Walt pretended to be thoughtful. "I might," he conceded.

The cocktail waitress was showing the autograph to the maître d'. "Either she is Marsha Stone, or else she's impersonating her. But I doubt that; no one could impersonate Marilyn Monroe either."

The hotel manager, who had joined the conference, weighed the matter. "I don't think an impersonator would have the nerve," he said. "Besides, it's actionable. I haven't seen her, but she's supposed to be sensational."

The cocktail waitress gave her judgment. "Looks like that come once in a generation. Who could ever look like Garbo?"

"All right," the manager said. "We'll assume that it is Marsha Stone, though why she picked here to reappear I'll never know. See that complimentary champagne is served. And the best of everything, of course. But don't overdo it; tell the help not to ogle her and discourage table-hopping."

"Of course," the maître d' agreed.

"I'll take care of the rest," the manager declared.

Walt had always known that the dining room was a good one, but it seemed to him that the service had never been as outstanding, which he could well understand, or the food itself so excellent, which apparently was their good luck. When the champagne came, he accepted it with quiet dignity. When they were alone again, he gave his full attention once more to his companion. "Marsha, I know what the swami said, but have you considered the implications of your appearance here this evening?"

She quirked a smile at him. "Have you?"

"No, and I don't care. I just wanted to be with you."

"As Bhakti?" She was clearly teasing him.

"Any way at all. Just as long as it's the same girl—Marsha Ellenbach."

She reached out a hand and laid it on his. "Walt," she said, "you are a genuine person. An honest-to-God man who knows how to act like one. I ran away from a whole phalanx of others who were nothing but front. I know you know that word, because I heard you quote Homer."

"There are a lot of solid types around," Walt said, deliberately tormenting himself. "There are eight in our department. Every one of them is right on. I hope you'll meet them some day."

"I'd like that," Marsha said.

They were almost through eating when the manager appeared at their table. "I hope you are enjoying your dinner," he said.

Walt knew to whom that question was directed, and he let her answer. "It's excellent, thank you," Marsha said.

The manager turned to Walt. "And you, sir?"

"First-rate. I've been here before."

"I thought I recognized you, but I didn't know your name."

"I'm Walter Cooper. Officer Cooper of the Whitewater Police Department." He did that deliberately, both to reflect any credit that he could on to his department, and to chill any possible "mystery millionaire" rumors that might spring up.

"We do appreciate your bringing Miss Stone here; we're most honored, of course." He turned. "Miss Stone, as you came in this evening you may have noticed some photographs we have displayed. Notable people who have chosen to eat here. If it isn't asking too much, would you permit one picture?"

Marsha was cool and self possessed. "If you wish, but I don't want too much fuss."

"Of course not." The manager turned and nodded. "We have our own photographer, and we'll be happy to send you some prints if you would like them."

"Perhaps, care of Mr. Cooper at the Whitewater Police?"

By the time she had finished speaking, a photographer had materialized beside the table. He focused quickly and took three shots. Then he spoke a fast, "Thank you, very much," and left.

The effect on the rest of the room was clear. The last doubt had been dissolved and the maître d' had to intervene personally to keep would-be table-hoppers from confronting his unexpected guest.

The manager expressed his thanks. "You've been most gracious, Miss Stone," he said. "Allow me to reciprocate by asking you and Mr. Cooper to be my guests this evening. And may I suggest our strawberry cheesecake for dessert; it's a house specialty."

In twenty minutes they had finished and were ready to leave. Walt asked for the check and was told once more that the dinner was on the house. "Next time," the maître d' said, thereby protecting himself from setting a precedent.

As they left the dining room, a solid line of people was waiting to see them as they departed. About fifty more were gathered outside on the parking lot. Grateful that he had remembered to wash his car, Walt quietly drove away.

On the return trip to Dharmaville, he put soft music on the radio and drove at a leisurely pace. "I'm sorry about all the publicity," he said.

Marsha turned toward him. "I'm used to it," she said. "But I did get awfully tired of being a prize exhibit everywhere I went. Have you got plenty of gas?"

"No problem; I filled up this afternoon."

"Then could we drive around a little? I like the moonlight."

He picked the most scenic drive he knew, and drove for well over an hour. During that time she said nothing at all; instead she looked calmly out of the window at the landscape in the pale moonlight that clearly did have an appeal for her.

At last she spoke. "Have you ever been married?"

"No."

"Why not?"

"Lots of girls, not enough real people."

"Am I real people?"

"I wish you were homely as a bat, so I could tell you just how much. I knew it when you served me tea, and you looked different then."

Marsha smothered a small titter. "You know, no one ever recognized me, not even the people I see every day. Before tonight, apart from Narayan, only Swamiji knew. He rescued me when I was desperate, and he never asked anything in return. I always feel safe and secure with him."

Walt desperately wanted to say either that she could trust him as well, or that he was not prepared to give any such guarantee, but he managed to keep quiet. "He must be quite a guy," he offered.

"Swami is, he's the real thing. And I'm an authority on fakes; I lived among them for some time, until I got fed up. People that come up to you and kiss you at parties before you even know who they are."

"And the propositions—I expect."

"Good God," she said, and put her hand on her forehead. "That's one of the great advantages of Dharmaville; I've been entirely free of that there."

"Marsha, may I ask you out again?"

"I'm hoping you will. And don't wait too long."

His hopes went into blazing orbit. He drove up a small rise where there was a viewpoint. In the thin moonlight a ghost world was revealed, misty and uncertain, timeless and still. He stopped the car and then sat still himself, letting her enjoy the unreal world in the moonlight. When she got out of the car, he followed and stood beside her, but not too close. His own awareness was screaming to him that one false move now would destroy both the immediate past and the limitless future. It was a freak of fate that he was with Marsha Stone and he knew it could not last.

Marsha turned toward him. "I'm waiting," she said.

He dared to reach out and she came to him. She rested her head on his shoulder for a moment or two, then she turned and put her hands on his shoulders.

CHAPTER 15

On the same evening that Marsha Stone was making her dramatic reappearance, Jack Tallon was sitting quietly in his living room, deeply concerned by the new information he had been given. He was thinking hard, putting together combinations and permutations, trying to see a ray of light that might filter through any possible cracks.

Jennifer had learned never to talk shop with him, but she was concerned about his mood. He had never acted quite the same way before and it worried her. She decided to take the plunge. Quietly she sat down beside him and said, "Tell me about it."

"It really wouldn't interest you."

"Maybe not, but it will give you a good chance to think out loud. That works pretty well, sometimes."

Tallon forced himself to come back to earth. "I can't really lay this one on you, Jen," he said, "but would you mind if I went to San Francisco for a day or two? There's a man there I have to see."

"Of course not. I'll miss you, but go if you want to."

His decision made, Jack got to his feet and went to the telephone. He called San Francisco information, got a number, and dialed.

As soon as a female voice answered mechanically, he knew that he had reached an answering service. "This is Chief Tallon of the Whitewater, Washington, Police Department," he said. "I need to speak with Mr. Mortimer Brown as soon as possible. Will you see if you can reach him for me?"

"Normally, sir, we're not supposed to do that. Is this police business?"

"Yes, it is."

"Hold on a minute."

After an interval the girl came back on the line. "If I may have your number, sir, Mr. Brown will call you shortly."

Jack did not like to give out his unlisted home number, but he had no choice. He supplied it and then sat down beside the phone. Less than two minutes later it rang.

"Chief Tallon?"

"Yes. Mr. Brown?"

"That's right. The service said it was urgent."

"It's quite important, Mr. Brown, that I see you as soon as possible," Tallon said. "How does your schedule look for tomorrow afternoon?"

"I don't have my calendar here, I'm at home, but I'm usually clear about four."

"Four it is, then, tomorrow afternoon. If I have any trouble with reservations, I'll call you."

As soon as he was finished talking, he called Northwest Orient regarding a morning seat to San Francisco. The reservations agent offered him a choice of flights and rapidly confirmed the one he chose. One more call secured him a hotel room in San Francisco.

That done, he called Sergeant Hillman, advised him that he was going out of town, and put Hillman in charge of the department until he returned. Then he went into the bedroom to pack his bag.

The office occupied by Mortimer Brown was large with a panoramic view of both the bay and the Golden Gate. Everything about it had been designed to be impressive and to make it clear to the visitor that money had been spent to enshrine more money. It stopped just short of ostentation.

Brown himself was a little under six feet, stocky, and jowled. In his fifties, his hair was deserting him, but enough wisps remained for him to brush them in a conventional manner. His complexion was ruddy enough to suggest a possible medical problem. The diagnosis was reinforced by the fact that he seemed incapable of sitting or standing still. He kept his body in almost constant movement, doing things with his hands, changing the position of his legs, or shifting his position in his elaborate chair. His attention, however, remained fixed; his eyes still.

"There's a great deal I could tell you about the land development business, if there was any point to it," he said, keeping his eyes fixed on Tallon's face. "One of the basic requirements is vision, and that is what Willie Sullivan did not have. Would you care for a cigar?"

"No, thank you."

"Would it bother you if I light up?" The question was not meant to be answered; in his own office Mortimer Brown was the controlling force and he intended to keep it that way. "I'll tell you a little story," Brown continued as he extracted a cigar from an imported pack and flicked a gold lighter. "Years ago, when I was just a kid ready to try and make my way in the world, I happened to stand next to a man who was wearing a very luxurious, dark blue topcoat. I'd never seen one like it, so I asked about it. He told me it was cashmere. I asked him how well it wore. It was very soft, but it could also fall apart. I still remember exactly what he said: 'It wears well enough, but it's not for a salaried person.' Right then and there I learned that no one would ever get anywhere working for a paycheck. That's for people who think they have security and want to keep it."

Tallon let out a little line. "I already know that you're very successful," he said.

"Moneywise, yes, but that isn't all. There are other things. I've taken raw land and turned it into productive real estate. Over the years I've given ten thousand people a view of the ocean with efficient, compact modern housing. They paid for it, of course, but the point is, they wanted to. Nobody forced them. I created the option and they took it. Anybody can take a vacant lot and put a house on it. They can even hook in some solar panels and cut the heating bills. But to look at a piece of raw soil, see it as a shopping center, and then make it a reality, that takes the kind of vision, and the kind of money, I can supply. I know where to get hold of whatever I need for any sound proposition, and no other kind interests me."

Tallon decided that it was time to start baling the hay. "You know, of course, that Mr. Sullivan was murdered by person or persons unknown. We're conducting an intensive investigation."

"Naturally, but Willie was in trouble most of the time, and he got a lot of people mad at him."

"I'm aware of that. Right now I'm particularly interested in the last deal he concluded, or tried to conclude, with you."

Brown leaned back in his chair as though he had to consider that matter carefully. He puffed at his cigar so that the acrid odor reached Tallon and annoyed him. He had no idea what kind of a cigar it was, but something made the aroma thoroughly distasteful. All the time Brown kept up his incessant shifting of his body; it seemed to Tallon that it was less pathological than an oversupply of nervous energy he could not dissipate.

"Willie made a damn fool of himself," Brown said at last. "He hated that name, by the way, because it belongs to blacks. His mother should have thought of that."

"Do you have a son?" Tallon asked.

"Yep, one son, three daughters, two married. The third is going for her PhD at Berkeley. My son's coming into the business. He's a little too eager right now, but he'll learn."

"You were going to tell me about Sullivan."

"Oh yes, sure. I've known Willie, somewhat, because he came to me from time to time for help in locating materials or some specialized help. I lent him a hand because, while he was only a builder, he was trying to turn a buck, and that's the name of the game. Well Willie got greedy. I had a little piece of land that came to me as part of a package deal and I let him have it for a fair price. He was hard up for something to do, so I sold him the property and advised him to put up condominiums. That's the only way to go now: twice the profit on half the land. But he didn't listen; he went for single family homes."

Brown stopped and relit his cigar. Tallon noticed that it was still burning, but apparently Brown was not satisfied.

"Now here is where he made an ass of himself," Brown continued when he was ready. "The plot was good for six, possibly seven, houses and they would have sold right now. But not being a developer, he decided to milk the last drop of profit. He put up ten houses: well, actually five, he never got the rest started. They were too close together, yards too small to even park a tricycle, and second- or third-grade materials throughout. You may think that the public doesn't see a thing like that after it's been covered with a coat of paint. But they do. Like they kick the tires on a car, they wiggle the garage doors to see if they're stiff and firm. I always make garage doors extra firm because of that. Just the way they dip oranges in dye and paraffin so that they'll look good and feel smooth. You understand why I'm telling you these things, of course."

"Of course," Tallon agreed.

"Well, Sullivan screwed himself. He put up those matchboxes, with knotholes in the side paneling you could put your fist through, one practically on top of the other, and then called them, 'A new approach to gracious living.' He couldn't give them away. He dropped his price after a while until he was down to two or three thousand dollars profit per house, and still he couldn't move them. So he came to me."

"And what did you do?" Tallon asked.

"I told him right out that he was going to have to take a bath. Condominiums he could have sold, but no—he had to have houses. More profit, he thought. Anyhow, he was up shit creek, and I needed a tax write-off. I offered to take back the property, cancel his obligation, and return what he'd already paid. The houses weren't worth anything: I don't know how he got by the inspectors, but he may have spread a little grease there. He was up against it because the bank was pressing him. He didn't have to take the deal, but I offered cash and he did."

"Let me be sure I understand," Tallon said. "You in essence took back the land and refunded his full purchase price."

"That's right."

"His loss was the houses he had put on it; the ones he couldn't sell."

"Yes, but there are risks in every business. He tried to reach too far over his head and he fell in. He had no other offer and he couldn't get one, so I bought his mistakes."

"Are the houses in Whitewater?" Tallon asked.

"No, not in your jurisdiction at all."

"And you still have them."

"No, three are sold and we have deals pending on the other two. My son did that. He put an ad in a swingers' journal announcing the development and making it clear that the homes would be sold to swingers only. Of course he made the price look right and I spent a few thousand fixing them up and covering the knotholes. I found some erotic wallpaper and put it up in the bathrooms. That became a good selling point." He paused to draw smoke from his cigar. "All I'm doing is picking up the profit that Willie could have had if he had used his own imagination. When you're stuck with a turkey, the way out is to make the public want turkey. You can sell anything that way."

Tallon had listened enough. It had all been helpful in assessing the man before him, but it was time to change tactics. "Now, Mr. Brown, I have something else to discuss. You aren't recording this conversation, are you?"

"Absolutely not—you got my word. And I know better than to lie to cops. We have to get along, you and I; that's why I cleared this time for us to talk."

That told Tallon a lot, but he was not about to show his hand. "There's a large, quite nice, piece of property that's partly in Whitewater. I understand that you want to buy it."

For the first time Mortimer Brown showed real interest in the conversation. "You mean the piece that the Jesus freak has at present? Yes, I intend to develop that."

"The man who owns it told me he doesn't want to sell."

Brown waved a hand through the air. "Chief, there's an old principle of business that you ought to know: every man has his price. I've talked to the owner, and all he's doing is holding out for more money. I know how much I'm going to pay him, and he'll make a neat profit out of the deal. I don't mind that; he's got the property, I want it, so he has a chance to cash in."

Tallon listened politely, then he made his own point. "Mr. Brown, I'm not accusing anyone of anything, at this time, but I want to line up some facts for you and see how they read—in your opinion. Sullivan took a heavy loss on the sale of the land and the five houses he had built. To a man in his financial position, it could have been a crippling loss."

"True," Brown agreed, still puffing his cigar and quite unperturbed.

"Next, he unexpectedly runs for the city council and gets elected."

"Irishmen are always running for public office. It's their mania."

Tallon was unfazed. "As soon as he takes his seat on the council, Sullivan begins to give the Dharmaville community every kind of a hard time. He tries to pass an absurd ordinance that would have required them to put a ten-foot fence around the entire property."

"That was only a gambit."

"I know that, Mr. Brown, but then he came back with the complaint that the community isn't meeting the requirements of the health department. Now he wasn't a big enough man, financially speaking, to take over that whole eight hundred and ten acres and develop it himself." Tallon stopped and let his host think about that one.

Brown took his time, rocking sidewise in his chair, but holding his head still. Then he took his cigar out of his mouth and looked at Tallon. "All right, I'll give it to you. You're a pretty smart guy. Sullivan had his back to the wall. Even with the bailout I gave him, he was still hooked for the cost of putting up those five houses and he dropped something around a hundred and fifty grand. He came to me in desperation. We weren't exactly friends, but I have a way of making things succeed—one way or the other. I made him a proposition. Since he had become a councilman, I agreed to pay him a commission if he ran the Jesus freaks off the property I wanted and made them sell."

"A big commission?" Tallon asked.

"By his standards, a very big commission. One that would have bailed him out completely and given him a good piece of change to put in the bank. A solid profit. Now you know as well as I do that business is business and politics has a lot to do with it. Yes, I wanted to force a sale; now I'll have to pay more to get the property."

"And you won't settle for anything else."

"No."

"Because of the legalized gambling," Tallon shot out.

For the first time Brown suddenly sat still. "How the hell did you find out about that?" he asked.

"How did you?" Tallon countered.

"I just told you: business is business and I have my sources. I pay for them. I battle local boards and various commissions all the time; it goes with the territory. Nobody wants to give away choice real estate; they all want to get their piece of the action." He stopped and leaned forward. "Now I believe in speaking frankly. Sooner or later I'm going to acquire that property, and that's going to result in a big increase in your local tax income. There'll be more money for your department, and for all the rest of the city. Strictly legally. I hire lawyers to do the arguing for me, and I hire the kind that win. You got me so far?"

"Yes," Tallon answered, and meant it.

"In fact, Tallon, I think it would be very much to your advantage if we were to work together on this. For the sake of increased revenue, and there can be other benefits closer to you personally. Understand that I'm not in any way suggesting any wrongdoing. Sooner or later I'll find something where that bunch of nuts has violated the law. When that's an established fact, then you can do only what's expected of you —enforce the law. When I take over the property, I won't forget your help; we can work out the details later."

"What if the people now on the land stay within the law and meet all their proper obligations? What then?"

Brown twisted his cigar in his fingers and once more an unpleasant odor drifted across his desk. "Don't worry about that," he said. "There'll be a violation."

For the last little while a slow fury had been building inside Tallon; now it had reached the point where he knew he faced a battle to control himself. He was almost shaking with anger, but he kept it hidden and not a trace of his emotions showed on his face. He had been a policeman for a long time and he knew his business.

"Before I leave, Mr. Brown," he said, his voice casual and relaxed, "I feel that I should give you a warning."

The man across the desk responded to that by tightening up and leaning forward with hard cold eyes fixed on Tallon's face. "And just what is that?" he demanded.

Tallon continued to play dumb. "Within the past two weeks, we have had two separate arson attacks in our city. In both cases houses were burned down; they were total losses. We have no idea at all who is doing this, or why. Arsonists of this kind are very hard to catch, almost impossible with the force I've got. Until this plague of fires is stopped, Whitewater might be a bad place to put in any new construction."

Brown leaned back and smirked. "That won't hold me up five minutes," he said. "I've got very good security people if I need them. Hey! You've got a big hippy colony right in your own town. There's your answer. Find the firebug there. I'm sure you can," he added.

"It's a thought," Tallon said.

Brown got to his feet. "Don't you worry about what might happen to me. I can take care of myself. A lot of people have found that out the hard way. Thanks for coming to see me."

Tallon was fortunate enough to make a connection that took him home that same evening. As the scenery of the Pacific Northwest unfolded in the gathering darkness, he fantasized that he had Mortimer Brown dead to rights on charges of grand theft and fraud. He was still angry that he had been treated as a child, that he had been assumed to be a "hick cop," and that he had clearly been offered a bribe. Obviously Brown did not know that some of the best policemen served small communities. It was not his business to interfere in civil affairs, but if Brown tried to take over Dharmaville on some legal technicality, he would get damn little cooperation from the Whitewater Police Department.

As he ate his airline meal, he mused on the matter and made a small decision: he would tip the swami off. Just as a friend. He finished all of the food he had been given without realizing it. The girl who was serving him was quite nice, and when she refilled his coffee cup for the third time, he thanked her.

"Did you have enough?" she asked.

"Yes, I think so," Tallon answered. "Where are all the passengers to-night?"

"It's a very light load. If you're still hungry, there are some extra desserts in first class."

"Is that allowed?"

"Absolutely not, but I hate to see things go to waste." She brought him a generous slice of a delicious cake that he polished off with relish. Then he felt just a little better.

For the first time he noticed that a newspaper was lying on the vacant seat next to the aisle. Having eaten well, and with a little more time to spend, he reached over and picked it up. He hadn't seen a paper all day and in his line of work, he had to keep up with all that was going on.

He did so very swiftly. The headline read: MARSHA STONE FOUND. That startled him somewhat because her whereabouts were being kept carefully secret. Then he noted the picture. It was four columns wide and for a newspaper photograph remarkably good. There seated in a restaurant booth and looking extraordinarily beautiful was the missing actress, her identity unmistakable. And seated next to her, looking like a youthful but very successful businessman, was Walt Cooper. Cooper, the one officer on his force who had, in the past, showed clear evidence of being bored with his job.

He looked far from bored in the picture. He sat as a man does when he is in full possession of himself, and he even contrived to appear handsome. His expression had no hint of a smirk or of triumph; he simply filled the role admirably of a suitable escort for the stunning Marsha Stone.

The editor had been resourceful. There was a reproduction of the autograph Miss Stone had given to the waitress. A local autograph collector had supplied another signature she had given before her dramatic disappearance. Clearly they were close to identical. It was a nice touch, proving her identity with evidence the public could see for itself.

The caption under the photograph identified the man in the picture as "Officer Walter Cooper of the Whitewater Police Department." That was all.

There was, of course, a long article about her dramatic reappearance, with a sidebar summarizing the details of her disappearance. Tallon read it all carefully to the point where he was told to turn to page seven. He did so and found more pictures. There was one of Marsha Stone in a highly successful motion picture, one at a party in Hollywood, and a formal studio portrait. There was a picture of the male star whose name had been linked with hers and a single-column head shot of Detective Francis MacNeil who had devoted so much time and effort in an attempt to locate her.

Deputy Sheriff MacNeil was clean-shaven; there was nothing about the picture that in any way suggested Narayan, the man at Dharmaville whom Tallon knew to be the same person.

When he had finished reading the whole thing, he put the paper down and thought until the seat belt sign came on. As he drove home from the airport, he was still thinking. He didn't know how it had happened, but his faith in his men was such he assumed that Walt Cooper hadn't done anything out of line. If Marsha Stone had chosen to reappear, it had been her decision; he was almost certain of that.

Jennifer welcomed him home with a warm embrace, poured him a cup of coffee, and exploded the news that Marsha Stone had dramatically reappeared with *Walt Cooper*. She put the italics into her voice. Jack just smiled at her.

It was just as well he did not know what was going on at his department or how valiantly his watch commander, Wayne Mudd, was guarding his unlisted home telephone number. The small lobby had never been so jammed and the media people who filled it were relentless. Two of them deliberately ran the few red lights on Main Street in the hope that by so doing they would manage to meet Officer Walt Cooper. Gary Mason stopped them both and issued citations. When he was questioned, he refused to say anything at all about his colleague Walt Cooper other than the fact they were good friends. On the subject of Marsha Stone he wouldn't open his mouth.

When Ed Wyncott came to work, to take over the midnight to dawn shift, he was mobbed until everyone knew that he was not Officer Walter Cooper and that he had nothing whatever to say to the press.

When Tallon arrived at his office in the morning, he caught the full blast. Most of the original reporters and would-be TV interviewers had left, but they had been replaced by an even more aggressive day shift. Huge trucks were parked in restricted areas with TV identification on their sides. There was no way they were going to leave until they had a story. They wanted to interview Officer Cooper, but even more they wanted him to produce Marsha Stone.

Tallon had dealt with the press before and understood the competitive pressures that every newsman faced. The people who were swamping his small facility were doing their job, as he was trying to do his. He managed to plow his way into his office by promising he would talk with the press shortly. As soon as he was alone and had the door shut, he called Harry Gilroy, the publisher of the local paper who had sat on the city council for so long. "Harry," he said, "I'm being bombarded up here."

"Naturally," Harry told him without sympathy. "What did you expect? And I'm not happy with you this morning: for the first time in thirty years I had a chance to break a major national story and you didn't tip me off."

"I'll level," Tallon answered. "I knew where Stone was, as of a few days ago, but it was police confidential. I had no idea she was going to reappear, and with one of my boys."

"How about an exclusive interview with the lady? All will be forgiven."

"OK by me, but you've got to earn it. As of right now you're the press relations officer of the Whitewater Police Department. Get your ass over here to your post of duty."

"Coming," Gilroy said, and hung up. From that moment forward Tallon was much relieved. Harry Gilroy was as good a newspaperman as there was and he would have all the answers.

Francie appeared, her hands waving frantically in the air. "Chief, it's like feeding time at the zoo, you can't imagine . . ."

Tallon actually smiled at her. "Hang in there," he advised. "Harry Gilroy is on his way over. He's our new press relations officer."

Francie returned to the lobby and informed the press that Chief Tallon would make a statement as soon as he had conferred with the press relations officer. That produced an immediate demand to talk with that official. The uproar was still going strong when Harry appeared and began to work his way through the crowd. "Are you Officer Cooper's father?" someone shouted at him, but he ignored it.

Once he reached Tallon's office, Harry came right to the point. "Jack, you're going to have to produce Cooper; there's no way out. They'll hound you until you do. And you'll have to make a statement. Now, for God's sake, fill me in."

Tallon did; a half a minute was all he needed.

"Where's Cooper now?" Gilroy asked.

"He's here. I've got him hiding out in the judge's chambers."

"How well can he handle himself, do you think?"

"He's done all right so far," Tallon answered. "Walt is pretty capable."

"All right. We're having a press conference in the courtroom in half an hour—you clear it with Judge Howell. Walt will have to show. How about Marsha?"

Tallon shook his head. "I haven't talked to the swami yet and I'm going to let him call the signals on that."

"Call him now, tell him what's happening, and wire him in. Someone may guess pretty quickly where she's been. From what I hear, he knows exactly what he's doing."

"That he does." Tallon picked up his phone as Gilroy went out to announce the press conference.

The media people went to work immediately. TV cables were strung, cameras and lights were hustled into the courtroom, microphones were set up, and from somewhere a large coffee urn was produced and plugged in.

Meanwhile Tallon had a short talk with Walt Cooper in his office. Calmly Walt told of his asking Marsha Stone out, but with the full expectation that she would wear her disguise as Bhakti. He had been floored when she had elected to go with him as herself, but he had followed through and hadn't failed to slip in a plug for the Whitewater Police. "I'm proud to be a member here," he concluded. "And, honestly, I didn't expect this kind of a reaction."

"How do you feel about meeting the press?"

"No problem, but I'd like to have a word with the swami first."

Tallon pointed to the telephone.

Cooper talked with Swami Dharmayana for two or three minutes. Tallon could hear only one side of the conversation, but it seemed to be going well. Quite clearly Cooper was getting some advice and all indications were that he would follow it. When he hung up, he seemed entirely satisfied. "It's all right at that end," he reported. "Whenever you want me to play St. George and face the dragons, I'm ready."

Tallon glanced at his watch and saw that the scheduled conference was three minutes away. "Let's go in," he invited.

It wasn't as bad as either had feared. Tallon made a short statement to the effect that Officer Walter Cooper was a member of the Whitewater Department in very good standing, that he was a student of the classics, and a most conscientious policeman. Then he introduced Walt and sat down.

Somewhat to Tallon's surprise, Walt handled himself splendidly. "Some attention was attracted by the fact that I had a date the other night," he began with disarming simplicity. "The lady I took out was Marsha Stone, the same Marsha Stone who disappeared from Hollywood a while ago. We are both unmarried and, up to a point, friends."

"Are you engaged?" a female voice interrupted.

Cooper ignored it. "The simple fact is, I invited Marsha out and she accepted. In the past she's sometimes done her hair differently and worn glasses so that people wouldn't recognize her, and they didn't. It was a surprise to me when she decided to appear as she did. That's all."

Of course there were questions.

"How long have you known Miss Stone?"

"Not too long."

"Are you in love with her?"

"I admire her very much."

"Are you living together?"

"Absolutely not."

"Where is she living now?"

"I won't disclose that."

"Are you the policeman who solved her disappearance?"

"No. A detective of the Los Angeles County Sheriff's Department found her. When it was determined that she was safe and needed no assistance, her wish for privacy was respected. That's the usual procedure in police work, unless a crime is involved."

"Are you going to take her out again?"

"I intend to ask her. Then it will be her choice."

"Is she going to resume her screen career?"

"I haven't the least idea; we never discussed that."

"What else can you tell us?"

"Drive carefully while you're in Whitewater. Our traffic regulations are reasonable and we enforce them. I'd hate to have to give any of you a ticket."

A half hour later the media people had all left with the exception of one very pushy female reporter who insisted on some exclusive information. Harry Gilroy handled her with quiet efficiency and sent her packing. Then it was back to business.

At the city council meeting that afternoon Harry Gilroy filled the vacant seat, by appointment. Jack Tallon asked for the floor and was given it immediately. "I want to report to the council confidentially on two matters. First, the arson attacks. We believe that they are the work of the same person. We obtained a good description and thanks to Officer Gary Mason, who chased the suspect across open country in his patrol car, we've identified him."

That caused a small sensation, as he had expected. Even city attorney Otis Fenwell, who became more testy each year, showed surprise. He would quibble and argue endlessly, but there was no question of his integrity or discretion in confidential matters.

"He is a very hard character with a record," Tallon continued. "He doesn't live in Whitewater and so far we don't have enough proof to go into court. We expect to get it. I've made certain arrangements with the police authorities in the place where he does live. If he ever heads this way again, and we expect him to, we'll be alerted and ready. We have a plan to nail him red-handed so that Otis can go into court with an airtight case."

Arnold Petersen, the mayor, put a question. "Jack, have you any idea about his motive?"

"Yes. It's possible that he's just a thrill seeker as so many of them are. However, I have good reason to believe that he's being paid. I have no hard evidence whatever, only grounds for suspicion."

"Can you say any more than that?"

"No, not at the present."

"And the other thing?" Petersen asked.

"This has to do with the murder of Councilman Sullivan," Jack said. "Ever since that crime was committed, our whole department has been working double shifts. We've gathered a great deal of data and uncovered some interesting information. Some of it, with respect to everyone here, I'd like to keep confidential for the time being. However, this does concern the council. There is a land developer, a Mortimer Brown of San Francisco, who I suspect may be at least indirectly involved in the circumstances surrounding Councilman Sullivan's death. Brown is trying very hard to acquire the land now occupied by Dharmaville and owned by the swami out there."

"Might that not be a good thing?" Otis Fenwell asked.

"I don't think so," Tallon answered. "I went to San Francisco yesterday to meet with Mr. Brown. I regard him as unscrupulous. Among other things, he baldly offered me a bribe to help him get hold of the land."

"Why does he want it?" Marion McNeil asked. She was almost always the person who went right to the heart of the matter.

"He wants to build a big recreation complex, to include condominiums, restaurants, shops, game courts, a winter sports area, and a lot more."

"That sounds pretty good to me," Otis Fenwell said. "All of that is taxable and it should bring a great deal of money into the city. You know that for some time we've been after nonpolluting industry to come here."

"That's true, Otis," Jack agreed. "But Mr. Brown also has some other ideas."

"Like call girls?" Marion asked.

"That wasn't specifically mentioned, but I would expect that would be part of it. You see, Mr. Brown is convinced that that particular location will be one of the few approved for legal gambling under the authority of the state legislature. What he really wants is to build a casino."

Bill Albrecht was listening carefully, then he came up with one of his usual cautious questions. "Suppose the swami doesn't choose to sell?"

Tallon turned grim. "So far Brown has approached the swami several times and the swami has said no."

"Good for him!" Marion said.

"The reason I'm bringing this up now," Tallon continued, "is the strategy that Brown told me he was going to use to force the sale of the property to him. He is hiring some legal eagles to find some infraction of our ordinances by the Dharmaville people. Then, he told me flat out, he expects me to force them out. He's a coarse man who's totally accustomed to having his own way and who intends always to win."

Dick Collins, the city manager, asked, "Jack, as of now, what are the chances that Sullivan's murderer came from Dharmaville?"

Tallon answered carefully. "We've conducted three separate investigations of the community using three different teams. All three have done outstanding work. One team concentrated on the swami himself. For the council's private information, he came up without a thing against him. He's a Harvard PhD, he is a genuine swami, and he seems to be in good repute everywhere.

"Our second team concentrated on a man known as Narayan who is second in command at the community. His background is impeccable. He's highly educated and he has a professional standing: he's a member of the bar in both Washington and California."

"In that case, why is he living at that crackpot place?" Fenwell asked.

Tallon turned toward the older man whose prejudices died hard. "Because he wants to, I guess. A lot of people retire to one form or another of the religious life and that's what he's done. Dharmaville is a religious center."

"What about your third investigation?" Mayor Petersen asked.

"We conducted that on the whole population of the community. We have a list of the full membership and our checking indicates that it's accurate. On the night that Mr. Sullivan was killed, there was a meeting at Dharmaville at which some films were shown. Almost everybody there attended. By checking and cross-checking, we have been able to establish that all but six of the residents were at the meeting. Of the six that remained, who did not attend, three have been accounted for to our satisfaction. Of the other three, one was Narayan, one was the swami himself, and one was a young lady who had been living at Dharmaville for some time under the name of Bhakti. This is positively not to be given out to anyone until she authorizes it, but we have known her true identity ever since it was discovered by Officer Walt Cooper."

"You don't mean *Marsha Stone!*" Marion McNeil gasped.

"Exactly. She wanted to get away from the public for a while and Dharmaville offered her sanctuary. Only the swami and Narayan knew who she really was. Why she recently chose to appear in public, I don't know."

"So she's been in Whitewater for some time," Bill Albrecht said.

"That's right."

"And she's back there now?" Dick Collins asked.

"As far as I know, yes. I talked to Cooper about it, of course. He had met her while he was investigating at Dharmaville and thought she was a nice girl despite the fact that she wore old-fashioned clothes, granny glasses, and kept her hair up in a tight bun. Since the girl was not under any suspicion of having murdered Sullivan, and since she's physically probably incapable of having committed that crime, he asked her out."

"Did he know then who she was?" Marion asked.

"Yes, he did, but he asked her with the expectation that she would pass as a very plain girl fortunate enough to have a date. When he called for her, and saw how she had prepared herself, he nearly fell over."

"So where are we now?" Otis Fenwell asked.

Tallon was honest. "With reasonable luck, we'll have the arsonist in the bag on his next try. And if my thinking is correct, he will try again. The investigation of Councilman Sullivan's murder is continuing. Quite frankly, we could use a break, but with one or without it, we'll crack it."

"Do you need any additional help?" Mayor Petersen asked.

"No, sir, not now."

As soon as the meeting was over, Jack took one of the official cars and drove to the large military base that was located not too far from Whitewater. He was shown in to see the commanding general who received him cordially; they had met a number of times before. The general offered coffee, which was standard procedure, and then asked what he could do to help the Whitewater Police.

Tallon laid out his problem without hesitation. Before he had finished, the general anticipated him and asked two or three questions. When he received satisfactory answers, he picked up his telephone. At his order a piece of equipment was put into Tallon's car; with it went the general's assurance of immediate assistance when it became necessary.

Much relieved in his mind, Tallon drove back to his office. As soon as he arrived he put in a call to Chief Smallins at River Falls and brought him up to date.

"Count on us," Smallins said. "As of now I'll put a twenty-four-hour watch on our friend. It won't be continuous, I can't afford that, but he won't get out of town without our knowing it. You'll be the first to hear."

"That's great," Tallon said. "We'll take it from there."

That matter concluded he knew that he had his trap set. If Wesley

Obermann were to attempt another arson attack in Whitewater, his balls would be in the wringer for sure. He sent for Ralph Hillman who reported promptly. Tallon noted with satisfaction that the dressings on his visible burns had been changed and that they were smaller than before. "How are you feeling, Ralph?" he asked.

"Much better, thanks."

"Are you up to doing a little electronics work?"

"Of course; what do you need?"

"There's a piece of military equipment in my car, number-two patrol unit. I borrowed it from the base. I'd like it hooked up as quickly as possible and tied in with our own system so that we can talk directly back and forth on the military helicopter frequency."

"That shouldn't take any time at all," Hillman said, "assuming that the equipment is in good order, and it certainly should be."

"If you need any help ask for it. And, Ralph, mum's the word."

"Of course."

In less than two hours Ralph Hillman reported that the military transceiver was on line and ready to go. At that point Gary Mason appeared and asked to speak privately with Tallon. As the young patrolman came into Tallon's office, he shut the door behind him. "While you were in San Francisco," he began, "we got an anonymous call. A female, middle-aged, but that's all we've got on it. She said that we might be interested to know that on the night of Sullivan's murder, the swami from Dharmaville was seen in Whitewater. That didn't sound like much until she added something more. She claimed that she positively saw him park his car and leave it less than a block from Sullivan's home."

CHAPTER 16

Dr. Arnold Petersen was not only the mayor, but also the very good friend of Jack Tallon. When Francie appeared in the office doorway to announce that Petersen was in the lobby, Tallon felt no concern at all.

It surprised him only mildly when, after coming in, Petersen closed the door behind him. As soon as his unexpected guest was seated, Jack asked, "What can I do for you, Arnold?"

The mayor by his relaxed manner made what he had to say easier. "Jack, this is no discredit to you or to your department, but I think we should call in the sheriff on the Sullivan case and do so immediately."

Tallon pushed his chair back so that he did not need to sit so stiffly at his desk. "Arnold, in all honesty I can't agree with that. And not because of any costs involved, or loss of face for our department. I've got other reasons."

"I certainly want to hear them." Petersen sounded if he really meant what he said. "But face the facts, Jack. It's been two weeks, plus or minus, and I'm getting some pretty heavy flack, despite what was said at the council meeting."

"I can understand that. People who don't know what's going on are often critical."

The mayor showed no signs of taking offense. "Jack, let me put it this way: you've got some fine men working for you, but none of them has genuine detective experience. I know that Asher is the official department investigator, but has he ever handled a homicide before?"

"No, he hasn't," Jack admitted.

"The sheriff has professionals who handle homicides all the time. He has a lab and a lot of other resources. Also, suppose that the case goes unsolved, which is a possibility. If we didn't call in the sheriff, we'd never hear the last of it. If we do call him in, then we've done all that we can and the onus is at least divided."

Tallon listened patiently and understood what lay behind it. When the mayor had finished, he allowed enough time to pass, several seconds, so that it would not appear that he was too quick to rebut. Then he spoke his piece. "Arnold, it's true that none of my people have had any homicide experience, but I have and I'm directing the investigation. I've given them all detective assignments and they've performed like seasoned pros. About the sheriff: if I'd felt that we needed him, I would have called him in during the first forty-eight hours. Now, frankly, it's too late. Sullivan's autopsy report is final and the crime scene was a city street that's been open for traffic since the day after the murder. Sherlock Holmes couldn't find anything there now. We have a large amount of data that I'm confident is accurate. And we're not through yet; we're working on it right now."

Petersen raised a point. "Otis Fenwell insists that you have a piece of hard evidence that proves a Dharmaville connection to the killing. I know that he was a friend of Sullivan's and that he got him on the council, but is there any truth to that?"

"As I said before, Arnold, we do have something, but it isn't conclusive or we'd have somebody under arrest right now. We're covering all bases. For example: not for publication for obvious reasons, but we learned that Sullivan had a regular girl friend on the side. We located her and she's been interviewed. I did that myself."

The mayor pursed his lips slightly. "Well I'll be damned. I never would have expected that. Is she involved?"

"Possibly, but I'm almost certain she didn't kill him, and there's no jealous husband in the picture. Now about Dharmaville: you heard what I told the council. It's all true. The swami doesn't even have a current traffic record. Now I'm going to give you something only for your own information: you recall my mentioning that three of the residents hadn't been alibied."

"The swami and Marsha Stone are two of them."

"Right. The third had already undergone a thorough check; he's an ex-policeman who resigned to go into corporate law. He was a missing persons detective with the Los Angeles County Sheriff's Department; he worked on the Marsha Stone case for weeks and he found her. Still, we'll go back to the mill on him until we know where he was at the time that Sullivan died."

"OK, now what is this piece of evidence?"

Tallon filled him in on the ankh. "Now I want to point something out, Arnold. The Egyptian cross is a fairly substantial piece of jewelry which means that the cord or chain that held it had to be fairly strong."

"But it could still be broken."

"Yes, but hear me out. Sullivan's body, while he was still in the hospital, clearly showed that he had not put up any kind of a fight. You can check that with Lindholm. Yet when Sullivan was brought in, he was clutching the cross in his hand."

"He might have grabbed for it when he was going down."

"Certainly, I considered that. But think of this, Arnold: the man who attacked him laid him low. *If* Sullivan had torn the ankh right off its cord or chain, the attacker would have felt it, even under the emotional stress of the moment. But there's absolutely no way he would be so idiotic as to leave the scene with that clue in Sullivan's hand. And one more thing: Sullivan was still clutching it when he was brought into the emergency room. You're a doctor; how does that hit you?"

Petersen saw it. "It had to be a plant," he said. "And Sullivan himself had to be in on it."

"You're right about the first part," Tallon said. "But Sullivan may have been handed that cross and he hung on to it for dear life. Dr. Lindholm told me that that was quite possible."

"How about that van fire? Any hookup there?" He glanced at Tallon's hands which were still partially covered with light dressings.

"No, that was a separate incident, and it was the sheriff that handled it for us."

"And the arsonist?"

Jack leaned forward once more. "That's another matter. He may very well be tied in and, if he is, I think I know why."

It was late in the day, but there was urgent work to be done. Jack sent for Walt Cooper who was just coming on shift. Jack asked, "Are you set for patrol?"

"Just going out. I'm working a double shift to cover Ralph. He can't drive yet."

"I know. Who's around that could take the car out for a little while?"

"Gary can do it."

"Good. I want you to call Dharmaville right now and get hold of your girl friend. Tell her that I'd like to meet her, and see if we can come right out. Also I'd like to get Narayan in on it and the swami too. Official call; make that clear."

Cooper hesitated for a bare moment, then he remembered his duty. "May I use your phone?" he asked.

After his call, to which Tallon tried not to listen, he told him, "She's there and she'll be glad to see us. She'll check with Narayan and the swami. When we get there, we're to go to the swami's dome; she said you had been there before."

Tallon drove. His hands were still a little tender, but he wanted to be at the wheel for what he considered a very good reason. He cleared the small downtown area and then settled down to a steady pace, but a slow one.

"Walt," he said, "you know that I came from the Pasadena Police; I was with them for several years. That isn't exactly Hollywood, but it's close enough that we had a lot of contact with the film community. I know it reasonably well and how it operates."

Walt turned toward him to indicate that he was listening.

"Now to the best of my knowledge, Marsha Stone is a very fine girl; I've never heard a word to the contrary."

"She is that," Cooper ventured.

"I assumed that was your feeling, or you wouldn't have asked her out. Your invitation, as I see it, was not to notch up the fact that you had dated a film star, but because you liked her as a person."

"Right on," Cooper said.

"Now, I want you to prepare yourself for something. In show business everyone is Miss—every female I mean, regardless of whether or not she happens to be married, or how many times."

"I know that."

"Looking at it dispassionately, Walt, Marsha Stone is a very attractive woman and she's fully mature. She was also extremely popular. You know that Narayan is actually Francis MacNeil, the sheriff's detective who put in weeks of hard work trying to find her."

Tallon stopped as he guided the car around a slow curve, letting his man take his time.

Cooper understood. "What you're saying, Chief, is that the odds are that Marsha and Narayan are if not married at least living together."

"Something like that. It's customary for film people to keep their private lives very much to themselves, or to appear as single for purely professional reasons. MacNeil had a very good start on an outstanding career, then he threw it all up and came to Dharmaville."

Cooper had been listening carefully. "I see. It adds up."

"Yes," Tallon agreed, "it does. I'm not saying it's so, but I thought I ought to mention the possibility to you."

Cooper was in a brown study. "To be honest with you, Chief, I thought of that and I asked her, indirectly. She said that she was single, but that may have been a figure of speech."

That was a load off Tallon's mind. Technically, Cooper's personal life was not his concern, but he hadn't wanted to see as good a man as Walt Cooper run blindly into a stone wall. The fact that Cooper had come to the same conclusion on his own was a vote for him. He had his feet on the ground and that was what was essential.

At the entrance to Dharmaville he turned in and chose the proper road up to the swami's dome. He pulled up and parked where he had been before and, with Cooper beside him, he walked up to the door and knocked.

Narayan opened the door and invited them in. He was courteous, but both men detected a certain reserve. In the main room the swami was waiting, in a pair of slacks and a turtleneck sweater this time, and beside him was Marsha Stone. It was the first time Tallon had seen her in person and he admitted instantly to himself that she was breathtaking. She wore a very simple dress and virtually no cosmetics, but that made little difference.

He said the proper and polite things and then noticed carefully how the young lady greeted Walt who was, of course, in uniform. She took both his hands for a moment and welcomed him with just the proper amount of warmth.

Since Tallon had asked for the meeting, he began it as soon as they were all seated. "I'm very sorry to disturb you at this hour," he said. "I hope it's not too inconvenient."

It was Narayan who responded. "It's quite all right, Chief Tallon. How can we help you?"

Tallon did not mince words. "I'm sure you already know that Santosh supplied us with a complete list of your membership here."

"On my instructions," the swami said.

Tallon nodded and continued. "Since we received it, we have made a thorough investigation and to my satisfaction all but three of the people here are accounted for at the time of the Sullivan murder."

"And we are the three," the swami said.

"You are," Tallon acknowledged. "Now, you have been very cooperative and I want to reciprocate. We have learned that Mortimer Brown, to whom you refused to sell this property, offered a large commission to Councilman Sullivan if he could force you off. Sullivan had made a very bad investment; Brown took it over, but on terms that left Sullivan with a disastrous loss. His financial situation was bad—we know the exact details of that—hence his almost desperate efforts to get you to leave."

The swami listened with patience. When Tallon was through, he spoke. "I had guessed at part of that, Chief Tallon, but I very much appreciate your confidence in confirming my suspicions. Sullivan was, after all, quite an obvious person."

"Was he ever on the grounds here to your knowledge?" Tallon asked.

"Yes, on several occasions. He had made such a point of describing us as a sex colony, I invited him to come and see for himself. He professed to take a considerable interest in our dome construction and he came back two or three times on his own. He was received each time and allowed to look about as much as he wished."

"Is it possible that he could have helped himself to Narayan's ankh?" Tallon inquired. "I don't need to explain why."

Narayan answered. "No, it's obvious why he would take it if he could, since it's so clearly identified as something that might come from here. Yes, it is quite possible he could have taken it. I assure you that someone did."

Tallon came back to the principal business of the call. "On the night of Mr. Sullivan's death, Swami, you were reported seen in Whitewater near the Sullivan home. Would you care to comment on that?"

"No," the swami replied, "I would not."

"On what grounds do you base your refusal? I don't need to point out its importance."

"No, you don't. As we discussed once before, I am a properly qualified spiritual leader and my confidences are therefore privileged."

During all of this Walt Cooper sat very quietly, giving most of his attention to Marsha. She caught him at it several times, but he found the temptation irresistible.

Tallon carefully shifted his position as he sat. "Respecting that fact, Swami," he said, "I'd like to ask you certain other questions that will not violate your professional confidence, but would be of considerable help to us."

"I'll reply if I can."

"Were you in Whitewater the night that Mr. Sullivan was killed? I realize that this is technically Whitewater, but I mean the city proper."

"Did I understand you to say that I was seen there?"

"Yes."

"Then that would be your answer, wouldn't it?"

"All right. Now, only in general terms, were you there in your spiritual capacity?"

"I think that's also been answered, Chief Tallon."

"I'll accept that it has. I won't probe into the nature of your errand that night, but I will ask you this: have you ever met Mrs. Wilson Sullivan?"

Tallon watched to see if the swami would glance at Narayan who was unquestionably his legal adviser, but the swami only looked upward for a moment toward the top of the dome. "I have met Mrs. Sullivan," he said finally.

"Swami, allow me to propose a theory to you. Mr. Sullivan was in a very difficult financial position, one he could escape if he could persuade or force you to leave this property. Mrs. Sullivan presumably was aware of this: there are several children in the family and the household budget would be a major consideration. Therefore, when she sees her husband's rather crude efforts to get you to sell, she decides to try herself. She asks you to call in the hope that, by laying the whole matter before you, you would be compassionate enough to sell to Mr. Brown and thereby allow her husband to receive the commission he had been promised."

The swami did not hesitate this time. "Most ingenious, Chief Tallon; my compliments. However, I will state categorically that your theory is not correct. You have my word on that."

"Accepted. But did Mrs. Sullivan invite you to call?"

The swami shook his head. "I have gone as far as I can," he said.

Unexpectedly Walt Cooper spoke up. "I think I've got it," he declared.

The swami gave him his full attention. "I'll be glad to listen," he offered.

Cooper looked toward his chief. "May I reveal something about Mr. Sullivan's private life?" he asked.

It was Tallon's turn to think for a moment. "I believe so," he answered.

Cooper spoke with quiet self-possession. "Mr. Sullivan had a girl friend and Mrs. Sullivan discovered that fact and let her husband know. However, Sullivan gave her no satisfaction, so she conceived a revenge. She phoned you, Swami, invited you to call, and confided in you. Not for guidance, because she's Catholic and would go to a priest for that. In essence, she told you about her husband's mistress and gave you that information as a weapon. Then you would be able to tell Sullivan that if he didn't stop his persecution of you and your community here, you would make his immorality public. I'm not suggesting that you would do that, Swami, but she might think that you would. I know that would lose all chance of his getting the commission, but she could have guessed that that was already a lost hope. Then she could inform her husband that she had confided in you and use it as a lever to force him to give up his girl friend. A little complicated, but it fits."

There was a silence of several seconds, then Tallon spoke. "Will you buy that, Swami?" he asked.

The swami gave his full attention to Walt Cooper. "Bhakti told me that you were a very intelligent young man. I have great respect for her opinion."

Tallon's heart seemed to leap inside his chest; that hadn't ruled the swami out, but it had answered many questions. He took up the conversation. "Let's drop that matter," he proposed. "Now, simply for the record, Narayan, I'd like to know where you were when Mr. Sullivan was attacked. I met you here the next morning, but I don't remember asking you that question."

"I was on an errand for Swami," Narayan answered.

"I will confirm that," the swami said. "He was not in Whitewater. I trust you will accept my word."

"I'm not sure that he can," Narayan said. "Not officially. I was in Spokane until after twelve. If necessary, I can produce a credible witness."

"Was Miss Bhakti, or Marsha if that's more proper, with you?"

"Yes, she was."

"And your witness will attest to that as well?"

"Certainly."

"It may become necessary for me to interview that witness."

"I understand that. If it becomes necessary, I'll personally introduce you."

"Fair enough. Now, one more thing. This is not directly pertinent to our investigation, but it would be helpful to know. You and Marsha are good friends, I take it."

"Yes, we are."

For the first time since the meeting had begun, Marsha spoke. "Chief Tallon, I feel sure that you wish to know whether or not Narayan and I are married. Or, whether we are on intimate terms."

She looked at Narayan who spoke for them both. "For reasons I would prefer not to discuss, our friendship has remained precisely that. I have a deep affection for Marsha, as I have for many people, but it has not advanced beyond that point."

Marsha spoke again. "Walter asked me if I was married and I told him I was not. I'm surprised he didn't tell you that, but perhaps he considered it a strictly private matter. I'd like to think so."

Tallon stood up. "Thank you all for your time," he said. "We don't like to make nuisances of ourselves, but we've got to keep at it until we find the answer."

"I understand," the swami said. "We all do. However, I venture the thought that the answer you're looking for will not be found at Dharmaville."

On the way back, when they had been on the road for several minutes, Walt Cooper asked a question. "Chief, do you think we can write off the Dharmaville people as suspects in the murder?"

Tallon thought carefully before he answered. "By inclination, Walt, I'd like to very much. But facing hard facts, I don't think we can just yet."

CHAPTER 17

Jack Tallon dropped Walt Cooper off at police headquarters and then drove home. Jennifer was waiting for him, glad for once to see him at something approaching a civilized hour. To celebrate, she took two steaks out of the freezer and put them into her microwave oven to defrost. By the very way that Jack walked across the floor on the way to prepare himself for dinner, she knew that the day had been productive.

When Jack came into the kitchen to join her and to fix drinks, she did her best to let him know how much his presence was appreciated. "How did it go?" she asked. It was a safe question became it was so general.

"Not too badly," he told her as he busied himself with bottles and glasses. "I was out at Dharmaville with Walt Cooper to see the swami."

Jennifer took a quick breath. "Did you meet Marsha Stone?" she asked.

"Yes," he admitted. "She's a knockout, no mistake. I think Walt already has a case on her, which is too bad."

"Why?"

Jack took some ice cubes out of the refrigerator. "Because I'm afraid he's in over his head. He can't really play in that league."

Jennifer paused and looked at him. "*I* married a policeman," she said.

Jack was very fast in fielding that. "Yes, thank heaven," he said. "But on his salary, which isn't that bad, Walt probably couldn't keep her in nylons—or is that a platitude?"

"It is. But hasn't this unreachable orchid been staying at Dharmaville? That doesn't impress me as too lofty a standard of living."

Jack stopped, walked three steps to her, and gathered her into his arms. "She isn't an unreachable orchid, dear; she's just a nice girl, like you. She certainly has looks, but remember she had it made in Hollywood and she chose to give it up. Now, when do we eat?"

"Soon." She knew just by the tone of his voice that she had nothing to fear from the glamorous Marsha Stone. But she had seen the picture in the newspaper and she couldn't help letting it get to her just a little.

When the meal was over, and Jack had helped to clear the dining table, he went to the telephone and put in a short call. When he had finished, he duly reported to his wife. "I'm going out briefly," he told her. "I've just made an appointment to see Mrs. Sullivan. I have two or three questions to ask her."

"Tonight?"

"Yes, tonight—while I have the chance. It isn't far and it won't take long."

"All right," Jennifer conceded. "Come home as soon as you can."

"I will," he promised and left. Ten minutes later he was ringing the Sullivan doorbell.

This time Mrs. Sullivan let him in herself. Apparently she had sensed his purpose because none of the several Sullivan children was in sight. There were sounds coming from other parts of the house, upstairs a TV was playing, but the living room was clear. Jack noted at once that his hostess had made a good recovery from her initial shock and grief. She was reasonably poised and she received him with a more relaxed manner. She seated herself and folded her hands, prepared to face whatever was coming. Jack read the signs clearly; they were about what he had anticipated.

"Mrs. Sullivan," he began, "we are making good progress in our investigation of Mr. Sullivan's death. I have three or four questions; I thought it best if I came to see you myself."

"I appreciate that," she said.

At that point a diplomatic gambit was necessary and Jack had his well prepared. It invited the information he needed, but it also gave nothing away on the chance that his hostess was still ignorant of her husband's association with his bookkeeper. "Mrs. Sullivan, through very careful investigation, we have now completed a full picture of the last forty-eight hours of your husband's life."

"Then I presume you know about . . ."

"Yes, we do. If at all possible, it will not be publicized."

"Thank you."

"No thanks are necessary, Mrs. Sullivan. However, if you will, I'd appreciate it very much if you will help us with some answers. First: Are you acquainted with Swami Dharmayana, the director of Dharmaville?"

"Yes, I am."

"Our investigation has indicated that he may have called on you on the night that Mr. Sullivan was attacked. Is that correct?"

Obviously his hostess didn't want to answer that question, but she must have sensed that he already knew what she would say. "Yes, he was here," she said.

"On your invitation, I assume."

"Yes, that's correct."

"How did he impress you?" He wasn't really interested in the answer to that question, but he wanted to give her an easy one, something with which she could feel comfortable.

"Well, he surprised me a little. He's a very cultured and educated gentleman. Of course neither of us knew at the time what was going to happen."

Tallon nodded. "I fully understand that. Your impression of him, then, was favorable?"

"I would have to say so."

"And I presume he waited a reasonable time for Mr. Sullivan to come home."

His hostess shook her head. "No. When Wilson went out, he didn't tell me where he was going, only that he would probably be out for some time. I thought I knew where he was going, but I said nothing."

Tallon nodded to indicate that he accepted all that she had said, but inwardly he noted one new piece of information. "There is no question whatever of the propriety of the swami's call here, but simply for timetable reasons, could you tell me when he left?"

Fortunately, his subject took the question well. "I don't recall exactly," she said. "I know it was before I was called from the hospital, but I don't really remember." Her voice faltered and a sudden tear rolled down her cheek. "It was the most terrible night of my life."

Without thinking about it, Tallon reached out and put his hand on hers. "Thank you. I'll be all right, it's just hard sometimes."

"Of course it is. One last question before I go. You know that Mortimer Brown offered your husband a payment if he could manage to get the Dharmaville people to give up their property."

"Yes, I knew that."

"Did you consider it possible, or likely, that Mr. Sullivan would succeed in earning that fee?"

She shook her head. "No, Chief Tallon. It was simply another way that Mortimer Brown victimized my husband. After cheating him out of almost all of our cash, he made that offer knowing that Wilson had no legal means available to get Swami Dharmayana to move. It was an outrageous thing for him to do, but Wilson was so desperate he tried every way he could think to succeed. I knew from the very beginning he had no chance."

"Do you blame the swami, Mrs. Sullivan?"

She raised her head and looked directly at him. "No," she answered. "I do not. He could have sued Wilson for the things my husband said about his community, but he didn't. The man is a saint."

Tallon thanked her and rose to go. As he did so the phone rang. Since it was close to her chair, Mrs. Sullivan picked it up. A moment later she handed it to Tallon. "It's for you," she said.

Tallon took the instrument and gave his name; he knew who would be calling. Sergeant Wayne Mudd was the watch commander. "Chief," he said over the line, "we've just had word from River Falls. You'd better get down here right away."

Wayne Mudd was the newest sergeant in the department, but he was already well on top of his job. As soon as Jack was in, he briefed him concisely. "Frank Smallins called personally. Wesley Obermann left his place about a half hour ago. He was on his bike. He stopped at a filling station, got gas, and filled a spare two-gallon can he was carrying. It was a legal can, painted red, and properly labeled. Obermann took off and was spotted twice before he left town, headed this way."

"Call the sheriff," Jack directed. "Brief the watch commander and ask to have Obermann spotted if possible. But I don't want him followed or tipped off in any way."

Mudd actually smiled, which was rare. "Already done. The commander has notified all his units in the field to be on the lookout for Obermann, but not to spook him. Whenever he's spotted, I'll get the word immediately."

"Good work, Wayne," Tallon said. "You'd better call in the troops. Get hold of everyone you can and pass the word."

Mudd was still smiling. Behind Tallon the door opened quickly as Brad Oster, Jerry Quigley, and Gary Mason came in. Nothing had to be said, they all understood. "Who's on patrol?" Tallon asked.

"Ned Asher. He's in uniform."

"You've called him."

"Yes. He's handling a call, but it's minor and he'll be in directly."

Within the next ten minutes every member of the Whitewater Police Department had reported in. Mary Clancy was among them; she was in uniform. Tallon noted that she had a new hat of standard police design; she was taking her duties as a reservist seriously.

Tallon gathered them all in his office. "Wesley Obermann, the arson suspect, is reported headed this way. River Falls notified us and we called the sheriffs; they'll try to spot him and trace his route. If he's coming here it's a change in his pattern. Both of his previous hits were in broad daylight. I had it set up to have a helicopter follow him, but at night it's a different matter."

Ralph Hillman spoke up. "It's already airborne, Chief, and we've been in radio contact. There's a half moon that will help a little. The chopper will stay behind the suspect and he won't hear it over the sound of his own motor."

"That kind of cooperation is priceless," Tallon said, "and I'm damn glad that you're that much on the ball. We don't know if Obermann is armed, but I'm going to assume that he is. Let me remind you that he's about six feet four and almost three hundred pounds. It isn't fat, it's muscle. He claims to be a karate black belt which I doubt like hell because he would never stand for the discipline, and no authorized *dojo* would take him with his background. But he's dangerous, don't mistake that for a moment. He's a street fighter. I want every one of you to observe maximum caution and under no circumstances is any one of you to try to handle him alone."

He stopped when Mudd, who had been listening outside, answered a radio call. In a moment he was in the doorway. "Obermann was just spotted by a sheriff's unit. He's still headed this way. ETA, twenty minutes."

Tallon took incisive command. "I want Ralph Hillman to take over the desk and communications; he still hasn't the full use of his hands. Ned Asher and Wayne Mudd in car one, Wyncott and Quigley in car two; myself and Gary Mason in car three. Oster and Cooper, you drive Ned's car; it's radio equipped. Mary, you'd better keep out of this."

"Like hell," Mary said, "I've been shooting on the sheriff's range. I'm up to expert."

"No way," Tallon declared.

Mary squared off. "Am I a cop or not?" she asked.

There was only one possible answer and Tallon knew it. "You're a cop."

"Then I want my assignment."

"We'll take her," Wyncott volunteered.

Tallon realized almost instantly that Wyncott and Quigley, two of his most seasoned officers, would know what to do. "All right," he said. "Car one spotted out of sight, but close to the highway on the north side. If Obermann shows, put it on the air immediately and then run a parallel course. Car two in the downtown, same procedure. I'll be in three on the south side. The unmarked unit parked on Main Street pointed south. By the drive-in so you look like customers."

"Got it," Brad Oster said. "We'll hold coffee cups to cover."

Tallon had one last instruction. He turned to Hillman, "Ralph, vector in the chopper if you can and for God's sake keep us informed."

"No sweat," Hillman said. "If you need me, yell."

"Get going," Tallon said.

The room emptied very quickly. Tallon stopped just long enough to take a small backup piece from the bottom drawer of his desk and to snap the leg holster in place. Then he ran outside; Hillman handed him the car keys at the door. Gary Mason was already in the unit, behind the wheel.

"I'll drive," Tallon said.

"No, sir," Gary contradicted. "Your hands aren't well enough yet for pursuit driving. And I know how; you taught me." He turned the key and brought the engine to life. It took him less than ten seconds to complete an equipment check. "Suggest you unlock the shotgun," he said.

Tallon knew he should have thought of that himself. He bent over and opened the lock that held the weapon in place. He pumped a round into the chamber as the car pulled away from the curb. As virtually his whole department went into the field, silently and without moving his lips he prayed that none of his people would be hurt—or worse.

A minute later Hillman came on the air from the station. "The chopper has spotted the suspect and is following. He's still headed this way."

Tallon picked up the mike. "Radio check," he ordered.

Ned Asher's voice came immediately. "Whitewater One. All set."

Jerry Quigley followed. "Whitewater Two. We're ready."

Tallon gave his own call. "Whitewater Three. We're fine."

Brad Oster was calm as always. "Whitewater Four. Set and carrying a shotgun." That was Ned Asher's car which had no police equipment other than the radio, so Oster, or possibly Cooper who was with him, had done his thinking before he left the station.

Gary Mason carefully drove down a side street to avoid showing too many police cars on Main Street at one time. He picked a suitable place and stopped. The car was in deep shadow under a huge tree, but from that point there was at least a partial view for almost half a block to the left.

Within two minutes the other three cars reported themselves in position and waiting. Tallon took a deep breath, knowing that there was nothing more he could do. He still didn't like the idea that Mary Clancy was riding in car two, but the last thing he had wanted was any kind of an argument. The department was functioning beautifully and up to full professional standards. Mary would just have to take her chances, but that was what she had wanted.

Calmly Hillman reported over the air that the suspect was an estimated six minutes north of the city. Tallon acknowledged and thought that in the darkness the helicopter was doing a remarkable job. He settled back in his seat, waiting as he had waited so many times before when he had been with the Pasadena Police. In the still quiet the whole case unrolled itself before him, from the time that he had learned of the attack on Sullivan up to that moment.

It was clear and sharp, like a well-projected film. The scene came alive and the information his people had so carefully gathered was in the forefront of his mind.

Then it happened. Two links that he had suddenly snapped together. He had not consciously thought about it, it just came to him. He drew a breath and held it, considering quickly the sudden idea that had flashed into his mind. It fitted. In some ways it was a long shot, but an easy answer he would have had long ago.

"Suspect ETA, five minutes," came from the radio.

Still struggling with the sudden insight, Tallon acknowledged automatically. He allowed himself one more minute to consider what he had just put together. As he did, he remembered one more thing and that single, unsupported fact changed an outside possibility into a strong probability. He would have to ask the swami one key question; if he got the right answer, he had it. Excitement began to flow through him and he was ready for whatever was coming.

"Why didn't you put Ned Asher in his own car?" Gary asked.

"Because he's in uniform. I wanted plain clothes in the unmarked car."

"Stupid question," Gary said.

"Not at all. If you hadn't been thinking, you wouldn't have asked it."

"White Three."

Tallon had the mike in his hand at once. "White Three, by."

"White One. Suspect in sight, coming straight down Main."

"White One, take up parallel pursuit one block west. Keep out of sight."

"Ten four."

There were ninety seconds of dead silence while Tallon held his microphone ready, waiting.

"White Two," Quigley reported. "He's stopped for the light. Gear on the side of the bike. I can see a gas can."

"Good work," Tallon said into the mike. "Follow four blocks behind. Don't use lights or siren."

"White Four," Brad Oster followed. "We've got him behind us."

"White Four, stay on station," Tallon directed.

A long half minute dragged by.

"White Four, suspect has passed us, headed south. It looks as if he's going straight through town."

Tallon waited no longer. "Hillman, call the swami now and advise him that the suspected arsonist may be headed for Dharmaville, ETA, ten minutes. Have him keep his people out of sight; we are covering in strength."

"Got it," Hillman responded.

Gary started the engine of the newly repaired patrol car; he was ready for action.

"White Four," Tallon directed. "On signal, speed past the bike. White Two, pursue with lights and stage a fake traffic stop."

"White Four; we copy."

"White Two; will do."

Tallon held back until he saw the motorbike coming south, still on Main Street. The huge rider was staying carefully within the law—or close to it, taking no unnecessary chances.

Tallon pressed the mike button. "Execute."

Within a few seconds he saw Oster and Cooper speed past in the unmarked car, fast enough to be well over the limit, but not too much so. Unconsciously he counted until Wyncott and Quigley, roof lights on, dashed past in supposed pursuit.

"All right, Gary," he said to his temporary partner, "follow, but not too closely." In response Mason put the car in motion and turned smoothly onto Main without crossing his hands on the steering wheel. He set an even, steady pace that matched the speed limit.

"White Three."

Tallon answered. "White Three, by."

"White One. Advise."

"White One, follow five hundred feet behind us. Low profile."

"Ten four."

Ahead of him Tallon could see that Wyncott and Quigley had pulled over the unmarked car. Jerry was walking over toward the supposed offending driver. The motorcycle rider went past the scene and continued on his way.

"Why did you do that, Chief?" Gary asked as he drove.

"Nothing makes a motorist feel more secure than seeing someone else getting a ticket. He knows that the patrol unit in that sector is tied up and probably will be for several more minutes. And he's the lucky one, he didn't get stopped."

"So Obermann on the bike feels now that he's out of the woods."

"Exactly."

Within five minutes the built-up area of Whitewater began to thin out rapidly and open country lay ahead. Technically the city limits went on for several more miles, but normal road speeds were allowed once the city proper had been passed. The big man on the motorcycle picked up to sixty plus and rode on, staying on his side of the road and not pushing his luck. Tallon heard a sound, listened, and detected the presence of the helicopter overhead.

"White Three."

Tallon took the mike. "White Three, by."

"Swami notified. He's taking precautions, but will keep his people out of sight."

"Good. I hope he has enough time."

"White Two and Four," Jerry Quigley cut in. "We're behind you."

"Following units close in," Tallon ordered, knowing his voice would be recognized. "If the suspect turns into Dharmaville, stay outside until I signal. If I do, come in fast and ready for action."

Three crisp responses assured him that his troops were on the edge and ready. "Can you drive with your lights off?" he asked Mason.

"I'll give it my best shot."

"Good." Once more Tallon used the microphone. "Hillman, if the suspect does turn into Dharmaville, call off the chopper; he might hear it if he stops."

An unexpected voice cut in on the air. "Air cover here. We copy and will do. Will stand by a mile or so off just in case."

"Thank you," Tallon responded. He remembered again that Ralph Hillman was a wizard with electronics; he had rigged it so the chopper could read them out directly.

It was silent for almost five minutes. Gary drove evenly, holding a steady sixty and knowing that the darkness would hide the markings and outside equipment on the police car. Behind him three sets of lights followed in procession. It could all be a false alarm, but he didn't think so. His heart was pounding a little harder than usual.

"Air to White Three: your subject is turning off the road to the right."

"That's Dharmaville!" Gary said.

"Right," Tallon responded. "Now hang in there and keep cool. We're going in behind him without lights. Try to avoid being seen or heard. If you'd like, I'll drive."

"No way, Chief. This is my baby." He reached to the panel, cut the lights, and accustomed himself to the near blackness. There was some moonlight, enough to see by on the highway. When he reached the Dharmaville entrance, Gary turned in smoothly and quietly. He drove ahead two hundred feet, but nothing appeared to move and the motorcycle was out of sight. Tallon rolled his window down and raised his hand. Gary cut the gas immediately to make the car as quiet as possible. Tallon heard the bike and realized at the same moment that the rider had also slowed down.

In the near absolute quiet of Dharmaville at that hour, Obermann could hardly expect to get off his motor, park it, and set a fire without his presence being detected. Possibly, Tallon thought, he could be counting on the fact that he was nowhere near the residential areas, assuming that he knew the layout of the community. Tallon did not know it too well himself, but he recognized an intersection coming up. "Stop," he told Gary.

As soon as the car was still he got out rapidly and checked the posted signs. They were barely readable in the very poor light, but he was able to make out Business Office and saw that the motorcycle track went that way. He got quickly back into the car and pointed. "Close in," he ordered. "This may be it."

Ahead of him he saw a short, illuminated arc, swift and shallow. Even before it landed he had the microphone in his hand. "All units close in," he directed. "Molotov cocktail just thrown."

A spurt of flame shot up ahead of him, revealing the corner of a sizable building. "Lights?" Gary asked.

"Yes." He seized the mike again. "Air cover, are you there?"

"Air cover, go."

"Stay on the bike if you can. He may take off cross-country."

"Relax; we won't lose him."

Three seconds later a brilliant spotlight came down from the sky. Almost at once it fixed on the motorbike and its rider. Tallon hadn't known that the military chopper was equipped with the police light, but he was fervently grateful that it was. There was a roar of engine sound and the motorbike began to gain speed. The rider whirled it around, left the road, and cut across the open ground toward the reception center. At that moment the light in the sky abruptly went out and he was caught traveling at relatively high speed with his visibility cut off.

Somehow he found his way toward the dark and silent building, drew back his arm, and threw another flaming bottle a good sixty feet. It crashed against the structure and the spilled gasoline burst into flame.

One of the Whitewater marked units, Tallon couldn't tell which one from his position, threw its headlights onto the motorcyclist and began pursuit as fast as the roadway permitted. Again the motorcyclist turned off the road and headed down the gentle slope toward the entrance drive. When he saw a sudden fence he swerved abruptly and took up an almost reverse direction, back toward the second fire he had started.

Gary Mason spun his car around in a tight bootleg turn and made the best speed he could. "Fire extinguisher in the trunk," he barked.

"Take the first fire," Tallon answered quickly.

In response Gary spun the car expertly in the right direction and headed toward the flames. As he closed in, he saw that several people were suddenly in view, fighting the blaze. He knew at once that they had been concealed inside, waiting.

He jerked the car to a stop, yanked out the keys, and had the trunk open in seconds. Tallon grabbed the extinguisher and ran toward the fire. When he was as close as he could possibly get, he triggered the extinguisher and aimed it at the hot point where the flames had started. As he did so, he saw that others were throwing water, but that was not much help against a gasoline fire. The extinguisher put out a foam that was.

He heard a burst of sound behind him, so close he had to turn for an instant. As he did so, a pair of capable hands took the extinguisher away from him and carried on. Two cars were closing in from opposite directions, between them the motorcyclist was caught in their headlights. At that moment the helicopter light came on again and the whole scene was revealed. The motorcyclist swung to the right to cut past the car coming toward him. It was a daring maneuver executed by an expert, but a second too late, he saw a log that had been laid down to mark the end of a parking space. When the bike hit it, it bucked and the rider was thrown forward over the breakaway windscreen.

With remarkable agility the rider thrust out one arm and rolled as he fell. He went over once quickly and then was back on his feet, an enormous man with lightning-fast reflexes. He broke into a dead run behind the building he had set afire. Tallon ran at his own top speed behind him, his gun in his hand, but wary of using it. Shots fired at night, even with the bright light overhead, could be wide, and he had no way of knowing whether or not other Dharmaville people might be coming, unseen, toward the fire.

Obermann rounded the second rear corner of the building and, running flat out, made for a patrol car that stood with its front doors open directly in front of him on the roadway. Tallon was putting on his best burst of speed when he saw someone jump directly in front of the fleeing suspect. Obermann knew his own size and power; he lowered his head and charged like a bull.

There was a blur of motion, almost too fast to be seen, as the two men collided. Then he saw the near impossible: the massive motorcyclist suddenly left his feet, his huge body turned in the air with his right arm trapped in a hold, and he slammed with a smashing impact flat on his back.

The man who had thrown him, still holding his arm, gave an additional twist and turned him over, pulling the captive arm up into a completely effective Aikido wrist lock. Tallon was there in four seconds; he whipped out his handcuffs and locked one side of them around the suspect's oversized wrist. At that moment he realized that the man who had made the capture was Narayan.

Obermann made a sudden attempt to get up when a voice barked, "Freeze!" Tallon looked up and saw Mary Clancy, her feet properly apart, holding her gun dead on the captured arsonist. The movement stopped.

Gary Mason grabbed the suspect's other arm and tried to pull it up into cuffing position; with Narayan's help he succeeded.

Almost out of breath, Tallon checked him none too gently for possible weapons. Strapped to Obermann's leg he found a lethal throwing knife; on his left side concealed under his leather jacket there was a four-inch, stainless steel-barreled .38 revolver. In the groin area he found a tiny derringer in an ingenious washed-leather holster that was taped to the skin.

Tallon got to his feet in the glare of the light that was still overhead. He looked at Narayan and said, "I just remembered that you were a cop. Where did you learn Aikido?"

"In the *dojo*, on my own time. The academy didn't teach it then."

"You were damn effective."

"Thank you."

They were interrupted by Quigley and Wyncott who came running up, not knowing that the principal action was over. Tallon looked and saw that the fire was almost out. There was some damage, but it was minor; the fire-fighting had been fast and effective. He turned toward the second blaze and saw that it too was almost completely knocked down.

A panting Santosh came up, his face smudged, and his trousers torn. "God, thank you!" he said. "We would have had it for sure."

Narayan explained. "As soon as Swami got the word, we put our defensive plan into action."

"Plan?" Tallon asked.

"Yes. Swami had figured out that the first two fires might have been just a cover for a possible attack on us. There was no visible motive for the others, you see, but a very good one for us. So we laid out a plan, just in case. Everyone knew in advance what to do and we had fire-fighting equipment, of a sort, ready in every likely building. Some buckets of water and some sand. They helped."

Tallon watched while the last of the short-lived fire was put out. He noticed that women as well as men were on the job and he wondered if Marsha Stone was among them. He let the prisoner lie where he was; Mary had him covered and he wasn't going anywhere. He wanted a few seconds to recover himself.

Narayan spoke again. "I've no right to ask this, but could I be around during the interrogation?"

"I think so," Tallon replied. "We might need a witness."

"Good enough. By the way, Chief, do you have any reserves in your department?"

The prisoner interrupted in a harsh, bitter voice. "You broke my Goddamned back!"

"You're all right," Narayan said. "I saw the roll you did, so don't give me any of that bullshit." He looked at Tallon. "Shall we put him in the car?"

"We'll do that," Jerry Quigley said. "It'll be a pleasure."

Tallon had not seen Wyncott and Quigley come up, but he recognized the desirability of letting them have their part in the capture. "Go ahead," he said. He stood and watched while the job was done.

As soon as the car doors were closed and Obermann was locked inside, the high tension that had been in the air suddenly evaporated. The helicopter pilot cut off his light and flew away. Tallon saw someone else coming and waited while the swami joined him. "I'm sorry to be late," the swami said, "I was staked out in the temple with our crew there."

Tallon looked around once more. "I think you have only minor damage," he reported, "and no one seems to be hurt. Your plan was certainly effective."

"You and your people did it," the swami retorted. "I've already had a quick account. Thank you; thank you very much."

"You're more than welcome," Tallon said.

"Then I guess that's that," Narayan added.

"Not quite," Tallon told him. He turned to Santosh. "Robert Brown, you're under arrest for the murder of Wilson Sullivan. Take him, Mary, and read him his rights."

CHAPTER 18

A small procession made its way back to the police headquarters in Whitewater. In addition to the four cars that had responded to the scene in Dharmaville, there was a fifth driven by Narayan with the swami beside him. Tallon had invited them to come along, knowing that he might very well need statements from them both.

Ed Wyncott and Jerry Quigley transported Obermann who, despite his bulk, offered no resistance. He had been in similar situations before and he was already trying to give himself the best odds that he could. Santosh was badly shaken, but he did as he was told and reacted visibly only when a cell door was finally slammed shut on him.

As soon as the prisoners had been secured, Tallon held a quick, informal meeting in the lobby. It was crowded, but with Ralph Hillman at the front desk his entire department was present in full strength.

"Thank you all," he said, omitting any dramatics. "It's over. We've got the arsonist, and the murderer of Councilman Sullivan, because you all did a superb job. There wasn't one weak link, and that's why we succeeded. The only thing I didn't like was leaving the city uncovered while we were all out at Dharmaville. Who's supposed to be on patrol?"

"I am," Jerry Quigley said. "I'll change and get right to it."

"Good," Tallon responded. "Who takes over at midnight?"

"I'm the watch commander," Wayne Mudd answered. "Walt has the patrol shift."

"I'll take it now," Cooper volunteered. "There's no need for Jerry to get dressed and go out for the short time he has left." He went back down the corridor to change into uniform.

Tallon surveyed the rest. "As of now the double shifts are finished and we'll go back on a regular schedule. You'll all be getting overtime pay, Mary included. Those of you who are now off duty, go home and get some rest. Say as little about the cases as you can because we don't want to run into a pretrial publicity hurdle. If we get confessions, I'll let you know."

There was a general exodus except for Ned Asher who waited. "I thought you might need some help with the prisoners," he offered.

Tallon made a decision. "If you'd care to stick around, it might be a good idea."

Narayan, who with the swami had been keeping in the background, spoke up. "I'm no longer a peace officer, but if the arsonist is a problem, I'll gladly lend a hand too."

"His name is Obermann," Tallon told him. "As soon as I get a chance I'll swear you in as a reservist. You have your certificate, so it's a lateral transfer. Your first duty will be to teach Aikido to the troops."

"Gladly," Narayan said.

"Let's go in back," Tallon proposed. "Swami, you can come along as chaplain; that's an approved function."

"I'm honored," the swami answered.

After proper precautions had been taken, Wesley Obermann was brought from his cell into the rear office that doubled as an interrogation room. As the prisoner sat down, he overflowed the plain wooden chair he had been given. Tallon sat on a desk opposite him.

"I'll tell you exactly where you stand, Wesley," he began. "We made you on your second job, when you burned down Professor Weintraub's house. The River Falls police cooperated fully, so when you started down here tonight, we had the word almost at once."

The prisoner sat silently, without moving.

"You know the score, Wesley: you're going to prison; there's no way out. We've got witnesses galore and you can't plead incompetence. You were caught red-handed, so there's no chance whatever to try for mistaken identity. You're in the bag."

The prisoner looked up and spoke for the first time. "What about my bike?"

"The police property division will look after it. My advice is to sell it, because by the time you get out, it will be shot anyway."

Tallon stopped, but Obermann offered nothing further.

"Now," Tallon continued, "just to be sure there's no slipup, we're going to read you your rights once more."

"Skip it," Obermann said. Tallon looked at Asher who took out his Miranda card and read off the legal phrases. It was an absurd procedure, but the courts required it and it was properly done.

"Do you want to call your lawyer?" Tallon asked.

"I don't have a lawyer."

"We'll appoint one to represent you, if you'd like. I can have him here shortly."

"Forget it."

"That's up to you. Perhaps you'd like to call the man who hired you —Mortimer Brown. You'll have to reverse the charges because he's in San Francisco."

Again Obermann remained silent.

"You know what you're up against," Tallon continued. "The best you can hope for is a lighter sentence than you deserve. We know that Brown hired you, and why. If you want me to report you as cooperative, suppose you tell me what he paid you for each job."

Obermann turned his broad, sullen face toward him. "What does it get me if you report me cooperative?" he asked.

"It helps. At the trial and later before the parole board. Right now you'd better take anything you can get."

"Five thousand dollars," Obermann said.

"For each job?"

"That's right. But he won't pay me for this one now."

"No, I don't think he will."

Obermann was put back into his cell.

Santosh was brought in with no difficulty and put in the same chair. His open breezy manner was gone; he was deathly frightened and it showed in every breath he drew.

Tallon did not speak to him. Instead he waited until the room was still, then he picked up the phone. When the exchange answered in San Francisco, he asked to speak to the supervisor. A moment later she came on the line. "This is Chief Tallon of the Whitewater Police Department in the State of Washington. I have very important information for Mr. Mortimer Brown and need to speak to him immediately. This is official."

He held the phone for a full half minute until Brown came through on a phone patch. "Mr. Brown," Tallon said. "I regret to tell you this, but we have your son here, in custody."

"I don't know what he's done, or what he's accused of," Brown declared, "and I don't know a competent lawyer in that vicinity. Whatever his bail is, I'll put it up. What's the fastest way to handle that?"

"If you need a good lawyer for your son, I can recommend James Morrison very highly. He lives here and he is our best defense attorney."

"I'll take your word for it; get Morrison. And how much is the bail?"

That was what Tallon was waiting for, because he wanted the suspect to hear his reply. "The charge, Mr. Brown, is murder in the first degree and for that there is no bail."

A near explosion came over the line. "I'll be there in the morning, as soon as I can arrange a charter. I'll have my attorneys with me. Meanwhile, get Morrison on the job."

"I'll give you his number, Mr. Brown," Tallon said. "I suggest that you talk to him and give him any instructions you wish. You're at liberty to tell him that I gave you his name."

"I'll do that immediately. Give me the number."

Tallon supplied it from memory and then hung up. He turned to Santosh. "Have you been read your rights?" he asked.

"Listen, man," Santosh protested, "this is crazy!"

"Read him his rights, Ned," Tallon directed. Asher obliged and then put the card back into his pocket with grim satisfaction.

"Let's clear up some preliminary points," Tallon said. "Do you deny that you are Robert Brown, the son of Mortimer Brown of San Francisco?"

"No, he's my father. All right, now you know. But there's nothing wrong in that. It was all part of a business deal. What's that got to do with accusing me of murder, for God's sake?"

"It's very simple, Santosh; you killed Wilson Sullivan to shut him up. He threatened to blow the whistle on your whole operation and you panicked. Now I'm very much afraid that you're going to have to pay for it."

Unexpectedly the swami spoke up. He had been so quiet, Tallon had all but forgotten that he was there. "The giving of the name Santosh implies acceptance into our community family. I'd appreciate it very much if hereafter you refer to this man only as Robert Brown."

"I'll be glad to," Tallon said. "If it hadn't been for your practice of using Sanskrit names at Dharmaville, I might have tumbled much sooner. I did see the name Robert Brown on your membership roster, but it's so common it didn't register at the time."

"I made a mistake," Ned Asher said. "When Wayne and I took on the job of checking out the whole Dharmaville community, Brown here told us that there had been a meeting on the night of the murder and that almost everyone was there. That was all perfectly true. Then he supplied us with the names of twenty-four people that he had seen there. We fell for it because it was such a good list. He simply gave us names of people he knew would attend; if he missed on one he could always claim that he had made a natural mistake—that he had thought he had seen that person there. So we faithfully checked everyone out from there on, but we didn't check back on him. Because he was our starting point, his name didn't even appear on our checkout list, so we didn't notice that not a single reliable witness reported him as present. I'll never make that mistake again."

"You guys are crazy," Brown said. "How soon does my lawyer get here?"

"Pretty soon," Tallon answered. "You see, Brown, you attracted attention from the very beginning. Dharmaville is a quiet place where things like meditation are encouraged. But you came on hot and heavy, so very different from the rest I couldn't help noticing it."

"So because you didn't like the way I talked, or how I went out of my way to make you feel welcome and to help you, you think I'm a murderer."

"Do you remember the day you came here and picked me up?" Tallon asked. "On the way out you told me that you weren't a member of the Dharmaville council, but you hoped to become one. After that I had a private talk with the swami about a very confidential matter. I didn't tell you what it was, of course, just that we had talked. But you said, 'That's all the swami needs, something else to worry about.' Swami told me specifically that the matter being discussed had not been known to the membership. After that, I started checking."

Brown sat in his chair, shaking his head as if he were confronted by irrational imbeciles.

"Take him in and book him," Tallon said. "Prints and the lot. By the time you're through, Jim Morrison ought to be here."

Asher and Mudd took Brown into the next room and put him through the booking process. Just before they finished, James Morrison arrived at the station. "I got a call from a Mortimer Brown in San Francisco," he told Tallon. "He tried hard to impress me that he was a big shot. He said that his son's in trouble here and he asked me to represent him. What's the charge against him?"

"Murder one; he's accused of killing Councilman Sullivan."

Morrison drew a deep breath and let it out slowly. "I had no idea it was that heavy," he said. "Has he confessed?"

"No, we didn't question him until his attorney was present."

"Then may I see my client."

"Come with me," Tallon said, and led him toward the back. When they entered the booking room he made a brief introduction. "Mr. Brown, this is your attorney, Mr. James Morrison. You will find him highly qualified. We'll clear the room and you can confer with him privately for as long as you like."

"Don't try to shit me; the room's bugged."

"No it isn't. I won't take that chance because, if it were, it might be possible grounds for acquittal. No one will overhear you." With that he left.

Tallon went into his office and phoned Jennifer. She had already heard the news. "When will you be home?" she asked.

"I haven't any idea. If the suspect wants to talk, then I'll have to stay here and listen."

"Well, do the best you can. I'm glad you've got him."

Narayan appeared at the doorway. "Are we welcome?" he asked.

"Of course," Tallon answered. "Come on in."

Narayan did, followed by the swami. When they had sat down, the swami spoke. "When you came to see me, I told you that you would have to look for your murderer somewhere other than at Dharmaville. I apologize."

"Don't," Tallon said. "You acted in completely good faith. Sit where I am, Swami, and you'll find out how much the good people in this world—those who like others, who are willing to help out when they're needed, and who operate on a basis of mutual confidence and trust—are imposed upon, abused, and victimized. Their goodwill and basic decency are exploited as weaknesses and the fact that they are honorable only makes them easier to rob. A lot of unscrupulous stockbrokers have made fortunes by knowing that."

"Amen," Narayan said. "I put one of them in prison."

"I think I know most of what has been going on," the swami said. "A large percentage of our people come from upper-class homes; that's something that isn't generally realized. When Robert Brown came to me, some months ago, he simply said that he came from a high-powered home where he felt himself lost, that he wanted to find more meaning in his own life. On that basis we accepted him. He was very high strung and we thought that we had calmed him down quite a little. I never sensed that he was an impostor."

"Actually," Tallon said, "he was a spy; the industrial variety, but a spy nonetheless. It's obvious that he was trying to find something that he could feed to Sullivan on the council and, by that means, discredit your operation. I don't doubt that he was sure he would succeed within a short time. But he didn't. However, he kept on trying, worming his way into the confidence of the council members, I presume, and waiting for the moment when he could uncover something juicy."

"I had to tell him to stop pressing his attentions onto some of our female members," the swami commented. "They complained to Narayan and to me."

"How did Sullivan fit into this?" Narayan asked.

Tallon loosened the knot on his tie. "He was the Browns's fall guy," he said. "They trapped him. He was a fairly small-time home builder who was elected to the city council on a platform of saving money—that's always a popular cause. When he took office, the Browns saw an opportunity. Young Brown showed him a piece of property his father owned and offered it at an attractive price. The proviso was that Sullivan would engage an architect specified by the Browns. They told him the man was very good, but needed the work and could be hired for a reduced fee. Sullivan was greedy and fell for it."

"Stupid," Narayan said.

"Definitely," Tallon agreed. "Following Brown's instructions, the architect laid out houses on the property, crowding them so closely together they would be unsalable."

"Didn't Sullivan see that?" the swami asked.

"Yes, but the architect convinced him he would make much more profit that way. Five houses were up before Sullivan finally woke to how he had been had. He tried to unload the houses, but even at cost he couldn't move them. At that point Mortimer Brown stepped in and offered to buy the land back, but on his terms. Sullivan had no other prospects, the bank was pressing him hard, so he was forced to take the offer that ruined him.

"As soon as Mortimer Brown had Sullivan in a desperate position, he offered to pay him a generous commission if he could force you to sell, Swami, and move out."

"Poor man," the swami said.

Narayan was thinking. "I wonder, Chief, if that wasn't a frame up too. The Browns never expected him to earn that commission. The real plan was to have young Brown get something on us, or fake it if necessary, and then hand it to Sullivan who would follow through with the council, claiming righteous indignation. For that they would pay him something, probably enough to keep him quiet, and promise him more in the future."

"You're right on," Tallon said. "We dug up the architect and he admitted the whole thing. He'll probably lose his license."

The swami supplied the next piece. "When he came to us, he put on a tremendous act about his devotion to the yoga and pleaded with me to give him a Sanskrit name. I did in the hope it would motivate him to really earn it. I didn't sense at the time he only wanted it to conceal his identity."

"Sullivan was a dupe," Tallon continued, "but he employed a very good and loyal bookkeeper. She's a highly intelligent lady, so it didn't take her long to put the thing together. Not all of it, but enough. And she told her employer what was going on. She had the foresight to suspect that Dharmaville might be located in an area picked for legal gambling. In that case, Swami, your property could be worth millions as a casino and resort site. Mortimer Brown was determined to make that huge profit. To him it was just a case of that old excuse for dishonesty, 'business is business.' You heard young Brown claim that a few minutes ago; he said it was all just part of a business deal."

"I feel sorry for him," the swami said. "His only real deficiency is morality, and that can be acquired."

"I see the rest of it, I think," Narayan said. "Sullivan realized that the information he had could be valuable. He probably saw young Brown and told him that if he weren't paid, he'd blow the whistle on the whole thing. After that he would go home confident that he had outsmarted the Browns at last, and that he would be back on his feet again shortly. He didn't allow for the fact that Robert was so insanely determined he wouldn't draw the line at anything."

"Please don't use that word 'insane,'" Tallon said with some feeling. "I don't believe that he was ever out of his mind for a moment and I don't even want to suggest that idea. There's some construction work going on at Dharmaville, isn't there?"

"Our new meditation center," the swami said.

"Then Robert probably found the short piece of re-enforcing rod at the site. Also, I'm positive that he took Narayan's ankh."

"He had the cabin next to mine," Narayan supplied.

"So, armed with the rod and the piece of jewelry, he went into town to meet with Sullivan once more. He probably tried to talk his way out, but Sullivan had had enough promises from the Browns and he wasn't buying anymore. Based on the medical reports, Sullivan probably turned his back on Robert and tried to walk away. He was hit from behind with a blow that was supposed to kill him outright. Robert planted the ankh on him, to be sure that Dharmaville would be blamed, and then hid his murder weapon where he was sure it would never be found. He didn't figure on Gary Mason."

"I can't compete with professional detectives," the swami said, "but I know something about human nature. Clearly Mortimer Brown is totally ruthless; he tried to make sure we would sell by hiring Obermann to burn us out. A direct attack on our property would be too obvious, so he had Obermann destroy two homes in Whitewater before he went after us."

Tallon nodded. "That's Mortimer's style: he put in his son to do the worst he could, then he backed his bet by hiring the arsonist when he wasn't getting results fast enough. I hope he can't buy his way out of this one."

"He doesn't have a chance," Narayan said. "Obermann will hang him to save his own hide. The heavy muscle types are all the same: they end up in the joint every time. They aren't bright. Right now Obermann is planning how he will try to con the parole board. And he may; a lot of them do."

The intercom light flashed on Tallon's phone and he picked it up. "Yes," he said.

"I've finished talking with my client," Morrison reported. "That's all I can tell you right now, except that he has asked to see his spiritual adviser."

Tallon knew that was the prisoner's privilege. "Did he specify?" he asked, to make sure.

"He asked to see the swami."

Tallon led the way back, the swami following behind him. "I don't envy you your job," Jack said as he unlocked the heavy door.

"Nor do I," the swami answered. "To so many people religious help is something to be called upon only as a last resort. We tried so hard to help him." As Jim Morrison came out, the swami went inside.

Jack went back to his office, leaned back in his chair, and shut his eyes. He had had about all he could take in one day. He felt a slight drowsiness, then he was asleep before he knew it.

Ned Asher shook him awake more than an hour later. Tallon rubbed his eyes, and sat up with his feet on the floor. "What is it?" he asked.

"Brown has asked to see you," Asher told him. "I should have told him you'd gone home to bed, but I didn't think fast enough."

"The swami?"

"Still with the prisoner."

Somehow Tallon found the energy to get to his feet once more and to go back to the cells.

It was after nine when he awoke in the morning. As soon as he was conscious of the hour, he jumped out of bed and called to Jennifer as he literally ran into the bathroom.

She appeared as he was beginning a hurried shave. "Take your time," she advised. "You were dead beat last night and I turned off the alarm so you could get some rest. I just talked to Wayne and everything is under control. I'll go get your breakfast."

"No time," Tallon snapped at her as he ran the electric razor over his face. "I have to be there; people are coming in." In a flat eight minutes from the time he awoke, Tallon was out of his house and literally running to his car. When he hurried into his department, he found everything calm and Francie at the front desk filing reports. He was almost annoyed that no one seemed upset at his tardiness.

At his desk he plunged into work, unconsciously driving himself to make up for the time he had lost. Ed Wyncott appeared, in uniform, carrying a tray. "Jennifer phoned that you missed your breakfast," he said. "I hope this will be all right." He put down the meal from the fast-food stand.

Tallon forced himself to stop, draw breath, and thank Ed for his trouble. He had never been late before and he did not intend to let it happen again. The fact that he was the chief made no difference; he expected his men to be on time and the same obligation rested even more heavily on him. That was something he would have to make clear to Jennifer when he got home.

He was two thirds of the way through the meal, going over paper work as he did so, when Francie appeared, hands aflutter. "There is a Mr. Brown to see you," she announced. "He has two other gentlemen with him."

"Tell Mr. Brown that I'll be with him shortly. Then ring Jim Morrison and suggest that he stop over."

"Yes, sir." Francie wasn't often that formal, but she was fully aware of Tallon's mood, having just spoken with Jennifer by phone.

Tallon finished off the last of the hot coffee and then shoved the remains of his hasty meal in a drawer. As soon as he had brushed the crumbs away, he called Francie on the intercom and told her to bring Brown in.

The land developer came storming in, brimming with indignation. He seated himself without invitation. The two men who followed him were so obviously lawyers that introductions were hardly necessary. They, at least, spoke their names and shook hands briefly before they drew up chairs and joined their client. Through all of this, Tallon remained virtually silent, largely because Brown was putting on too much of an act.

"Now, what's this all about?" he demanded. "I got here as soon as I could. Had to charter a Learjet and that costs money."

"That's your problem," Tallon answered calmly. "As I told you on the phone last night, your son is being held here on a charge of first-degree murder, specifically the murder of Councilman Wilson Sullivan. That's what it's all about. We also have in custody Wesley Obermann who's being held on a charge of arson and arson for hire."

Brown waved a hand through the air to indicate his total lack of interest in Obermann. Then one of the lawyers leaned forward and spoke in a normal, rational tone. "Chief Tallon, my partner and I have been retained by Mr. Brown to represent his son. However, we are from California."

Tallon was just as calm and collected. "I didn't get your name, sir."

"Higgins."

"Mr. Higgins, last night I advised Mr. Brown by phone that his son was in custody and of the charge against him. Also, of course, Mr. Robert Brown was advised of his rights. Mr. Brown wanted an attorney to advise his son and I recommended Mr. James Morrison."

"We'd like to meet with Mr. Morrison very much."

"I've already directed my secretary to call him and I expect that he will arrive shortly."

The other attorney spoke up. "You realize, Chief Tallon, that to accuse Mr. Robert Brown of murder is an absurdity. Besides which the young man has not been himself for some time; he's been taking refuge in a religious camp."

"And your name, please?"

"Fineberg."

"Mr. Fineberg, Mr. Robert Brown stands accused of first-degree murder. His innocence or guilt is something to be determined in a court of law. However, we have sufficient evidence to hold him on that charge, and as you are fully aware, there is no bail. His preliminary hearing will be before Judge Howell who has his chambers in this building."

As he stopped, Jim Morrison appeared in the doorway. Tallon performed the introductions and waited until Morrison was seated. A chair had to be brought in for him.

Mortimer Brown was unable to contain himself any longer. He pulled out a cigar, but Tallon shook his head. "I'm sorry, Mr. Brown, but for health reasons, there is no smoking in any part of the police station, including my office."

"I think you can make an exception," Brown countered, and reached for his lighter.

"No, I won't make an exception," Tallon snapped, "and furthermore there are no ashtrays. This is my office and I don't allow any smoking here. If you must smoke, go outside to do it and come back when you're finished."

Brown had not expected that kind of reception and very clearly didn't like it. He put the cigar away, got himself under control, and then nodded to Higgins. "You take it, Ted," he directed.

"Would it be possible, Chief Tallon," Higgins began, "to give us a summary of the evidence on which you're holding Mr. Brown's son?"

"I don't have to, but I will," Tallon replied. He gave a brief rundown.

Brown barely let him finish. "Why Goddamn it, that's insanity!" he stormed. "All you've got there is circumstantial evidence that won't hold up five minutes in court and you know it." He leaned forward and shook a fat finger in Tallon's face. "Now, you listen to me and you listen good. You came to my office and tried to cut yourself in on the deal I'm making; you wanted your piece of action. And when I told you that wasn't ethical, you told me that I'd find out about you the hard way. Well, I have." He stopped to let that much sink in. "My secretary was listening in on the conversation and she'll testify. Now you sign whatever paper is necessary and release my son or I'll lower the boom on you so Goddamned hard you won't know what hit you."

"I think what Mr. Brown means," Higgins cut in quickly, "is that the evidence as you've presented it is inadequate even for a preliminary hearing. You must excuse him, but you will understand that he is a very concerned father."

Brown drew breath, but Fineberg punched him quite openly in the ribs with his elbow.

Higgins went on. "You see, Chief Tallon, we understand your position completely and are sympathetic to it. But you've got the wrong man. Mr. Sullivan was a big, burly man of considerable physical strength. Mr. Robert Brown is hardly half that size. Also, as I understand it, you have no witness to the crime, no witness to your claim that Mr. Brown, Jr., was even in the city of Whitewater that evening when he was killed. In fact the only thing you appear to have is the fact that he is Mr. Brown's son and that cannot possibly be grounds for detaining him. I believe that if I talk to Judge Howell in his chambers, he will certainly see it that way."

Brown sneered openly. "Now will you get my son out of the can, or do I have to take legal action?"

Tallon slowly shook his head. "No, Mr. Brown, I will not release your son. His detention is completely legal and he has been given the advice of a competent attorney. He also asked for spiritual guidance and he was given that."

Fineberg spoke. "He must have been tremendously upset to ask for spiritual help. I know the young man well and that isn't his pattern of conduct."

"It was last night," Tallon responded. He looked at Morrison who nodded his head. "He named the minister he wanted, and that gentleman counseled him."

"That's correct," Morrison said. "He made the request to me and I saw that it was honored."

"Who did he ask for?" Brown demanded.

"Swami Dharmayana," Tallon answered.

Brown almost threw his arms into the arm. "That crackpot!" He turned toward his attorneys. "He's the Jesus freak who runs that place I told you about. Minister, hell, he's a fake from the ground up."

"Mr. Brown," Morrison said, "an accused is entitled to see a religious adviser whenever practical and your son specifically asked to see the swami who is a fully recognized spiritual leader. Also, sir, I would suggest that it would be most helpful if you would temper your attitude so that this meeting can continue on a more positive note."

"I second that," Higgins said. "With the note, as I mentioned before, that Mr. Brown is a very upset man at the moment, and for very good reason."

Brown took a deep breath, held it, and then let it out very slowly. "All right. I'll concede that my temper sometimes does get the better of me. Let's go back to square one. You don't have a case and you know it. I'd like you to release my son here and now. Failing that, I'll ask my attorneys to see your Judge Howell and we'll get a court order to spring him."

Tallon reached into the top-center drawer of his desk and drew out a document. He laid it before him and then rested his hands on it. "I believe this has gone far enough," he said, "and I don't want to waste anymore of your valuable time—or mine. I have here your son's full confession to the crime of murder, with all details supplied, properly witnessed, and signed. He gave it voluntarily, without our asking, after conferring with Swami Dharmayana. He stated in my presence that he wanted to relieve his mind, and he did. And, as is usual in such instances, he supplied a number of details that had not been made public and which would only be known to the guilty person."

"May I see that?" Fineberg asked.

Tallon passed it over.

It was very quiet in the office as the San Francisco attorney read the document. It was printed in ink on ruled paper, by hand, and contained all of the necessary legal phrases concerning the absence of duress or any other improper persuasion. As Fineberg was nearing the end, Ed Wyncott slipped in and laid another paper on Tallon's desk.

Fineberg handed the confession back. "In view of that," he said, "I will concede that you have the right to hold Robert Brown while his defense is being prepared. Mr. Morrison, did you advise your client to make this confession?"

"No, I did not," Morrison answered. "Our conversation was privileged, but I will state that definitely."

Mortimer Brown had turned an almost stark white. His distress was so evident, Tallon quickly picked up a phone. "Get a doctor here, fast!" he ordered.

Slowly Brown shook his head. "I'm all right. But I don't believe it; I don't believe a word of it. It's a frame up—it's got to be." Visibly he began to recover. "Of course that's it: he was framed and now this. What time did you get it?"

"About four o'clock this morning," Tallon answered. "It was completely voluntary and, before he signed it, your son had another meeting with Mr. Morrison. I was not present, of course, but after that meeting Robert told me that he wanted to confess and he insisted on doing so."

"At four o'clock??" Brown's indignation began to return. "He was dead on his feet. And you kept after him: that's a defense right there. Goddamn it, I'm not going to stand for this any longer!"

Tallon glanced at the fresh document that had been put before him, then he punched a button on his phone. In response Ed Wyncott and Wayne Mudd appeared in the doorway.

"Mr. Brown," Tallon said as calmly as though he had not been up most of the night, "it's a good thing that you've brought your legal advisers with you, because you're going to need them. Wesley Obermann has given us a complete statement implicating you in the crime of arson. Since you hired him to commit the crime, you are by law equally guilty. By coming here you've saved me the trouble of extraditing you. You're under arrest. Officer Wyncott, read him his rights."

Brown sprang from his chair, his face flaming with rage. For a moment Tallon thought he was going to lunge across the desk, but Mudd effectively prevented that. When Brown was taken out of the office, he was in handcuffs.

Jennifer checked one more time, looking around her kitchen to be sure that everything was just as it should be. The dips had been prepared, the bottles for drinks had all been lined up on the counter, and the cheese was ready. There was so little in the way of entertainment in Whitewater, the excuse to give a party was always welcome. The 8 percent raise that had just been given the Police Department, while less than had been hoped for, was a suitable occasion to celebrate.

Jack came into the kitchen. "Gary and Ralph will be coming early," he told her. "They'll have to leave to take over from Wayne and Jerry, who'll be in later."

"Can't they park the patrol car outside and respond from here if anything goes down?"

Jack shook his head; Jennifer knew better than that. "The watch commander has to cover the station, and one car, at least, has to be rolling in the field." He didn't add that law enforcement was a twenty-four-hour affair for every policeman and, like telephone operators, the holidays were usually the busiest times.

Mary Clancy, who had come early to help, set out the dips around the living room. She was just finishing when Ralph Hillman and his wife, Betty, came to the door. "Are we too early?" he asked.

"Right on time," Tallon assured him. "Come on in."

Five minutes later Gary Mason arrived alone. "No date?" Tallon asked as he opened the door.

"I'm hitting the bricks tonight, and I can't ditch a date to go to work. Besides, Mary's here."

"Indeed she is," Tallon agreed.

Half an hour later most of the expected guests had arrived. The swami appeared with a lady whom he introduced to Jennifer. "This is Kumari," he said. "She met Jack at Dharmaville and wanted to know you too, so I invited her to come with me."

"I'm glad you did," Jennifer approved. "Come in and enjoy yourself."

When Narayan appeared, he was unexpectedly escorting Marion McNeil, the councilwoman. "I decided that we MacNeil's should stick together, regardless of spelling," he explained. "So I asked her."

"Right on," Jennifer told him. "Come on in, Marion. And congratulations, Francis, I hear you're our newest reservist."

"Working with Jack will be fun," Narayan said. "I'm going to like it. And once a cop . . ."

"Don't I know it!" Jennifer told him. "I live with a cop. Come on in, and make yourself at home."

When Jennifer answered the next ring, Walt Cooper was on the doorstep. She took a quick look at the stunning girl he had with him and for a moment felt completely inadequate. Then she rallied.

"Jennifer," Walt said. "This is Marsha Stone."

"As if I didn't know. I'm so glad you could both come." After letting them in, she went back to her kitchen wondering how any girl could ever manage to look like that. It was unfair, and she wondered if Mary Clancy thought so too.

The appearance of Marsha Stone in the living room quieted conversation to the point of embarrassment. Jack Tallon richly enjoyed the spectacle as Walt took his date around the group and introduced his colleagues. The reactions were about as he expected them to be. Within a few minutes Marsha was simply one of the guests. He gave her high marks for being such a good mixer.

He caught a fragment of conversation when she was talking with Brad Oster. He had said something about her visit to Whitewater to which Marsha replied, "Actually, Brad, I'm living here, and I like it very much. If I can manage it, I'd like to stay for a while."

Tallon glanced at Mary Clancy and moved her a notch even higher in his esteem when he noted that she did not seem to mind at all being overshadowed by Marsha Stone. Mary herself was strikingly attractive and she also seemed to be that rare thing: a girl whose every thought isn't given to competition. She was secure in herself, as she had every right to be, and it brought her his genuine admiration.

Before long, Marsha and Mary were talking together as though they were old friends. That, Tallon decided, was class.

Ralph Hillman and Gary Mason spoke their thanks and left to take over at the station. A half hour later Wayne Mudd and Jerry Quigley, their shifts completed, came by together. Jennifer produced fresh plates of finger foods from her refrigerator. As she set them out, and Tallon busied himself in preparing drinks for the newcomers, he noticed that everyone was making an effort to suggest that the party had just begun. It was that kind of subtle understanding that made him so proud of his department. As far as he was concerned, the Whitewater Police could serve as a model for the nation.

After she had been asked several times, Marsha talked a little about her life in Hollywood. She said nothing at all about her disappearance, or why she had decided to come back into public view, but she did discuss some of the strains and tensions that went with the making of a major motion picture. She spoke as though the same things could have happened to anyone in the room. A circle had formed around her, but none of the fabled movie industry ego appeared to have rubbed off onto Marsha; it seemed almost as though she was asking those who surrounded her to consent to be her friends.

For the first time, Tallon began to understand how a girl of her gifts and talent had been content to sit in the reception center at Dharmaville and to live so simply as part of the community.

The phone rang.

Tallon picked it up. Ralph Hillman was on the line. "Chief, Gary found a front door open on Nestor Avenue and checked it out. The whole place was wrecked. Furniture smashed, everything ransacked, apparently a lot of stuff missing. He's standing by."

"Right away," Tallon said, and hung up.

He turned toward his guests and spoke just loudly enough to be heard. "There's been a major burglary and vandalism in the high-rent district."

Before he had finished speaking, the members of his department were getting quickly to their feet.

"Let's go, gentlemen," he said. "We've got work to do."

This is John Ball's second novel about Chief Jack Tallon. Mr. Ball is also the author of the popular Virgil Tibbs series, which includes *Then Came Violence* and *In the Heat of the Night,* the film version of which won five Academy Awards including Best Picture. He is also widely known for such works as *The Killing in the Market, Miss 1000 Spring Blossoms, Last Plane Out, Rescue Mission, The Winds of Mitamura,* and *Police Chief.* He lives in Encino, California.